ISBN-13-987-0-9792622-4-1
ISBN-10-0-9792622-4-0

www.jsiwicki.com

SLABYPRESS
W25952 State Road 95
Arcadia, WI 54612
U.S.A.

Technical, Cover, and Book design by JBS.

For information contact:
slabypress@yahoo.com
infojsiwicki@gmail.com

Special thanks!
-To everyone who helped with the production of this book-

DREAM KILLER

—Bedtime Stories and Dreams—

Memories of Michael Colt - I

JOHN SIWICKI

—A dream may not be—what you think a dream to be—

JOHN SIWICKI

SPATIAL ZONES

The ocean, sky, and mind are places we're still learning about, and these spatial zones fill us with wonder. Life exists in the sea, on the planet; stars remain steadfast above as ideas go in and out of the mind. The sea and sky are free areas from birth for all to study and explore, but the mind is the one place that we discover on our own. It's a place of experience: we process things we see, hear, smell, taste, and feel, with one added intrinsic component—it's where dreams are created. We travel to other dimensions in sleep, and after waking perhaps a small memory of it remains. During a sleep episode ideas come, and occasionally all of us go to some of the same places in our dreams. So are we really one mind, our mind—or part of many?

The practice begins at different times, but for most this usually comes when darkness falls and our eyes close. Our brain activity increases, imagination and vision overwhelm reality. Colors of day become shades of night, and a prism of light connected to some hidden dimensional shift opens a door to an enlightened awareness. It's believed that this feeling grows into a world created from the thoughts of the mind. If that's true, where do these thoughts originate? Similarly like black is to white, hot being the opposite of cold, unconsciousness being within consciousness, the two worlds of the mind co-exist, and awareness of each is separated by time, repose, and dimension. Whether the mind is awake, cognizant, at rest, or in sleep mode, imagination seems random and able to take control at any time. But is it imagination, or something else? A more fundamental question becomes clear: what is *it*, and where does *it* come from?

Is the world an illusion filled with phantoms, ghosts, memories and apparitions that distort like water, rising up to where they melt into clouds that float effervescently above as ever-present vapor in the atmosphere? Maybe this door to the unknown is how moody spirits sidle in, out, and through dimensions. In this place up high they abide for a time, waiting, watching, planning, and floating until at the precise time that they connect to people and control fate through chance, or by a planned encounter in the physical world where the outcome is, or isn't, known beforehand. Unexplainable things happen again and again no matter how well one plans. And even though goals are mapped to rope a path we hope comes true someday, surprise is always lurking to inflict the best or worst outcome. But as life would have it, even the best laid plans require adaptation, and modification, to ensure an expected result.

So what is time and space? Is it just an empty black hole of endless moments that become filled with countless activities of enjoyment, work, failure, success, and entertainment? Does it exist to enable control to exact revenge? Is it the place where all things of and about life as we understand it abides? Do ideas just lie dormant until jarred, then become alive, building momentum, expanding on their own power until eventually having a mind of their own? Off they go then on the hunt, returning to what they know, and leeching on to random bodies. Are we essentially multiple parts of ideas or are we individual thoughts created from dark places searching for a light to shine upon us, enabling growth for a life of imagination controlled by our actions?

In an unconscious state of dream activity people travel to places believed to exist only in the mind. After some dream bits are remembered, they may have some meaning or give us an idea of what the future holds. The question is how to decipher these dream bits so that they make sense. Voila, there is a dictionary for this called the *Beatty Papyrus*, the oldest known dictionary in existence for interpreting dreams. It was used by priests called "Masters of the Magic Library." Later, another book called *Oneirocritica*, written by Artemidorus Daldianus, also told the secrets of dreams.

It's during the sleep stage when memory shuts down to create a dream world similar to reality. Without memory, the ideas and dreams are soon forgotten, but then on occasion a part of the dream is remembered, and in a quirky way it somehow stays with us. With this concept in mind, it's believed by some that dreams *are* actually reality, and that the time we're awake, not. Are both connected in some unique way? This cycle of being awake and asleep can be compared to reincarnation, or rebirth. So in a way, we die when we sleep, and are re-born every time we wake. By enabling the understanding of dreams and who we are, our role may become clear with time. In the end we may know and see purpose while our time fades into darkness for the very last time. As we search to find the way to the light on that final path of no return, we look for the answer to everything.

Today Gods are worshipped, revered, and feared, but it was more so in ancient cultures. It's written that Morpheus, God of Sleep, shapes dreams in such a way that the actual time of a dream might last anywhere from mere seconds to an eternity, because in his world, there is no accurate way to calculate time. Hypnos, the cave dweller, never sees the sun rise or set while lingering alongside the river of forgetfulness. This river flows endlessly to a place we never could imagine; a place where the only sliver of light reflects from the water. Pasithea, the creator of hallucinations that appear and vanish before our eyes, uses a magic trick of *now you see it now you don't* that convolutes the perception of reality with shadows that move all around. Nyx, the ruler of darkness, this realm you enter at the cost of never leaving, trapped forever in a never-ending search for a way to escape from a realm black as coal. And finally, there's Thanatos, who lives in the underworld where everything ends, where all thoughts, ideas, and memories remain a fog of the past, just footprints of time, sleeping, hoping to someday escape and become reality. Thanatos, the dream killer, holds the key to the door that leads to the place of memories, and he's the one who keeps the world of the mind captive.

If there is a key to the door to where dreams originate, that door can be opened, allowing some thoughts to escape through vibrations that alter time, space, and lives.

THE ENCOUNTER

"Look over there," Sue said. "See that thing floating out there?" She walked closer to the shore, her anxious eyes probing the water. "What do you think that is?"

She was with Michael on an early morning walk along the river, and there was always something floating in the water, so Michael wasn't paying attention; he was in a hypnotic trance playing with his dog. With a robust throw the Frisbee went flying, and the dog jumped to retrieve it. Buster loved that Frisbee. At first Michael fought with Buster to get it back, but the dog finally let it go, and he tossed it again. It was summer vacation; they had just finished the first year of high school, and were walking next to the river talking about . . . things.

"Out there, see it?" Sue walked to the shore, kicked off her sandals, stepped into the water without hesitation. She usually dressed like a Bohemian, but it was summer, so she was wearing cutoff jeans, and a Red Dirt t-shirt she'd gotten in Hawaii. She waded out until the water was knee-high to get a better look at the floating hulk.

Now Michael noticed Sue, wondering what she was pointing at, then he looked out at the river, and said, "What are you talking about?"

She turned, and said, "Over there!" Frustrated, she kicked water at him, then repeated, "Over there, can't you see it?"

"Over where? What?"

"That thing way out there," Sue said, and raising her sun glasses, her burning gaze aimed at Michael. "See it? Are you messing with me? You see it, don't you? There's a bundle of something floating way out there, and it doesn't look like a log."

"Yeah, I see it," Michael said, laughing. "You know, there's always some junk floating out there. Whenever I walk by the river I always see something floating along. Can't make out what that is though." But then Michael stopped playing with his dog, and a haunted look crept across his face. "Wait a second! Are those arms and legs bobbing up and down?" Michael stood, walking to the edge of the shore behind Sue, focusing, staring out at the water. "Hey that's a body!"

"You really think so," she said, then turned to watch the dog charge to the shore line. "Is that why Buster's barking?"

"It's definitely a body," Michael said, "and Buster's picked up the scent, he smells it!"

"Where would it have come from?" Sue asked. "And how does it end up in the river?"

"I've heard of it happening," Michael said. "Someone falls off a boat, gets caught in the current, and they're dragged under."

The dog was a black and brown mixed collie given to Michael by a local farmer, and smart, so clever that he always looked both ways before crossing the road. Now he was barking like crazy, and not letting up because he sensed something odd happening.

Something that resembled a body was definitely floating out there in the water. Buster showed no sign of letting up with the barking. Michael and Sue watched the blob floating and bobbing around in the waves. It more or less stayed in the same place without coming to shore. The mysterious bulge just went back and forth, up and down, around and around.

"It must be caught on something," Michael said, "and that's why it won't wash ashore. Let's swim out, and see what it is. How about it?"

"What!" Sue said. "No way you're going to coax me into swimming out there," Sue said. "If it is a body, I don't want to see a dead person. This is crazy, Michael. Sure you really want to do that? I don't think it's a good idea. Look how far out it is. Can you pull it all the way back here? It's a body, a real person, not just an old log."

"We should do something," Michael said. "We just can't do nothing. It's stuck on something, or weighted down, so it'll never come ashore."

"Let's just go," Sue said, "and tell somebody. Let them get it. We're just kids in high school. What can we do about it? If it's really a body we should get someone. Let's tell your grandfather. He'll know what to do."

"If we wait too long it might float away by then," Michael said. "The river's pretty strong, and carries everything downstream. If it's a body we might be helping to solve a crime. You wait here, and I'll go out to get it."

"I don't know," Sue said. "I don't know."

"I have to see what it is," Michael said. "I can do it! It'll be fine."

"Okay, Michael, I'll wait here, but if you get in any trouble out there, wave or signal, and I'll get help."

"Don't worry," Michael said, "I'll be fine." Off went his sneakers, socks, shirt, and jeans. Then he took the star-shaped amulet that his grandfather had given him from around his neck, and said, "Sue, hold on to this for me." He stood there in his underwear grinning. "Sure you don't want to come?"

She laughed at Michael standing there in his underwear. "I'm not taking off my clothes. What if someone came along, and saw me?"

"They'll see a beautiful girl," he said. "And anyway, you're wearing shorts; just keep your clothes on." Michael stood for a moment, took a deep breath, then gingerly stepped into the water. "It's a little cold," he wheezed, and took a deep breath. "I'll be okay once I'm out farther," he yelled in a higher voice. The cold river water swabbed his body, and he continued ahead until it was chest high.

"This is a crazy thing to do," she said, and watched his body slip through the water as he swam out to the bulk that was bobbing in the waves.

After a few minutes Michael rolled on his back with his eyes turned up to the sky, focusing on the clouds that were hanging high above him, and wondered why they seemed not to be moving. As Michael looked around across the water the waves pitched over his head, but he swam farther and farther. He was young, tenacious, and a good swimmer. Michael turned back to give Sue the thumbs up. She stood on the shore's edge, and he watched her step back away quickly before the water wash over her feet almost afraid to let it touch her skin. Her hair floated in the breeze, and she brushed from her face as her hand went up giving him an intimate wave. She placed the amulet around her neck as Buster stood at her side watching Michael. He turn away toward the floating hulk, throwing one arm out, then the other, kicking his feet, and making his way out to the object.

Michael was almost there, and could clearly see the body. *It is a man!* he thought, and took a deep breath, then ducked under the water. When his head burst up through the surface he shook the water from his face. A few moments after momentarily resting, a peculiar feeling overcame him and strange things began to happen in the sky. A myriad of flashbacks from dreams appeared as he swam farther. The images increased, so he stopped swimming, and just floated in one place trying to orient himself. *What's happening?* he thought, blinking, then with his eyes wide open he seemed locked in a trance. A spree of images from different dreams he'd had flooded the landscape. They seemed to leak out of his mind, and appeared everywhere around him. He shook his head to clear them away and again heard the dog barking on shore. He whirled around looking back, sweeping the shore where Sue had been standing, but only saw Buster barking, jumping, agitated.

Where's Sue? he thought, and looked around perplexed because she was nowhere in sight.

He moved closer to see the floating hulk in front of him, then flipped it over, revealing the pale wasted face of a gray haired man. "This guys been shot!" he said, and focused on the large hole in the man's chest. *Looks like a shotgun did this.* The water had begun to wash the wound clean, leaving only traces of blood. "Wait till Sue sees this," he said, and grabbed hold of the body, then started back to the shore. Finally able to pull the body to where his dog waited on shore he dropped to his knees exhausted and wiped the water from his face. "Sue?" he yelled, then looked around at the trees, shore, and backwater. "Sue!" *Where is she?*

Michael's focus went back to the body that he'd dragged out of the water, then knelt next to it and rolled it over. He heard footsteps on the brush and his head snapped up turning toward the trees. Someone was walking through the woods toward him. *Sue must be coming back,* he thought. Buster turned toward the sound barking in an unbroken cycle. Michael grabbed his clothes, and threw them on quickly. As he put on his shoes he saw a slim older man of average height with slicked back gray hair exit the trees and stop at the edge of the forest. This man stood at the tree line brushing the chaparral from his black clothes. When the man looked up, Michael could see he sported a thin moustache with a face that bore determined stern features that projected a hostile look.

More images of places, faces, and sounds, flashed in Michael's mind, then the images spun around like a carousal becoming a blur. Generations of family went by, young people grew old, and he wondered how this could be. *What's happening? Who are these people?* "I think I know them."

Still at the edge of the tree line, the man cleared his throat, and said, "I see by the look on your face that you're beginning to understand and remember things." The man walked closer. "I'm here for the body you just pulled out of the water."

"The body?"

"Yes, that dead man has something I want, but have to take care of you first."

"Don't know anything about the dead man, but I do know who you are," Michael said, because he was remembering things from the past, or another time. Confused by all of this Michael moved away from the body toward the tree line, away from the man with Buster following at his side.

The man walked closer to the body. "I'm afraid you can't know that I was here, or what happened, so all of your memory has to be . . . wiped away. And there's only one way to do that."

"What are you going to do?"

"I think you understand what I'm going to do with you." the man said with a sinister voice followed by cracking laugh.

Michael backed away, and Buster's barking grew mad, "I can't do anything to you," Michael said. "I'm just a kid."

"I have to end this here," the man said. "And getting rid of you, and that grandfather of yours, is at the top of my list, and of the utmost importance."

Michael moved closer to the woods, stood still a moment and thought, *I've got to get out of here!* Without warning, he bolted, and ran with Buster close behind, breathing quick, hard, and deep, sprinting for his life. He turned to see if the old man was following behind, but saw nothing.

"Got to run faster," he said. "Faster, faster, faster," he repeated as his footsteps hammered the ground, branches brushing his arms as he pushed them aside. Buster took off in front of Michael and took the lead. "Buster wait!" he yelled. "Wait!" but the dog vanished from sight, and his barking faded. Michael stopped when he got to the edge of the woods, then fell to his knees, out of breath.

When he looked up he saw the cabin and his grandfather, Nick, on the deck with Buster. Michael jumped to his feet, running and shouting, "Poppi, Poppi!"

Nick turned when he heard the kid yelling for him, and stepped off the deck, then made his way toward Michael.

Michael yelled, "Sue's gone, and there's a man," he fell again, then stood looking back at the woods. "A guy in the woods is chasing me!"

"What man?" Nick asked, then he realized who it was.

Michael ran to Nick. "It's okay, Michael, it's okay. I'll take care of this, go to the cabin."

Then the man who'd been chasing Michael emerged from the edge of the woods, with a face expressing a feeling of recognition as he stopped and looked around. A moment later he spotted Nick, and said, "Well, my friend, it's been a long time, or seems that way, but we both know time is relative to us." He laughed as he walked following the tree line eyeing Nick, and grinning with pleasure.

Nick did know the man, and saw his hate emanating, a seething long time hate that had built up over the years, decades, and generations. "I'm not letting you go this time," Nick said. "You'll never leave this place, it finishes here. It's ends here!"

"I agree," the man said. "I remember your kind gesture years ago from another time. I haven't forgotten what you did for me back then, but I'm afraid it doesn't count for anything now. I must say that you look so much older, almost respectable with the gray hair and beard. I feel that I should show you some respect, but let me be blunt, I won't let you or the young lad go. I'm afraid this is the end for both of you!"

"So, let's get to it, then," Nick said, and approached the man. Nick grabbed and held a star-shaped amulet that hung on a chain around his neck. Nick was surprised when the man did the same, but was pushed back by the heat emanating from Nick's outstretched hand.

Thoughts and memories from both their pasts flooded the sky, flashing all around backward in time, to the present, then forward in time. They approached each other, circling, closer. A glow of color pulsated, roaring air-waves moved outward into the trees creating a wind that bent them to the ground. Then both men rose above the ground, higher and higher, spinning slowly, then faster at a dizzying hypnotic speed until they were a blur. Michael stood on the deck watching them turning faster, then rising upward and downward, attracting and repelling.

Then a chime sounded, the peal of a bell flowing 360 degrees out through the air like a clapper striking the soundbow marking a baptism. One loud toll that echoed and resonated on and on, like it would never end. It broke the waves of space, the ground vibrated, sending flocks of birds flying up into the sky and animals running in a panic. Michael turned from watching them at each others throats spinning in the clouds to seeing where the ringing bell sound was coming from, but it seemed to be everywhere and all around. It rang on and became so loud Michael covered his ears, but still felt the vibrations going through his body. Now Nick and the man had also become aware of the ringing echoing bell toll, they separated, and fell to the ground. Soon the sound faded, and there was only silence, a peaceful moment in time. A moment later, high above in the sky from behind pulsating glowing clouds, the shadow of another man appeared.

THE COLTS

Michael Colt sat up in bed like he'd been struck by a bolt of lightning, dazed, with rills of sweat running down his face. He felt tired, and he sat blinking and looking frantically around the room like he'd just come back from a long trip and wasn't quite sure where he'd been or now was. Just like a traveler who had gone through time and space exploring distant worlds that only exist in the back of one's mind, and totally exhausted after partying the night away.

"Man, now that was a party," he said as he felt his head throb in time with last night's music still ringing in his ears. Michael Colt closed his eyes, fell back onto the bed, and moaned, "A long . . . night. That it was!"

Michael was at a birthday party for Sue's dad, the owner of Outsider's Inn. They went there early, stayed late, the result being a hangover he wished he didn't have.

"All I remember is pouring lots of drinks for people, and more than a few down my own throat. Did I do anything stupid at the bar? I did a lot of toasting, played pool, then Sue came back here with me." He sniffed the air. "I can still smell her perfume," then he looked around the room, "but she's not here. Is she's downstairs? Don't hear anything. I guess she's left?"

Sitting quietly, he looked over at the window. "The ferns look happy soaking in the light," he mumbled. They were a gift from Sue, and hung on either side of the bedroom window, glowing in the sunlight. "Do they look out of balance, or is it just me?" he said. "Me, I guess. I'm out of balance from too much booze last night, they look fine now." His focus changed to the cactus on the desk, then to the dog, a black and brown collie sleeping on the rug. During a brief time of silence, he organized his thoughts, and things around him finally came into focus. Using the one hand he could move, he swept back his curly brown hair and ran his fingers through a beard that had grown longer. While he sat quietly still half asleep, he mumbled, "Man, sometimes when I wake up in the morning, it feels like coming back from the dead," then he let out a gasp. "But how would I know how that feels? I'd have to die and come back to life, but that's impossible." It was quiet in the room, then he whispered, "The days seem to go by slowly, but then before I know it, a whole year's gone by."

He yawned, and his lungs wheezed as he inhaled the stale air that had been trapped in the room. After releasing the carbon dioxide in one breath he said, "That should keep the plants by the window happy and drunk for a while." He clinched his teeth firmly together while grinding them, then with the same hand he wiped grains of sleep from his glossed over eyes, then coughed to clear his clogged throat. He tried lifting his other arm, but it was numb because he'd been sleeping on it. He yelled, "Damn," and groaned while shaking it trying to clench his fingers into a fist, then growled, "C'mon, wake up!"

because it felt like it had been numb forever. When the pins-and-needles feeling floated under the skin, he knew he'd massaged the muscles back to life. "Now, I'm awake," he said, "and so is my arm." Then as if an electric switch had been turned on, power returned, and his fingers moved. He watched his calloused hand clench into a fist, then release, extending his fingers outward a couple of times, squeezing tighter and tighter each time.

Glancing at a beer can he'd left on the night table he said, "Let's see how well it works," then reached out, grabbed the can of beer from the desk, and drank what was left from the night before. "Swill," he said after a sip, then gulped and swallowed all the slag left in the can, coughing. "That is some skunk-piss," he said, gagging and coughing, then shook his head in disbelief as he looked at the can. "I knew it was going to be some warm shit, so why the hell did I drink it? The mysteries of life . . . we never know why we do certain things." He squeezed the can flat between the palms of his hands and eyed the metal trash can on the other side of the room. Up the can went in a high arc, spinning like a Frisbee. A moment later there was a flat thud, a kind of dead-bell sound when it hit the inside, then some tinny clatter as it fell on the other cans. "Score one for me," he said.

He closed his eyes and remembered the long night he'd woken from. "Of all the dreams I could have, why do I keep having the same ones over and over? And why are parts and pieces missing? It's a crazy puzzle with everything all mixed up, and I don't get how things jump from time to time and place to place. Normal, I guess, and the same for all who dream. I could stop drinking, maybe that would help," he said. His gaze turned downward to the small triangular-shaped amulet hanging from a thin silver chain around his neck. He reached down and held it in his hand, rubbing it with his fingers and thumb, finally squeezing it in his fist. The longer he held it, the warmer it became until it was so hot he had to let it go. "Why did Poppi tell me to wear this thing all the time? I still wonder why. It's just a piece of glass with some drops of gold liquid inside. What is this thing?"

Michael recalled asking his grandfather about the amulet with the gold liquid. "King's water," he told me. "I think king's water is used to test if gold is real or not," Michael whispered, then held the amulet up to the light that flickered through the window. He shook it, and watched it glisten. "What is this thing?" he said, and finally let it go. He rose and stretched his arms high in the air, clasped his hands together, then lowered them behind his head slowly. He turned his head to the left, which instigated some synchronized bone cracking in his neck, then twisted his back to the right with the sound of more popping and cracking. Michael was in pretty good shape, but he was a mason, and all the lifting he'd done up to now was catching up. Aches and pains in the morning were part of the routine.

"Nothing wrong with hard work," he said, "and I like building things with stone, but don't want to do it for the rest of my life." He turned to the computer on the desk. "Got to finish my book and find an agent to help sell it." His eyes panned the room. "My life's here in front of me because most everything I've grown up with is in this cabin, hanging on the wall, in the closet, under or behind something." Of course the things in the room brought back incredible memories: old baseball glove and bat, baseball cards, comic books, clothes, shoes, fishing poles, books, miscellaneous odds and ends of no value to anyone else. Even things that had belonged to his father and grandfather seem to hold a stronger-than-usual sentimental value.

"Why do I keep all of this junk?"

And, on other the other side of the room he kept the rejection letters from book agents and publishers. He had pinned them on the wall next to the bookshelf as a reminder of his goal: to finish and publish his book. There they were arranged like avant-garde art wall paper, a sort of memorial to failure, and he had a belief he would overcome it. Hanging just above them to protest this failure, a quote he'd found.

> 'Live in the past and regret,
> Live in the future and worry,
> Live in the present—and be!'

Michael thought about the book *Being and Time*, written by Martin Heidegger, and what he said,

> 'The possible ranks higher than the actual'.

"Sometimes it doesn't take much to make the possible happen—only the decision to act," Michael said, then stood, and marched to the bookshelf on the other side of the room.

"Just acting on a thought can change everything, either for good or bad."

He grabbed a book from the shelf, opened it, and read another quote. This one was from Henry Ford, the inventor of the assembly line.

> 'If you think you can or can't you're always right'.

"He was definitely right about that. Maybe I'm too negative in my thinking. I wonder if I'll ever find an agent to help sell my book. Got to think it's possible, got to think positive, got to think it can happen."

But then all of the letters and emails he received basically repeat the same old story that boiled down to, sorry, but we're not interested in your book at this time. We wish you the best of luck in your endeavors. When read between the lines, it really meant "screw off," we don't need your crappy book, or care about a nobody.

"I'll bet most of them never looked at or read any part of my book," he said. "And that one agent in particular probably didn't. He seems to really have it out for me. His letters are downright nasty."

Some were so negative that Michael kept them in a special place on the shelf.

"Why do I keep writing back to this guy, and why does he keep replying?"

He grabbed the most recent one from the shelf and read it again.

```
Mr. Colt,
Your manuscript, and I'm being
generous when I say that, has found a
new home in my circular file. Why I'm
even wasting my time writing you even
has me baffled, so the only reason must
be to save the world from seeing or
reading it.
     The collection of drivel you've
written, and I'm saying that loosely,
needs to be burned! The words must be
purified and cleansed from pages that
had better been left blank, so more
proficient writers could use them
instead. You've abused the English
```

```
language by writing sentences of
complete nonsensical gibberish.
```

```
     So please stop the mind-bending
pain for all of us who are readers/
writers of genuine literature. Tell me
you'll pursue whatever else it is that
you do to make a living, and discard/
delete this pile of pulp that you call
writing.
```

```
     Perhaps digging ditches is more
in line with your talent, or perhaps
sweeping streets. Thankfully this paper
can be recycled, so all is not lost.
```

```
     R. Lee
```

"I hate that guy, Michael said. "Mr. R. Lee doesn't know what he's talking about, and I won't give up because of what he thinks of my book. I'll keep making improvements, and sending him letters until he chokes on them." Then he ripped the letter into tiny pieces and threw them into the air. Michael raised his eyes to the ceiling and smiled as the pieces of paper floated down all around him to the floor. "I'm going to finish my book," he said, "and publish it myself if I have to!"

Looking out the window he watched the trees swaying in the breeze like they were painting clouds on a blue sky, but his thoughts soon went back to publishing the book. "I'll keep trying to find an agent; there's got to be one out there that likes my story. So how do I find that one agent and get a book deal? I've tried everything I can think of— or have I? Need to get some interest going about the book. Just have to find the right person."

He opened the window, leaned out, and took a few deep breaths. "Maybe I'll have to do the whole thing myself," he said. "Maybe there's no other way. I've worked on it off and on for years, written and edited whenever I've had the chance, day and night. I've put so much effort into this thing." He turned and looked at the pieces of the rejection letter on the floor, then scraped them into his hands. "Just have to keep tweaking and polishing the story because it's more or less finished. Hell, I can't stop now, can't just quit after putting so much time into it. Making a living as a writer is the goal, expressing what I know and feel into a story." He dropped the small bits of paper into the trash can, and while watching them glide down, said, "I wonder if it'll always just be a dream."

Michael went outside and stood on the deck looking at the truck he used to haul stone and tools to jobs. "I can't believe that old thing still runs." It was beat up, and he'd had it a long time. He stood where Sue always parked her car, but there was no car. "I guess she's gone home," he said, then thought, *Why do I do this kind of work?* "Just have to bide my time for now, and settle for being a stone mason like Poppi," he said. "It's an honorable line of work, and it seems to come naturally to me. Maybe it would be easier to find an agent if I wrote about masonry work and laying brick? It's what I do."

Michael's phone rang, and he knew the caller. "Yeah, morning," he said.

"When are you bringing the stone for the fireplace? I'm waiting at the Vortrich place."

"Hey, Moses, sorry," Michael said, "got a late start this morning. I stayed at the party way too long. I'll bring the stone tomorrow; let's take the day off today. How are you feeling this morning? You were there pretty late too?"

"I feel fine," Moses said. "Okay, I'll do what I can here, and see you at the shop later. Want to finish up this job and get paid. But, okay, let's work on it tomorrow for sure!"

"Don't worry," Michael said. "I'll be there. Say, Moses, let me ask you something. I'm thinking about writing a how-to book on being a mason. You know, stuff like laying stone and brick. Maybe add techniques on mixing mortar, dry set masonry, and grouting. Choosing the right trowel; how to grip, load, and butter joints. Tricks on using a mason hammer to split brick, maybe write about the chisels needed, using the six-vial level, and brick mason's folding ruler for spacing."

"Good stuff to write about," Moses said. "Masons go way back in history. They've left their mark in stone everywhere on earth. People are interested in building. What's happening with the other book you're writing? You finished, right? You said you were. When can I read it?"

"More or less," Michael said. "Just some editing left."

"I'll help you anyway I can," Moses said, "and as much as I can. Well, you rest up today, and make sure you get that stone here tomorrow, so we can finish this fireplace. We can talk about books later."

"Take it easy, Moses."

Michael knew about mason work and building structures with stone, blocks, and brick because he had worked with his grandfather, Nick, since he was a kid. He called him Poppi as long as he could remember. Michael looked up to Nick, a robust outdoorsman who hunted, fished, and celebrated with drink on occasion. And later Michael worked with Moses, Nick's partner, after school and during summer vacation. Michael sometimes called him Uncle Moses, but there was no blood relation. Moses was from parts unknown, and from what Poppi had told Michael, he was a guy who just showed up one day looking for a job. Nick hired him, and they got along from the very beginning.

Moses worked with Nick after being discharged from the Army; Nick showed him the art of building with stone, then became a partner. Nick had put time in the service too, so they got along even though there was an age gap. Michael learned many things from these two guys. Nick and Moses were always talking about masonry, the Army, and guns. Nick and Moses always had beards, and were tall and stocky, so when Michael was young he thought they both looked like grizzly bears.

When on a job, Nick and Moses always told Michael he had "pattern", which meant he instinctively knew how to put or place each stone for the best visual configuration. They told him that even though every stone was randomly broken into odd shapes and sizes, they could be put together like a puzzle. They said he had a gift he was using without knowing, without thinking, doing it almost like magic, and one day he would understand why. It was like telling a story and leaving a mark that would be around for years to come. Not only did Michael learn how to lay stone and brick, but he got stronger after years of lifting it. Soon Michael could hold and toss bricks like a juggler, and would look like Nick and Moses: brawny, powerful, like a grizzly bear.

Every morning Nick made coffee and cooked breakfast after he showered and got dressed. He always sat at his desk and checked his schedule for the day. Working outside in rain or shine all the time gave them all a rough outdoor Viking look. Being a Hungry Point resident and having the name Colt meant guns, hunting, fishing, and camping on the river. Nick wasn't sure if he actually was related to the famous gunsmith, but liked to let on that he was, and would tell stories that made it seem so at the only bar in the area.

SCHOOL DAYS

After a day's work they sometimes stopped by Outsider's Inn, the bar in Hungry Point that was owned by a man called Jeremiah Kick, the son of a man with the same name, and the previous owner. Like his dad, Jeremiah was the talkative sort, short, stout, had a crew cut and handlebar moustache. Since this bar was the only place to get a drink, business was always good. The building was a log structure, solid, quaint, old, and stayed open way after midnight. Kick had an adopted daughter, Sue. She went to school with Michael, and they became quick and close friends maybe because both had lost their parents when they were young. Sue's parents had died soon after she was born, just as Michael's had.

They grew up discovering life together. They rode bikes to the same meeting place every morning to catch the bus to school, and talked about what they were going to be when they grew up. The bus stopped a few times to pick up more kids on the way, and took thirty minutes to school along a scenic road that stretched along the river to a town called Dodge. On occasion they'd skip school and spend the day at the river talking, fishing, and exploring. Michael kept some fishing gear in a hideout they'd built from branches and other miscellaneous material collected from the river. He built a makeshift grill from wire and river stones, while Sue brought some pots, pans, and dishes from home.

Once they found that wine made them feel good, she would occasionally lift a bottle from her step dad's bar, and their weekend getaways became something to look forward to. They would imagine and dream they were spies on a mission in a foreign country after Michael would re-tell some of Poppi's bed-time spy stories. He bought a transistor radio that could pick up some of the local radio stations. The sounds of drums, guitars, and piano echoed through the woods. They'd gather driftwood, embrace nature, and listen to the flowing river until late at night under the moonlight.

"I've always wanted to ask you about that thing you have around your neck. Where did it come from?"

"It was a gift," Michael said.

"A gift? From who?"

"My grandfather gave it to me a long time ago. He told me to always wear it, and never take it off. That it was special, and someday I would know why. "

"What's so special about it?"

"I really don't know. It's just what he said to do, so I listened to him. I know he wouldn't have told me to do it if it wasn't important."

"Can I see it?"

"Sure," Michael said, then lifted it from his neck, and handed it over to Sue.

"So light," she said surprised, "but looks heavier than it really is."

"Yeah, I guess. Go ahead and try it on."

She dropped the amulet over her head, and once it had settled around her neck, she held it. "Wow, it's hot!"

"I know," Michael said, "it gets that way after holding it."

"Amazing," she said, and let it go. "Where did he get it from?"

"Don't know, he's never said where he got it."

"It sure looks interesting," Sue said. "Here, better put it back on," and handed it back to Michael.

"Poppi said he'd tell me more about it when I'm older."

"It looks and glows like a star," Sue said.

"It does, doesn't it?" Michael said, and they relaxed in the calm of the evening, resting on the ground, listening to the river, and watching the night sky glisten above.

Outsider's Inn was where and how Hungry Point news got shared. Nick Colt was a mason, but he did carpentry work when asked. Nick made the sign that stood in front of the bar, and did repairs if they were needed. He built the huge stone fireplace that stood off to the side of the bar. Inside, hanging on the walls of the bar, were mounted trophy bucks and fish. An old pool table with leather pockets sat parallel to the bar. Scattered around the room were some wooden tables and chairs that Nick Colt had built from wooden pallets that the brick and stone were delivered on. Some nights a game of poker was played until the sun came up the next morning.

If you looked out the window of the bar you could see the building that housed the Post Office across the street, and that's where the Game Warden's office was located. Hungry Point was too small to have a sheriff, and wasn't even classified as a town, just a sleepy village on the Mississippi River. It had a small restaurant; breakfast and lunch were the busiest times of day. Jim's

Hardware was a chaotic place filled with nuts, bolts, and odds and ends for fixing whatever was broken. Jim had a machine shop in his garage, and could make parts for just about anything.

All anyone knew was that Nick Colt ended up in Hungry Point working as a stone mason after a stint in the Army. And before Michael was a year old his parents were killed in a car accident, or at least that's what he had been told by Nick. He had no memory of his father or mother, and only knew them from photos. Michael's first memories were fishing and swimming in the Mississippi. When his grandfather thought Michael was old enough to understand, he told him how his parents had died in a car accident. But as time went by, the story changed. First they were driving home from a fishing trip, then it was after a Christmas party, and finally after having dinner at a restaurant. Michael wondered why the story changed again and again, but shrugged it off because Poppi was getting older. But sometimes he wasn't sure, and thought there was some other reason for the contradictions.

On occasion, at home alone, he'd look through family photo albums that were kept in a trunk in a closet. In most of the pictures, the guy Nick had told him was his dad looked young, clean-shaven, stocky, and resembled his grandfather Poppi. In some of them he wore an Army uniform posing with other soldiers at different places. It looked like a few photos were taken near water, a river or lake, sometimes sitting on the bank holding fishing poles. In others there was a woman with short wavy hair who seemed to be too fashionably dressed for a fishing trip, and she looked to him to be a little out of place. He later learned that this was his mother.

In a few of the pictures there was a German Shepard, and scribbled at the bottom was the name Buster. There were pictures of them in mountains, skiing, riding horses, and sitting in front of cafes. He'd heard stories about his parents from Nick, and wanted to find out as much as he could about them. Looking through the album he thought, *We will never meet, and these pictures are the only way I'll ever know you. I feel as if we've met, almost like I've been to the places in these pictures and that we are close. But why?*

At school Michael wanted to learn all he could about writing. There were two English classes with teachers whose nicknames were Big C, a rotund woman, and Little A, who was petite. Both were competent teachers who held classes that were interesting and occasionally fun. Michael read everything in the school's library and anything else he could get his hands on to improve his writing. When he felt ready, the work on his book began. He'd been outlining it with pen and paper, then got a computer from and the process sped up. The book slowly grew in size, page after page, little by little, day by day, using Poppi's stories. Then the editing process began.

Sometimes he would write with Sue in the room, and he would notice how she was growing into quite the young woman, so there were a lot of pauses. She'd always been slim, and now Michael could see how her body was changing. She never changed her simple straight hair. It brushed her shoulders and occasionally covered her face to give her a mysterious aura. In the right light she looked like a picture he'd seen of Greta Garbo. Sue supported Michael, but she was interested in business, and usually talked about the customers who came into the bar. She could talk to anybody about anything while memorizing them with a wide entrancing smile. She wanted to change the place to make it more modern, so she carried a notebook, filling it with ideas and sketches of the way she wanted the bar to look. She had plans, and was determined to make them a reality.

Michael put on weight and started to run on the trails to the river, and ride his bike more and more. Lifting concrete blocks and stone had built his body into a frame that was lean and muscular. There was one spot at the top of a hill next to the river that he would climb, and could see the whole river valley. Once in a while he would drop by the bar and help Sue with cleaning after the place got trashed the night before.

They were together a lot, before, during, and after school, sometimes passing time just sitting on the grass near the cabin Poppi built, just watching the trees waver in the breeze. They went for walks to the river on every trail they knew, and blazed some new ones as well. Just passing the days, talking, singing, and laughing. Time had stopped it seemed, and it would stay this way forever. At least that's what he thought.

In high school Michael gradually seemed to think he lived in two worlds: one where he was a kid growing up learning new things, and another where he was older watching his life from a distance. *If I could see what was going to happen in the future, I could change the outcome.* The future became an important issue for him, and he talked about it with Sue at school whenever they were together more and more. "What do you think happens to us after we die?" Michael asked.

"I think everyone would like the answer to that," she said. "I guess it depends on what you believe. I really haven't thought about it that much, too busy with school and stuff. We're young, so why think about death and dying?"

He looked at Sue, and said, "You must think about it a little. It must have crossed your mind at some point. Haven't you ever been in a tight situation? Ever think, once my eyes close for the last time, I'll never see this world again?"

"So far nothing that serious has happened to me. If I do think about what happens when we die, it's for other reasons."

"I wonder if it's over after we die," he said. "You know, like cutting down a tree. I know our body stops working, but what about all of our thoughts, ideas, and what happens to our consciousness? There's a lot of energy there, so what happens to it? No one knows if we go to another place, world, or dimension. See that tree over there. We can only see the branches, but it has roots below the ground, and that's a whole different world."

"Let's go for a walk down by river," Sue said, wanting to change the topic.

"Okay," he said. "You know the river is kind of like a tree, we only see what's on the surface, but there's a whole different world under the surface, and it keeps flowing around and around."

"I like walking next to the river," Sue said. "I feel at home here."

"Me too," Michael said. "Let's go to our shack. We haven't been there for a while."

They walked down the trail in the forest and came to an opening. "There it is, still standing," Sue said. "We've had some good times there. Let's go inside."

"What are you doing after graduation, Sue?"

"I guess I'll help dad with the bar. I really want to make it into something special."

"You're staying in Hungry Point?"

"I don't know," she said. "I like it here, and I think he's expecting me to help him. What about you?"

"Guess I'll stick around and help Moses with the business."

They sat on the floor of the hut and watched the river flow by, then Michael leaned over and kissed Sue on the cheek. He took in her aroma while he embraced her. They kissed again, and felt each others warmth. "I love you, Sue."

BEDTIME STORIES

As Michael went back into the cabin he looked up at the old clock that hung above the kitchen door. *That's been hanging there since I was a kid.* "Six thirty," he said. "Boy, that clock sure is old."

At that moment memories of when he was growing up, and how he'd always gotten up early came back to him. He'd check the time on that clock and, after eating, go for walks to the river with Buster and Nick. It was fun, but it was also a time for learning about nature. Nick knew a lot about plants, animals, fishing, and the river. There were trails and high points where one could get a good view of actual size of the river. Nick said the name came from the Ojibwa word, Misi-Ziibi, and, translated, it literally meant Big River. He talked about the source at Lake Itasca, the tributaries, and the mouth where it emptied into the Gulf of Mexico. Poppi said the river was 2,340 miles long, and it bordered states all the way from the Canada to the gulf. The people who lived on or near the river used it as a highway to transport goods by boat, so trade grew up and down the river. Some of the first cultures in the area thrived on what Poppi called the three sisters: maize, beans, and squash. Two famous French explorers, Marquette and Joliet, traveled the river and found it the quickest way from Canada. Soon after more explorers arrived, then steamboats and the stories from Mark Twain's book *Tom Sawyer*. It was an exciting time of growth. The music that was played had its own flavor too, along with numerous songs about the river, and people who lived along it.

Even though the Mississippi is lined with trees that aid in stopping erosion, many roots of trees are visible when you take a boat ride down it, and you can clearly see where the water has washed away the soil. There are pine trees, cattails, moss, water-lilies, duckweed, and a variety of frogs, toads, catfish, turtles, spiders, and bugs. The river and the banks of the river teem with life, and waterfowl use it for migration. Everything that falls into the river eventually flows out into the Gulf of Mexico and into the oceans of the earth.

Now that he was awake Michael went through his usual morning routine: out to the kitchen, made some coffee, fried a couple of eggs, then grabbed his schedule book. His head still throbbing a bit, he checked what jobs he had lined up for the week. At the same time he tried to remember the dream he'd had that morning. It was like a vague event that actually happened years before and all the small details were muddy like the river. One thing he did remember was a shadowy figure that walked in hallways, on the street, or stood still, waiting for someone or something. In one hand the figure carried a bag that resembled a briefcase. This image melted and blended into an unrecognizable figure. He wasn't sure what he held in the other hand, but it could have been a gun.

Michael sat at the old oak desk built by his grandfather. He reached out, touched the top, and ran his hand over the wood. He was amazed by the fine work and how it all fit together so well. This was where Poppi had always done his paperwork, and when Michael sat at the desk, he couldn't explain it, but he had this strange feeling that he'd always belonged there. *It's like I had built it instead of Poppi. I think I remember watching him make it when I was young. It's a strange feeling.* He always sat quietly for a few minutes before he did any work there because that reaction and feeling never left him.

He turned on the computer, and opened a file labeled DK. It was an abbreviation for the book he hoped to write titled, *Dream Killer.* He wasn't sure why he called it that; the name just came to him one day when he was sitting by the riverside watching the sun set.

Every night without fail Nick would tell Michael stories at bedtime. Sometimes the stories would continue from the previous night, other times he'd start a brand new one, but they were all connected through the characters and the story. They were about a guy who could get out of any tough situation, a guy who always came through, who could solve and get out of the most hopeless of circumstances time after time. The bedtime stories were so real they were forever etched in Michael's mind. The ideas for the book he was writing came from the bedtime stories Nick had told him, and they were written like narration in his grandfather's voice telling Michael a bedtime story. He read from the first page thinking about what to change or modify, if anything.

"I really feel like I know this guy that Nick told me about in the stories," Michael said. He remembered it as if he were listening to Poppi, and almost like he was inside Michael's head.

Bedtime Stories and Dreams—Memories of Michael Colt—The Driver

"An iconic black car raced down a narrow cliff-side road chasing after a similar white sports coupe. A middle-aged burley man with a russet complexion and slick black hair rolled down the passenger side window. He balanced the barrel of a semi-automatic weapon out the window, and his hands were steady as he aimed." Poppi gestured as if he were holding a rifle.

"Burley means big, right Poppi?"

"Yes, it does, and husky or stout."

"What about russet?"

"Maybe dark and rough, like leather on a wear-worn shoe."

"You mean like if someone works in the sun or spends a lot of time outside?"

"Yeah, that's right, and it could be the reason for a russet complexion. Just imagine he's a rugged and tough looking guy like Moses."

"Right, Uncle Moses is always outside, lifting stones, concrete blocks, building walls, and fireplaces. He's a big tough guy; no one would ever mess with him. What's iconic?"

"Kid, you ask a lot of questions, but that's good. Well, it means . . . a symbol for something, something well-known. Could be a famous painting, like the Andy Warhol Campbell's Soup painting, an icon in baseball is Babe Ruth, and any famous emblem or logo is an icon."

"Is your Colt .45 an icon?"

"Yes, the Colt's iconic. It was and still is a part of a cowboy's and soldier's wardrobe."

"Tell me what happens next in the story?"

"Okay, right, well we got off track there a little, didn't we? Back to the story then, so after adjusting his sunglasses in a way that meant business, the man in the car with the weapon fixed his index finger on the trigger." Then in a low quiet voice, Poppi said, "He moved his index finger slowly across, and up and down, massaging the trigger. BAM-BAM-BAM!" Michael jumped, and Poppi laughed. "Gotcha! Sorry, I'm just trying to make the story more realistic."

"That did scare me, Poppi, but keep going because it does seem real, and sounds like a dream I've had before."

"Okay, kid," Nick said, and kept on with the story. "Gunfire exploded, shattering the rear window of the white car, and glass flew everywhere. The driver of the white sports car was swerving across the road out of control, zigzagging, trying to avoid the barrage of lead. After he was back in control, he brushed off the pieces of broken glass from his leather coat, and kept driving."

"Wow!" Michael said, mesmerized, while watching Nick's wild arm and hand gestures.

"Then bam!" Nick punched his fist. "The white car slammed into, then scraped along the cliff-side concrete guardrail. The driver lost control for a moment while trying to check the damage to the front fender.

"Below, very far down the cliff, he watched the raging sea crash between large rocks jutting from the coastline."

"Did he drive off the road?"

"It looked like it was the last round-up for him." Then Nick stopped talking, smiled at Michael a moment, and waited a while, building tension.

"Did the car roll down the cliff? What happened next? Come on, tell me."

"Hold on, let me think" Nick said. "Okay, more bullets ricocheted through the interior of the white car, breaking out the windows leaving, shards of glass on the road, and all over the floor of the car."

"What are shards?"

"Sharp pieces glass from the car's windshield."

"Okay, I get it, then what?"

"The chunks of broken glass left hanging in the window frame looked like frozen icicles. Then, as the driver of the white car got control, the black car rammed into the rear bumper, snapping the driver's head back like the crack of a whip. The driver of the white car weaved and dodged on the road. Bullets glanced around, and through the white car as both of them crossed the center line many times and were on the verge of spinning out. The driver of the white car pushed the accelerator to the floor. He pulled away in control, and far enough in front of the pursuers to avoid the attack."

"Were the bullets coming from every direction?"

"This is just a story, so that can happen."

"What does verge mean?"

"It means on the line, a border, and the point at when something could go either way."

"So, anything could happen?"

"Yes, in a way, that's right. Sometimes what happens in a single moment determines the outcome, usually by the one who takes action first."

"Tell me what happens next."

"The cars raced side by side, bumping and smacking into each other as they approached a snow-capped mountain. At the base of the mountain was a tunnel that had been carved out years ago. The driver of the black car extended a weapon from his window and fired another barrage. Many bullets flew, but by some miraculous act of skilled driving, the white car avoided having its tires shot out."

"The guy in the white car is a pretty good driver?"

"Yes, he is, Michael. He's very good! Good at many things."

"Like what?"

"I'll tell you someday," Nick said, then got back to the story. "Around the cliff-side's hair-pin corners they pushed, shoved, and banged into each other more and more. They slowed to a crawl on corners, and raced out of the curves like being shot from a catapult. The dark tunnel opening grew in size, then a moment later they pierced the darkness side by side. The headlights of both cars switched on as engines echoed and reverberated in the cave-like space. Gunfire lit the tunnel like fireworks, and it cracked and echoed as an eruption of lead rained from the black car. The white car swerved back and forth staying in front, trying to hold off and block the attack. Using all the space of the road, he sped up and slowed down, but still returned no gunfire."

"What happened next?"

"Calmly and methodically the driver of the white car grabbed a round shiny metal object about the size of a tennis ball from the seat. He flicked a small lever on the top, and lobbed it out the window. The object flew up in a high arc, fell, and wedged in the grill of the black car."

"Wow!" Michael said. "Then what happened?"

"There was an explosion—flames, smoke, and a torrent of torn metal burst and splintered in all directions. Mangled bits from the explosion flew in all directions as the black car slid to a stop. The men inside the black car were burned, and unrecognizable. The driver of the white car opened a small brown embossed leather case. He removed and lit a cigar, blew the smoke out the window and said, 'That was a beauty,' then melted into the darkness of the tunnel."

"Who's the guy in the white car, Poppi? What's his name?"

"Good question, Michael," Nick said. "Let's see, what's the best way to answer that?"

"Poppi, you said you'd tell me who the driver is! C'mon!

"Well, it first started when he was a boy, and not much older than you, Michael. It happened after meeting a man who had some very special skills, so along with growing up on the street the world became his school, and from that point on he knew what his future would be."

"What future? What skills?"

"A future connected to the past, and skills that would involve him in dubious activity, and how he met the man who had helped him begin his journey. This boy, who'd grown into a man, had a change of heart, and got the idea of offering these special services he'd acquired during his life to the authorities."

"What did he do?"

"Well, crime was rampant at the time mostly due to him. He was alone now, and because he lived a life of crime, knew all the forgers, crooks, had their confidence, and was able to stop their illegal activity."

"What's rampant?

"Something out of control, untamed wild action that continues until it's stopped."

"Why did help?"

"Because he thought he could change the world, and make it a better place for all people. The authorities were so impressed at how efficient he worked that they asked him to create a special force."

"So he became an agent for them?" Michael asked.

"That's right, and the force he established was aggressive and successful. After working with them for many years, and creating this resourceful squad he wanted to resign, and publish his memoirs. He realized that he couldn't do this, because if the information in the book got into the hands of the wrong person they could destroy, and control everything. "

"What's in the book?"

"A sketch of his life, where he came from, and how he became the person he was."

"What happened to the book, and to him?"

"He went into hiding, and put the book in a secret place."

"No one knows where it is?"

"No they don't, but to this day there are some people who meet at different locations around the world talking about him, and the book."

"Where do they meet? What's the driver's real name? Where's the book?"

"Well, I'll save that for when you're older. Cover up now and go to sleep." With that being the last word, Nick pulled the blanket up to Michael's chin. He leaned over, brushed his grandson's hair back, and kissed him on the forehead.

"Good night, Poppi," Michael whispered.

"Good night, kid" he replied. "See you in the morning. Pleasant dreams," and switched off the lights.

MORNING RUN

One dream Michael had was not from a bedtime story, it was about one surreal morning when he was fifteen years old during summer vacation. When he dreamed about it Sue wasn't there, and he wondered why, because in his memory they were walking along the river together that morning. He'd never forgotten that morning, the time he walked to the river, and what he had found. The story was in the newspaper, on TV, and a re-occurring dream that never quit. He carried the incident in his memory forever.

This odd morning happened when he was a kid, and the day started as usual. First, he woke at the same time and spied his dog, a Shepard, sleeping on the floor next to his bed. Buster was given to him by a farmer, and was a puppy when he got him. When the dog was a pup, Michael always put the food in a Frisbee to train him to catch it, something he'd read about in a magazine. All you do is replace your dogs dish with a Frisbee, and it'll jump to the moon to get it back. Dogs love their bowl.

Michael was so surprised that it really worked, he told his friends, and they tried it as well.

Michael whistled; the dog raised its head and ears ready for an early hike to the river. They followed the same routine every morning. Michael got dressed, then went into the kitchen and tore off a hunk of bread, just enough to munch on during the hike to the river.

"Okay, Buster, let's go!"

Usually when they set out, Buster was always the first to bolt out the door and hit the woods running, but not today. Instead he stood and waited on the porch for a time sniffing at the air. He'd definitely caught the scent of something in the breeze that morning. Then like a horse at the track fixed at the gate, he bolted off the deck, running like a mad hound hot on the trail, hunting his prey. Buster never acted this way, and the barking grew frantic, and faded as he chased after him. Michael ran faster, following the sound of his dog on what he thought would typically be a daily jaunt through the forest to the river. This was their morning ritual, but today was different, strange. Today was definitely odd!

Hungry Point was established as a trading post many years ago, and had a long history of explorers stopping there to refit on the way to somewhere else. It was in a place where rivers intersected leaving numerous backwaters and streams that siphoned their supply of water off the Mississippi. Anyone could walk the worn trails made by local fishermen and hikers, so you'd never know who or what you'd run into; there could be a surprise waiting at any bend. Michael followed the barking, stopping a few times to listen and catch which way it was coming from, then he was hot on the trail again.

Michael changed paths every morning, but he had several favorite trails, and the one he was on now was the best. That morning sunlight flickered on the dew covered leaves, and the flora produced an enchanting aroma with an enticing atmosphere. The sky was first light blue, being painted before his eyes by an anonymous invisible artist who had a vast canvas to work on. With the sun up, and rising fast, everything surrounding him rose from the earth, strong, vivid, and hearty in color. He walked briskly after his dog Buster as shadows floated freely, reappearing quarks controlled by some invisible magical force appearing, then vanishing, never to be seen again.

Michael's thoughts were broken by Buster's frantic and incessant barking. He picked up the pace and ran down the twisting path, pushing the thick overgrowth out of the way, curious at Buster's unusual behavior. Michael knew this path; he'd walked it on many occasions, and was familiar with all of its oddities. The dog's steady barking echoed, and bounced in the air, seeming to come from different directions. The dog was after something that had captured its attention.

"Is he after another dog, a cat, a squirrel or some other animal?" Michael said. "He's never wailed on like this."

Breaking out of the trees he saw the backwater, the river, then his dog standing on the shore barking at waves of water rolling in and out of the shore without pause. Michael thought he'd heard someone walking behind him, and scanned everything in the vicinity as he made his way closer, turning and checking the path behind to see if he'd been followed. The air was filled with the sounds of birds calling, an occasional jumping fish, and off in the distance the rumbling echo of a boat motor. Now he spotted what the dog had smelled before ever seeing: a floating gray bulge bobbing in the middle of the backwater just far enough away to make it impossible to identify.

"What is that?" Michael whispered. "Is that what you smell?" he said, then knelt on one knee patting and rubbing Buster's head. "It's not a log," he said. "Looks like it's got arms and legs, but that can't be." He looked at his dog, and whispered, "Can't be a person, can it?"

The floating hulk drifted and dipped under the surface as waves caught up with it, forcing it to bobble more and more. The dog continued to bark, and Michael stared, wondering how to get whatever it was ashore. Getting soaked wasn't in his plan for this morning, but he wanted to know what was floating out there—curiosity had captured him. He watched his dog jumping and barking, more and more. *What if it is a body? And if it is, how'd it get here?*

"Let's go see what it is," he said, then took off his pants, shirt and shoes, but the dog hesitated as Michael stepped into the backwater. He looked back at his dog, it wouldn't budge. "Come on, Buster," Michael ordered, but Buster stayed on the shore barking like crazy as if he wanted to frighten off something. "Okay, stay there. I'll be right back."

The water got deeper with every step, and soon it was waist high. *Should I stop? Turn back? Go home to tell Poppi?* "I can't stop now," he muttered. "I've come this far and can't stop now." He continued forward, turning back occasionally to see Buster still making a ruckus on the shore, and barking at the wind.

Now the buoyant lump was in front of him about an arms length away. He put his hands underneath, pulled and lifted. It flipped it over. And that's when he saw a pale face staring back at him, and he fell backward stunned. Buster was still barking on shore like a warning of impending doom. Michael took a few deep breaths, held the last one a moment, then let it out slowly. Now he was in control and feeling composed even though he stood in waist high rising water that was sloshing around his waist. He hesitated to examine the body, but began a visual inspection. The man's face was pale, his mouth wide open with a gaze of surprise in his lifeless eyes. Michael noticed a gold ring on the guy's left hand, then to the water gurgling around the big hole in his chest.

"Shot!" Michael said, "He's been shot, and the wound looks fresh; could have happened some time early this morning."

Michael hunted with Nick and Moses and had seen animals shot, but this was the first time ever to see a dead man, so his heart raced. He took a few deep breaths, then began the chore of pushing the body to shore where Buster stood pawing at the ground, uneasiness in his howling and barking. Michael handled the situation like someone who was a lot older, as if he instinctually knew what to do.

"I'm coming," he said wiping water from his face. "Hold on dog, I'll be there soon." He muscled his way back, treading water, and close to shore his footing gave way, and went under, swallowing what seemed to be the whole river.

"Almost there!" he said, then coughed, spit out the water, wiped his face, and cleared his eyes. "Reach the shore," he said, "I can do it," and spit out more river water. "Made it finally!" Exhausted and breathing hard he grabbed the man's arms and dragged the body out of the water. He fell backwards, and dropped to the ground exhausted. After catching his breath, he rolled over on his stomach. He was soaked, covered in sand and mud, then he noticed Buster had stopped barking, and was now moaning and whining. The dog kept his distance, either from fear, as a warning, or a signal that something bad was about to happen.

"It's okay, Buster," Michael said. "I've got him, no need to worry, it's okay."

Michael stood with his attention on the dead man, looking over the corpse carefully. He knelt next to the body wondering what to do next. "His eyes are cloudy," he said, "and that hole in his chest's been washed clean by river water." *Should I check his pockets?*

Impulse took over and he knelt down looking for some identification. There was a waterlogged notebook with some pages missing. He looked through it and thought, *Why do these names and dates seem so familiar?* In another pocket he found a wallet, money, but no identification. In the wallet there was a black and white picture of a young woman wearing a turtle neck shirt and a knit cap. The background was white, and the picture a little washed out. *Looks like it was taken in the winter?*

The woman in the picture had an inviting smile, like she knew the person who had taken the photograph. Small catch lights were in the pupils of her eyes, and her short dark hair was combed back and pinned. *I think I've seen her before.* Michael put the picture in his pocket, then continued rummaging through the dead man's clothes finding a key. *This could be for a locker.* "Number eleven," he whispered. "Maybe it's for something valuable?"

He put the key, notebook, and wallet back in the man's pocket, grabbed his arms, and pulled him farther away from the water. The body was water-logged and heavy. "That's far enough," he said, and sat there staring at the dead guy thinking of what to do. *I'll cover the body with branches, then go home and tell Poppi*, he thought. With his dog at his side, he looked over his handiwork, then glanced down at Buster.

"There, that should be good enough." The dog whined. "Okay, let's get out of here and tell Poppi, he'll know what to do."

NAMELESS MAN

Michael knew the trail and what was ahead, so he ran on automatic pilot faster than ever before. "I'll never forget this day," he said, "the day I saw a dead man, and fished him out of the backwater." He collected his thoughts and what he might say to Poppi. *I'll tell him I went for a stroll with Buster to the river, Buster was acting strange, and I saw something floating in the backwater. Not sure what it was, but after getting closer, found it was a body.*

Down the narrow backwater path, ducking, angling, and twisting through the trees to avoid branches whipping into his face. He repeated what he would say to his grandpa in his mind over and over.

As he ran, he turned and looked at Buster. "You seem scared, dog. Why? Are we running from a ghost?"

At first, the dog stayed close behind, staying right on Michael's heels. As they got closer to the house, Buster charged out in front, and led the way back, then disappeared into the trees. Arriving at the forest edge, breathless, he stopped and fell to his knees. When Michael looked up he saw Poppi standing on the porch holding a coffee mug and enjoying a morning cigar. Nick hadn't noticed Michael catching his breath at the edge of the forest, but turned when he saw the dog run to the house.

"Buster!" Nick said. "Where's Michael?" Buster jumped on the porch with his tail wagging, barking, then jumped off the porch, stopped, and turned, barking wildly again.

From Nick's vantage point the terrain that lay in front of the cabin faced the east edge of the woods, and was easily scanned with a quick look. Michael had just walked out of the woods when Nick saw him fall to his knees near the brick path that led to the house. Michael waved, got up, then headed down the path that he had helped Nick build. The bricks were laid on ground without mortar, uneven, and grass had come up through the joints. Nick stepped off the porch, concern etched on his face, then when he saw Michael walking quickly toward him, yelled, "You okay? Okay, boy? What's wrong, kid?"

Michael was fidgety, bent over and panting after running full speed from the backwater. Sweat dripped from his face, his lungs were sore from breathing hard, and he still had images of the dead body he'd found carved in his brain.

"What's wrong, boy?" Nick asked. "You okay?"

"There's a body at the river ... a ... man," Michael said, short of breath, in shock, not able to get the words out in complete sentences.

"Slow down," Nick said. "Just breathe, don't talk, breathe." After a few minutes he looked at Michael. "What did you see by the river? Tell me kid, what's the matter?"

"There's a body," Michael said, who then collapsed, and fell on his face exhausted, his lungs sucking in air like a vacuum cleaner turning on and off.

Nick picked Michael up, held him firmly. "Tell me again," he said. "What did you see? You said there's a body? Where?"

"Floating in the backwater near the rope swing you made, where we jump into the water. I saw his face! It was a milky pale color, his eyes were cloudy, and there was a big hole in his chest. Shot, Poppi, shot! Someone shot him, but no blood. It was washed away by the water, maybe it happened this morning."

Michael stepped back from his grandfather's arms, silent. "It's okay, don't say anything else. It'll be fine."

They sat on the grass wondering about the guy floating in the backwater. Nick raised his head, looking over the yard, and the exact spot in the woods where Michael had come out. He scanned the yard, senses aware, watching every movement around the perimeter.

"Got you under my wing kid," Nick said. "Nothing's going to happen to you. Everything's fine."

The sun was up now, and it was getting warm. The usual morning sounds were floating in the air, and after a moment Michael was his old self again.

"What about the dead guy, Poppi? What should we do?"

"Well if he's dead, he's not going anywhere. Just rest a moment, then take me there," Nick said. "I want to see this body!"

"Look Poppi," Michael said, "I found this picture. She's pretty, isn't she?"

Nick's eyes opened with surprised after he saw the picture, and whispered a name.

Michael couldn't hear what he said, but thought, *Does he know her?*

"Did you find anything else?" Nick asked, and put the picture in his shirt pocket like a memento.

"I found a notebook," Michael said, "a wallet, and a key."

"Do you have those things?"

"I left all that stuff there," Michael said. "I put it all back."

"Okay, don't worry Michael, but don't tell anyone about the key, the picture, or the notebook. It'll be our secret."

"Okay, Poppi. Why?"

"I don't want anyone to know about it. It's very important. You've got to promise."

"I won't say a word. I promise!"

"You ready? Let's go for a walk to the backwater, and take a look at this body you found."

Michael and Nick walked back through the woods to the backwater, down the same path, with Buster leading the way. This time they walked cautiously, exchanging looks with each other, knowing that they would soon see a dead body. Buster was silent because he had already sniffed the air that had been touched by death. He was on a new adventure, actively searching for rabbits or some other animals to run down. And for Michael it seemed like a whole new day had started all over again, and what he'd found floating earlier in the backwater was nothing but a dream like one of his grandpa's bed-time stories.

It would be lunch soon, but no one had an appetite, and food was not on their minds. Nick was in his late sixties, but moved at a good clip down the path through the trees. Michael did his best to keep up while turning back, checking and looking down the path at the footprints on the trail. Nick trudged on, moving branches out of the way, then stopped. "You okay, kid?"

"Yeah, fine, but it looks like there are lots of footprints here. Raising his arm and pointing straight ahead, Michael said "We're close. It's just ahead, behind that pile of branches over there. I covered the body with sticks and leaves so no one would find it."

"I can go on by myself," Nick said. "You can stay here if you want. I should be able to find it. No need for you to see it again?"

Michael looked up at Nick. "I'll be fine," he said. It had sunk in now. Everything had happened so fast and had at first felt like a dream. "I know this isn't a dream. I know it really happened."

"Okay, show me the place," Nick said. "Is it that way?"

"Yes, over there," Michael said as they cleared the edge of the forest near the shore of the backwater.

"There," he said, and pointed to a cluster of trees that had fallen nearby the shore.

"Remember the time we pitched our tents too close to the trees one summer?" Michael said. "That night there was a big storm, the wind knocked over a tree, and fell on a tent. It broke one kid's leg. That's where it is."

"Okay, I'll check it out," Nick said. "Stay here with Buster."

"Near that pile of branches," Michael said again as Nick walked forward.

Nick headed over to the fallen trees, and found the body right where Michael said it was. "With the sun climbing, and the heat rising, the smell's going to get unpleasant around here," Nick said. "The corpse's going to be a rotting magnet for flies by afternoon." Nick removed the branches and saw a gaping hole in the man's chest. After lifting the vest covering the body to the side, and seeing the man's face, he said, "This is not good."

"Do you know him?" Michael asked.

Nick turned to Michael, but waited a moment before saying anything. "No," he said. "No . . . I don't know him. You were right, looks like a shotgun slug at close range." Nick checked the man's pockets, found the notebook, opened it, and saw that the last five pages seemed to be torn out. He looked at the key, turned, smiled at Michael, then put everything in his pockets.

Michael watched Nick examine the dead man. *He's checking him over like a professional; like the police do on TV. But Poppi's a bricklayer, so how does he know what to look for?* he thought, and moved closer to get a better look.

Then Nick stood. "Okay, let's go home. I guess somebody didn't like him because he didn't do this to himself."

"Did you see the notebook?" Michael asked.

"Yeah, but it's been in the water a long time. Not sure what is salvageable."

"Did you take the key and the wallet?"

He knelt down, and looked at Michael. "You know the stories I tell you at night about the driver." Michael was calm, and quiet, as he listened to Grandpa Nick. "This is your chance to be like him, so when the police ask if we found anything, you say we didn't. Don't tell them about anything. Nothing about the notebook, the picture, or the key, just keep it between us. Don't say anything about any of it. Come to think of it, maybe I should tell them I found the body, then you won't have to talk to them at all."

"I'll do whatever you say, Poppi."

"That's what we'll do, then. We'll say I went for an early morning walk, then came back and told you about the body. We'll just change places, okay?"

"I won't say anything," Michael said. "But how'd he get here?"

"Well, I think he was on a boat, shot, and fell into the water."

"Who did that to him, Poppi?"

"Don't know, but the people after him were looking for something," Nick said. "That's why it's important to keep it a secret for the time being."

"Okay, Poppi."

They walked back to the cabin. Nick looked around, scanning the terrain. He was careful, and looked in the trees, then he would stop and stand quietly, listening. Occasionally, Michael felt a hand on his shoulder, and a voice whisper, "Stand still!" Nick did this a number of times on the way back to the house, and now Michael began to worry because he'd never seen Poppi act like this before.

Michael looked back at his grandpa. "What's wrong, Poppi?" Michael asked as he watched his grandpa's head turn back and forth, looking the woods over as if he had the feeling that they were being watched. The wind blew, trees wavered, and there was a clap of thunder, but no dark clouds in the sky. Nick always had a feeling about things, a gut feeling, and he was usually right. When Nick said it was going to rain, it rained; when he said a fish would jump, it jumped. Whenever he made a prediction it usually happened, so if he thought they were being followed or watched—they were!

Even though a terrible thing had happened that morning, it was turning out to be a very exciting day for Michael. He felt the same as when he listened to the stories his grandpa told him at bedtime. *I wonder why Poppi's acting like this,* Michael thought. After they made it to the edge of the woods, and the cabin came into view. They stopped a moment.

"Michael, I want you to wait here with Buster until I check the cabin. Stay right here. I'll signal you after I check the place out."

"Okay, Poppi, this is kind of fun."

"Yeah, exciting, just like the stories I tell you, right? If I don't come out in ten minutes, you run and go find Moses. He'll help you and know what to do. Tell me what I said."

"That I should run, find Moses, and tell him what happened."

"That's good. Go straight to Moses."

"Okay."

"When I come out, I'll signal, all clear, okay? Just wait here."

"Okay."

Michael waited with Buster at the edge of the trees as he watched Grandpa Nick carefully walk up the red brick path on guard, like the soldiers he'd watched in war movies, ready for an ambush. Grandpa Nick turned, and looked back at Michael. He gave a quick wave, and walked up the steps of the deck. He peered into the windows ready to move away quickly if someone was there, inside, waiting. He opened the door and went in.

THE SIGNAL

Michael fidgeted, and it was hard to keep still while he waited with Buster at the edge of the woods near the tree-line. Birds whistled, bugs squeaked, and the clouds above sailed by and changed shape. He listened for any unusual or strange sounds from the cabin, anything that might signal trouble. He sat crouched on his heels ready to bolt, quiet, alert, patient.

Then Michael and Buster both turned and looked behind at the same time after hearing the distant sound of a sputtering engine that was in need of repair. He looked at Buster, his hand caressed the dog's back. "It's probably a fisherman going up the river," he said. "It's okay, a lot of boats always sound like that." Again they both turned, but in the opposite direction to a motorcycle's hollow distant echo. "Love that sound," Michael said. "I want to get a bike like that someday." *A Harley Davidson,* he thought.

Other than seeing the dead guy floating in the pond, and waiting for Poppi to signal, it was a regular morning. Only a short time had passed since they stopped at the tree line, but now it seemed like an eternity. "What do you think Buster? Should we go to the house and check on Poppi? Well, Buster? Is it okay?" Michael said. "Should we wait a little longer?" He sat there talking with the dog. "What should I do? Grandpa Nick's not coming out. I'm starting to worry. How long have we been here?"

He looked at Buster. "Maybe the same man who killed the guy we found floating in backwater is in the cabin." Their heads jerk up when they heard a noise coming from inside the cabin, something thrown against the wall, then another crash—a broken window or glass shattering.

"Maybe he dropped a dish," Michael said. Then it sounded like something heavy fell to the floor, and everything went quiet. *What do I do?* he thought. "Poppi said to run, so that's what I'll do. I'll do like I was told to do." Buster took off at full clip after Michael. It was a repeat of an hour ago when he had found the body and told Poppi.

"Got to get Moses," he said, while running down the trail, slapping away branches and knocking off leaves. "Tell Moses, like Poppi said, about the body."

Nick had known Moses a good part of his life; they were like brothers, and he trusted him completely. They were stone masons who had worked together in the block and brick laying business for many years, and Michael was learning the trade from both of them. The shop where they kept their tools and equipment was next to a lumber mill owned by two brothers who logged the nearby forests. They cut up the logs and sold the wood to other lumber yards that refinished it for building materials. There were a few family businesses in Hungry Point who hired the locals, and that kept it friendly, so everyone knew everyone.

Michael saw the rows of logs stacked in ten foot high piles ahead. "Getting close, he said, "I hope Moses is around." He ran between the stacks of wood turning left and right, taking a short cut to the shop, he knew this place like the back of his hand.

"There it is," he said, and grabbed the door handle. "Locked, and Moses isn't here," then thought of the spare key under a concrete block out back. "I hope it's there," he said, then hustled to the back of the shop, found the hiding place and lifted the block. A smile covered his face when he saw the key. He went back to the front, then unlocked and opened the door to a silent vacant echo chamber. The only light in the dim shop seeped in through the clean parts of the dirty windows. Michael looked around and kicked at the gravel floor. "What should I do? When will he get back?" He locked the door and sat at the old wooden desk in the corner of the shop. He pushed down on the keys of the big brass cash register, and the cash drawer opened with a ding. "The bell still works." Inside he saw old coins, a few buttons, and some fish-hooks. "I wonder why they keep this old thing."

This was another place where Nick sat, working on plans of stone structures, brick walls, and fireplaces. Where he calculated bills, and listened to baseball games on the radio. Michael moved some papers around looking for something to read until Moses returned. He found a *Popular Mechanics* magazine and skimmed through it, then came across a picture and an article on how to make your own batteries. After he read the battery story, he flipped through more pages. He thought about Poppi, his bedtime stories. More memories bubbled to the surface of Michael's thoughts. He fell asleep in the chair, his arms crossed resting his head on top of his hands dreaming of the nameless man his grandpa had described. Poppi's stories were always in his dreams.

* * *

The first image he saw was a panorama of the room where he slept growing up. The round light that hung from the ceiling looked like a full moon through squinted eyes, and that's when odd things happen, on nights with a full moon. His room was like most kids who lived in Hungry Point, a little sparse, a bat and glove by the door, some fishing poles hanging on the bottom of a rack, and a tackle box on the floor at the base of the bed. There was a foggy full length mirror on the back of the door, a bookshelf with his favorite books, and a desk to study at or to put model cars together on.

On some nights he'd listen to the same story, and every so often Nick told a new one. The dreams came to life after he closed his eyes, and Poppi's voice came through loud and clear, deep and commanding. He was the narrator of Michael's dreams, and whose voice described moments and memories as they were just happening. At night Poppi would turn down the lights and set the mood to begin a story. Michael wrote this in his book.

Bedtime Stories and Dreams—Memories of Michael Colt—Unknown Figure

"Out of nowhere an outline of a man's shadow appeared on the road, then a door opened and the shadow floated across the wall down to the floor. The silhouette moved like it was alive or coming to life piece by piece, bit by bit. Then, the sound of footsteps walking down a narrow dimly lit hallway got louder and louder. The attention of the figure focused on the windowless doors on either side of the corridor. No longer a shadow, a real man came into the picture, and his left hand reached out and grabbed the door handles, turning, rattling, and pushing on the doors. In his right hand a revolver hung down at his side. He raised it when he attempted to open the doors, so if by chance one would open he'd be ready to pull the trigger if he had to."

"Is this the same guy who drives the car, Poppi?"

"You'll just have to wait and see, Michael," Nick said, and continued the story. "Now I see him more clearly."

"What does he look like?"

"He's wearing a dark suit, and his hair is short and sharp like a military cut. He's lanky, wide shouldered, but muscular. The way he moves is from all the training he's had, this man is a soldier. He continued trying to open each door, but found all of them to be locked. Down the hallway he walked trying the door on the left, then the one right, and each one after that."

"What's he looking for?" Michael asked.

"Just wait and see. I'll be getting to that soon. The corridors were endless, twisting passageways like in the belly of a ship. The only lights were mounted in the ceiling, and covered in metal-wire-mesh. Each footstep taken echoed so much so, it seemed like being in a tin can. He continued searching, and ready at any moment as a hunter tracking prey."

"He's a hunter?"

"Yes, Michael, he's a hunter. Finally, the man reached the door at the end of the passageway, turned the handle and opened it, a chess player not sure of his move, but not letting go too soon. Light bled out through the thin crack in the door, then turned to total blackness. A velvety low voice said, 'I've been waiting for you.' The man pushed the door all the way open, and dropped to the floor. Gunfire rang out, but he didn't return fire, and just waited in silence for a footstep or the sound of breathing. Then a clanging sound as something fell to the floor, or had been thrown. There was silence, then he caught a reflection, a flicker, and aimed in that direction. He fired, and shots were returned, then there was a thud."

"Who was shot? What happens next?"

"The faceless shadow man searched the room for something, maybe for secret documents."

"What kind of secret documents?"

"That'll be in the next installment, kid," Nick said, "time for bed."

"Oh, man, okay. Good night, Poppi."

"See you tomorrow, Michael, pleasant dreams!"

TIME TO WAKE UP

Moses slammed on the breaks and his truck skidded to a stop, then he backed up to the center overhead door at the shop. He was there to pick up another load of stone that was stored in the shop. But before getting out, he grabbed a sandwich from a cooler on the floor and sat in the truck listening to talk radio and eating. The shop was on a lonely road, so only a car or two cruised by blowing the horn, he waved back.

"Damn, what a nice day!" then said, "I thought Nick was going to be here. I wonder where he's off to today."

He looked in the side mirror to check if there was any food in his beard. After putting on his sunglasses, he lit a cigar and got out of the truck. He stood next to it a moment, then lowered the tailgate. Sunlight spread into the shop, across the floor, and up the walls as he opened the overhead door. There was a surprised look on his face as he thought, *What's he doing here?* after seeing Michael in the chair he yelled, "You asleep, kid? Michael, hey, Michael," he said a few more times, but there was no answer. Moses walked over to the desk, put his hand on Michael's shoulder, and shook him till he opened his eyes. "Wake up, kid."

Michael groaned.

"Wake up, Michael," Moses said again.

Michael opened his eyes after Moses rocked him back and forth once more. His magazine fell to the ground and landed between his feet. He propped up his head, startled, but after seeing Moses standing there he let out a sigh of relief. "Moses," he mumbled.

"Are you okay, kid? You seem edgy. What's wrong?"

"I came here to get you. Poppi told me to come get you if anything happened."

"To get me," Moses asked. "What happened? Is Nick hurt?"

"I don't know."

"Don't know? Now I'm confused, kid. Tell me."

"I went for a walk this morning with Buster to the backwater near the river. I saw something floating, and wondered what it was, so I swam out to see."

"What was it?"

"You're not going to believe this because it's hard for me to believe, but I found a man," Michael said, "a dead man!"

"You found dead man?"

"Yeah, he was floating out in the backwater off the channel. And he was shot, and had a big hole in his chest. I ran back to the house to tell Poppi about it, and took him there."

"You went back there together?"

"Yeah, and Poppi looked the guy over pretty good. After searching him, he found some stuff. I found a picture in his pocket, a picture of a pretty lady."

"What did you do with the things you found?"

71

"I left everything there, but I think Poppi took the stuff after we went back, and said, when we talk to the police, not to say anything. Told me to say he found the body, and not me."

"Where's Nick, now?"

"I think he's in the cabin. He told me to wait at the tree line, and he'd give a signal, but if he didn't, I was to run and get you, so that's what I did. That's why I'm here."

"What do you think happened, Michael?"

"I heard some crashing noises coming from the cabin."

"What do you think it was from?"

"It sounded like chairs crashing into the wall, and glass breaking."

"You didn't see anything?"

"No," Michael said, "nothing. Just ran here as fast as I could. It's what he said to do."

"You did good, Michael. Now listen to me. I want you to go to the town hall building and tell Carlo what you told me. Just that, okay? Use one of the bikes."

"Okay, but what about Poppi?"

"I'll head over to the house and see what happened. Wait here about twenty or thirty minutes, then go to the town hall. That'll give me some time to check things out."

"Are you coming back here, or staying at the house?

"I'll wait at the house."

"I hope Poppi's okay," Michael said.

"He's probably fine."

THE WARDEN

The quasi police station was in the building next to the post office, it was also where town meetings were held. Anyone could voice their opinions, complaints, or ask for help. Everyone was close, just like a family, and supported each other. As seasons changed so did the number of people who arrived to enjoy fishing and water-sports. Hungry Point was a river town, in summer the population tripled, and that's when most businesses made their living.

The room on the first floor was big with a make-shift stage, and a few rooms upstairs, one for the quasi mayor's office, a store room, and the game warden's office. Michael ran inside and up the stairs, and saw one guy working there, Carlo Black, the Game Warden. He was also the acting police officer of Hungry Point. He was friendly, knew his work, and never pushy, so people liked him. He was tall, only shaved for special events, mostly wore jeans and a kaki shirt with his gold and silver badge pinned on the pocket. There was an embossed image of a fish and bear in the middle of the badge, and imprinted above that was *Game & Fish,* and below, *State Warden*. His sidearm was a standard Army issue single-action, semi automatic Colt .45 that he shot weekly at a nearby rock quarry; he could hit anything. His truck was decked out with a gun rack on the rear window, radio gear, and a rebuilt hopped-up engine.

His grandparents had lived and died in Hungry Point. They ran a small hotel, but now it was operated by a family that moved from a city nearby. In summer they held concerts; bands that at one time were headliners, now performed at their summer festivals. Carlo's dad moved to Chicago, got a law degree, and ended up in the Army. That's where he met his mother who was a secretary in the same department. At first Carlo followed in his dad's footsteps and got into law, but, against his father's wishes, gave it up. He couldn't stand the notion of being inside an office all day. He loved the outdoors, and a rural setting is what he wanted. Using family connections he got the job in Hungry Point after he'd heard about the Game Warden position.

Now he was looking at a kid standing in front of him, out of breath, and who seemed to be in trouble. Something had scared the tar out of him.

"What's wrong kid?"

"It's, Nick, my grandpa."

"Yeah, I know you; I know him, the brick and stone guy?"

"Yeah, he works with Moses."

"I know Moses, we target shoot at the quarry."

"Moses told me to come and get you."

"To get me?" Carlo asked. "Why?"

"He said you would help."

"Help with what?"

"I think my Grandpa Nick's in trouble."

"What kind of trouble?"

"Poppi found a dead guy floating in the backwater, then on the way back to the cabin, he said to wait, and went inside, but didn't come out."

"He didn't come out? Who else was in the cabin?"

"I don't know," Michael said. "Moses said to get you."

"Did something happen to your grandpa?"

"I don't know," Michael said. "Grandpa Nick told me to wait, and he'd give a signal if it was safe, but didn't. And I heard some crashing sounds from inside the cabin. Before he went in he told me to tell Moses if something happened. Moses said to come here to you."

Michael was breathing hard reliving the events that had just happened.

"Your name's Michael, right?"

"Yes."

"I want you to stay here. Don't go anywhere, don't talk to anyone, and don't touch anything. Stay here. I'm going to your place to see what's going on. I'll be back as soon as I can. If anyone comes in, just say I told you to wait for me"

"Okay, I'll wait."

"Good, and don't worry. I'll take care of Nick. I'm going to drive to your place and check things out. After that, I'll be back."

Michael walked to the window and watched Carlo get into his SUV. *I hope Poppi's okay*, he thought, then sat in Carlo's chair. He looked around the office, then noticed some pictures on Carlo's desk and picked one up, and thought, *That guy next to Carlo looks familiar*. He sat back, closed his eyes, and remembered a bedtime story from Nick.

Bedtime Stories and Dreams—Memories of Michael Colt—Not Knowing

"With his face in the palms of his hands a strange and unfamiliar feeling rushed through the driver's veins, and he thought, *I don't know where, or who I am*, then rolled his hands over his face, and down the back of his neck. With his eyes open he could see where he was."

"Where was he Poppi? What happened to him? Why doesn't he know who he is?"

"Something happened to the driver, and he lost his memory," Nick said.

"How'd he lose his memory?" Michael asked.

"He was on a mission with his team, and tried using a new system predicting the outcome of a situation. Somehow this affected his memory."

"He knew what would happen?" Michael asked.

"He got a formula from a man who was working on logic and outcomes, and wanted to reduce the chance of a mission failure."

"How did he meet him, and how did the formula work?" asked Michael.

"The Driver met the professor at a conference where he spoke on logic, and they decided to work together. At first it seemed simple, and used a common-sense method, but became more complex, allowing the driver to make decisions based purely on logic."

"What happened next?"

"He collected formulas given to him in a notebook, information including names of people on the mission and his team. But for some reason on this day, things were not clear, his mind was in a fog, thoughts came slowly, and he didn't know his own name."

"So, what did he do?"

"He opened the notebook, read the formulas the professor had given him trying to understand them, but began to find that his memory was weak, like he was reaching at thoughts that were floating away into a black hole."

"What did he do?"

"He closed the book, and thought of who he was."

"Did that help him?"

"Yes, things began to make sense, and he remembered, but realized he had an object around his neck that wasn't there previously."

"What kind of object?"

"It was a triangular shape, more than one put together into a snowflake pattern. And, inside was a gold liquid."

"Was it gold?"

"Yes, it was gold, and he remembered what the professor, the man who'd been helping him with formulas to predict the future, called it."

"What was it called?"

"The professor called it the Bell."

"What did the thing around his neck do?" Michael asked.

"He didn't know, and couldn't remember where it came from or how he got it. He only knew that it was special, and held some kind of power that allowed him to do things no one else could."

"Where did it come from?" Michael asked.

"That's a story for another night, kid." Nick said. "Time for bed."

***

Michael woke after he thought he'd heard a door slam closed, and when he looked up, saw nothing, but he had the feeling of being in another place. *Maybe I wasn't awake and that was part of my dream*, he thought. A shiver went through his body, then he grabbed the amulet around his neck. *It's just like the one Poppi wears.* "What is this thing?"

CALL FOR BACKUP

Carlo grabbed the radio receiver after he got into his truck. "Dispatch . . . this is Game Warden Carlo Black. I'm at my office in Hungry Point, and heading to Nick Colt's place on Mill River Road. Can you send me some back up? There was a report of some trouble. I may need assistance. I should be at the location in fifteen minutes."

A voice on the radio replied, "Okay, Carlo, we'll send backup."

"Thanks! Carlo, over and out."

Carlo left the flashing lights and siren off. *What could have really happened at Nick's place?* he thought, and drove the speed limit, not racing, playing it cool, as if he were taking a Sunday drive in the countryside.

Then a call came on the radio. "Carlo?"

Carlo grabbed the radio. "Yeah."

"Just a call to let you know backup is on the way."

"Be there soon," Carlo said. "I'll keep an eye out for them, over and out."

Traffic was sparse on Mill River Road to Nick's place, and the few cars he met were people he knew, so he waved at them like usual. Just after a turn in the road to the cabin's tree lined road, he saw the driveway up ahead, and turned onto the narrow gravel road that led to Nick's. He pulled over to the side of the road at end of the driveway and parked next to the mailbox. *I should walk in,* he thought, *just to be on the safe side*, and turned off the engine. He took out his revolver, checked it, took off the safety, and got out of the truck. As he walked to the cabin he carried the weapon down at the side of his leg. Panning the area, he thought, It *seems quiet here, like any day, and nothing's wrong.* "Why did the kid come running to my office long-winded about his granddad being in trouble?" He stopped in front of the porch, and yelled, "Nick, you in there?" There was no answer, no sound.

He walked up the steps onto the porch, weapon in his hand, up at the ready. He glanced through a window. *Well, something happened here*, he thought. *Someone knocked over the chairs, and there are broken dishes on the floor. Where's Nick?* "Nick," he called out, but there was no answer. "Something's definitely happened here," he said, and shifted to the side of the front door. He grabbed the handle and turned it slowly, first looking inside, then he stepped in. "Nick," he said. "You okay?" There was no answer. "Where's the backup? Shouldn't they be here by now?"

He made his way into the kitchen, stepping lightly, avoiding the broken glass the best he could. From end to end all of the cupboards in the kitchen had been opened: dishes, cups, and things were scattered all around on the floor. A clock hung off-kilter on a wide timber beam header in an opening that led into the living room—the second hand ticking away. Carlo moved toward the living room, and looked through the opening. A roll top desk on the far side of the room had been ransacked, the cover rolled up, busted, and pieces were dangling from it. Bookshelves and cabinets were turned over, and every drawer had been pulled open.

"What the hell happened here?" he said, and stepped on pictures that had fallen onto the floor. When he removed his foot the glass was broken. As he stared at the picture, one man's face was familiar. "What's my dad doing in this picture with Nick?" Carlo said. He picked up the picture and put it in his pocket.

Then he heard a chime echo, and a bell toll that echoed. He peered through the window and saw men dressed in black walking into the yard from the trees. After they stopped, he watched a moment and tried to listen to what they were saying, but couldn't understand. *None of them look familiar.* Carlo thought as he walked to the front door, then out to greet them as they walked up the brick path. Holding his weapon he stood waiting on the porch, then smiled. They said nothing as they moved closer. "Wasn't expecting so much backup," Carlo said. "Is there something I should know? Where are you guys from?"

"What the hell?" he yelled as they raised their weapons and opened fire with their assault rifles, sending lead flying at the cabin. "What the hell are you guys doing? I'm on your . . . side!" Carlo yelled. Stunned and shocked, he threw himself back into the cabin landing on the floor. Bullets flew through the windows ricocheting, tearing chunks of wood from the cabin walls, and broke more windows.

"Why are you shooting at me?" he shouted. They answered with more gunfire. "I've got to get out of here," he said, and crawled to the back door. He poked his head up, and looked out the back door to see if someone was waiting there. Then after hearing footsteps on the porch, and banging on the door, thought, *I'm screwed! They'll be in the house, soon. The back door is my way out. Go now or I'm dead. Get the truck, it's not far. The trees are my best bet.*

He heard the front door break opened, then footsteps walking across the cabin's wooden floor that were getting closer. Metallic sounds of gun clips being locked and loaded into weapons was the signal that he should get the hell out of there now.

"I'll be okay once I'm in the trees," he whispered.

"But still have to be careful. Might be someone waiting in there to bushwhack me."

Carlo was breathing hard as he burst through the back door, then leapt off the rear deck landing square on his feet running, never missing a beat, his stride in time.

Now I know how that kid Michael feels, Carlo thought. *Hope the old guy's okay, wherever he is.*

RUNNING

Carlo raced to the tree line like an Olympian, then turned, and waited for a second while looking back at the cabin. After he heard the distinct sound of bullets ripping through the leaves, he hit the ground. With his head down he raised his weapon, and aimed at the two guys running toward him. He emptied half of the clip; they buckled and fell to the ground.

"So, how do you like it . . . bastards," he said. "Some of your own medicine back at you. Shoot at me? Assholes."

He jumped to his feet, running off the path, knocking away the branches, and deadwood breaking under his steps. "Who's that?" he said after seeing a truck parked on an old logging road ahead, then fell prone to ground. "Who's truck is that?" he said again. *Wait a minute! I've seen it around town*, he thought. "Moses."

Then a hand covered his mouth. "Quiet," a voice whispered.

The hand moved from his mouth slowly as Carlo turned around. "What are you doing here? What the hell's going on? Michael's at my office in Hungry Point. Told me Nick was in trouble. Never expected to be . . . shot at. I thought these guys were the backup that I called for. Where's Nick?"

"Don't know where Nick is," Moses said. "He wasn't here when I showed up."

"I thought the kid was pulling my leg about the body," Carlo said, "thought he watched too many detective movies or something."

"I only know what Michael told me. That they found a body in the river this morning, then dragged, and hid it under some brush. On the way back to the cabin Michael said Nick seemed to think there was something strange happening. He told the kid to wait at the edge of the forest behind the trees for his signal, and if there was no signal, to get me."

"What about the body?" Carlo asked. "Who is it?"

"I don't know," Moses said. "When I got here Nick was nowhere to be found, and the inside of the cabin was a mess. I saw Buster on the porch, and he led me to the body. The body's got a hole in his chest the size of my fist," Moses said, "and looks like he was shot point blank."

"That dog's pretty smart," Carlo said.

"Yeah, he is," Moses said. "I ran back here as fast as I could when I heard the shooting."

"Maybe the same people who've been shooting at me have Nick? They must have something to do with it. It's too much of a coincidence."

"I'd say the odds are pretty high," Moses said. "Things like this don't happen around here. We just don't find bodies floating in the river every day."

"What did the guy floating in the backwater look like?"

"You know, he looked a little like a guy I remember seeing in pictures hanging above Nick's desk in the cabin.

He told me some of them were taken when he was stationed in Europe. In one picture there are some guys in uniform sitting around a table in a bar or restaurant. Nick told me about it. He liked talking about the old days when he was in the service because I was too, just at a different time."

Carlo reached in his pocket. "I took this picture from Nick's cabin. Did the dead man look like any of these guys?"

Moses took the picture to have a closer look at the men. "Now, I don't know, could be one of them, it's hard to tell. Nick told me stories about working for the OSS. You know, the organization before it was called the CIA. He said it was nothing top secret, but interesting stuff none-the-less. Maybe these guys worked with him?"

"Do you think it has something to do with the guy who was shot, and the ones shooting at me?" Carlo asked.

"Wondering about that myself."

"Where do you think Nick is?"

"I wish I knew, Carlo, I wish I knew."

"Listen," Carlo said as sirens blared. "Must be the backup I called for. They're finally here," The distant wailing was getting closer.

"Let's go have a look," Moses said. They hiked back to the tree line, and saw a patrol car roar into the yard.

Two officers jumped out, guns at the ready.

"I know them," Carlo said, "they're from Dodge."

"Yeah, I know them, too," Moses said. "Have you been to the summer festival there? They have the grease pig catching festival in Dodge every summer, and it's the funniest thing there is to watch."

"I'm not so interested in pigs right now, Moses," Carlo said. "I was almost killed, and there's a dead man. I don't give a crap about catching . . . a pig."

"It's a good laugh."

"Okay, Moses, whatever you say," Carlo said and walked toward the cabin.

Moses and Carlo walked back to Nick's cabin, first to where Carlo had shot the two armed attackers. "Whoever those guys were, they cleaned the place pretty well," Moses said.

"What happened to the guys I shot?" Carlo said. "I know I dropped two of them."

"They took the bodies," Moses said.

"Can you radio the State Police, and tell them what happened," Carlo asked, then Moses and Carlo went into the cabin.

Moses whispered. "You know, Carlo, I'd appreciate if you wouldn't mention what I said about the guy in the picture you showed me. You know, looking like the corpse floating in the backwater. At least until we figure out what's going on."

"So, what should I say? And Michael's still waiting for me to bring his grandpa back. Once we start messing with the story it'll be hard to keep it straight later."

"I don't want to get you in trouble, so tell them what you think is right." Moses said.

"I don't know anything about the guy floating in the back water, but I've got to tell them about the kid, and how he ran to my office to get me."

"Like I said, tell them what you think is right. But we really don't know what's going on. Maybe the same crew who tried to get you had something to do with the guy getting shot at the backwater."

"I'll let them ask the questions, and try to find out more first," Carlo said. "What are you going to say?"

"I'll just say Michael came to the shop, and asked me to look in on Nick because he was worried about him."

"What about the kid?" Carlo said. "What's he going to say?"

"He knows what to say."

Bill Fritz became Sheriff of Dodge after a stint in the army as an M.P. He had grown up in the area, liked hunting and fishing, and sometimes went shooting with Carlo. He was a football player and wrestler in high school, stocky and well built. He joined the Army to see the world. They were friends, not close, but friends. "Hey, Carlo, what happened here?"

"It's pretty messed up. Nick's grandson showed up at my office and told me his grandpa might in trouble, so I jumped in my truck and headed here. Some guys started shooting at me. I thought they were the backup I called for."

"I heard about it, and that's why we're here."

"Yeah, called while I was driving here," Carlo said. "When I got here I found the house empty, some broken furniture scattered around, and no sign of Nick."

"I see you parked at the end of the driveway down by the road."

"Just being careful," Carlo said. "I walked down the driveway from the road, didn't want to scare anyone off if they were still here. You can't see the cabin till you come around that bend. And from there you can see the front deck. I stepped on the deck and looked in the window, saw the place messed up. I thought Nick might be in trouble, and was walking through the house when I heard this strange chime, then footsteps outside."

"What kind of chime? Where did it come from?"

"A ringing sound like a church bell that echoed. Then footsteps, I thought, they were the backup I'd called for. Some guys had weapons in hand as I walked out on the porch waving, thinking they were friendly. But after I said hello, all hell broke loose, and they started blasting away."

"Just like that?"

"Yeah, and I hit the deck because lead was flying all over, tearing chunks of wood and glass from the cabin. Look at it! I crawled back in the house on my belly, and figured my only chance was to run to the woods from a back door. I bolted, and just as I made it to the tree line I noticed a couple of them coming after me, so I fired back. I think I hit them because I saw them drop."

Fritz's partner walked around the corner of the cabin "I checked in the back, couldn't find a thing. There's nothing here, no bodies anywhere, and no sign of any tracks. Seems strange that you weren't hit with all the lead flying, don't you think?"

"Guess I was lucky," Carlo said. "The bodies must have been taken by the others. You think so too, right, Moses?"

"That's about it, I guess," Moses said. "Nick's grandson, came to the shop. He told me about Nick finding a body floating in a backwater near the river. Nick sent Michael to the shop to get me, and I told I told Michael to get Carlo. I thought Nick would be waiting here for me. The cabin was a mess, and Buster was on the deck. He took off running, and I followed him to the body. A little after that, I heard shots, and came back to the cabin, and found Carlo crawling on the ground over in the trees."

"Tell me more about the man floating in the backwater."

"I don't know anything about him," Moses said.

"Didn't recognize him at all?"

"No, just looked him over a little," Moses said. "I saw he was shot in the chest."

"Let's check that floating body you found. I'll have my partner call the State Detectives," Fritz said. "He'll stay here, and wait for them. You take me to the body, Moses? We can talk to the kid later. Where is he?"

"He's at my office," Carlo said.

"Carlo, why don't you head back, and tell him what's going on," Moses said. "I'll show Fritz where the body is. Make sure he's okay?"

"I'd like to see the body," Carlo said.

"Be easier and faster if I do it," Moses said. "I know where it is."

"Okay, I'll go see to the kid," Carlo said.

"Good, then maybe with a little luck, and some questions, we'll find out what's going here," Fritz said.

TRAILS AND PATHS

"Do you walk these trails a lot?" Fritz asked.

"Yeah, a lot of people do. And the fishing around here is fantastic if you know where the good spots are. And if you get on any path around here you'll always end up near the water."

"So what's the best way to get to where this body is located?"

Moses pointed toward the back of the cabin. "Let's go around back and take that trail over there, follow me. The body was dragged into the woods and covered with brush to hide it from animals and prying eyes; should still be there. It's about a twenty minute walk."

"We'll have to get the body checked before moving anything," Fritz said, "but I'll have a look at it first, then when the forensic team gets here, they'll take pictures and collect evidence. We should be able to put together a rough idea of what happened."

"I wish whoever's going to do that lot's of luck," Moses said, "because he was dragged out from the water to the shore, and covered with branches. The body has been handled and that makes a huge difference on how evidence is viewed, right?"

"I reckon the detectives will check it over, and do their best to find some clues as to how or why he was shot. Check if he was killed at another place and the body dropped in the water." Fritz said. "We'll just keep an eye on it for them until they show up, and do the same with Nick's cabin. They have to go through it, and check everything. Does the kid have any relatives in the area?"

"Not sure, just me, I guess," Moses said. "Well, we're actually not related, but he grew up with me teaching him how to lay stone and brick, so it feels like we're related. He can stay at my place until we hash everything out, or we find Nick. The trail on the left leads to the backwater, down this way."

"I vaguely remember this place," Fritz said. "I used to go fishing here with my friends. We'd stay on the river and camp the weekend."

"I think everyone around here's been fishing and camping on the river," Moses said. "Pretty crowded in the summer." They came to a well worn-path with animal tracks everywhere, and could hear the water washing on shore. "We're getting close to the backwater where Nick put the body. Keep walking. It's just that way."

Fritz followed Moses through the trees, then asked, "So, you recognize the dead guy at all?"

"No, never seen him before," Moses said. "Don't think he's from around here."

"What do think about it?"

"Could've been fishing?" Moses said. "Maybe the body floated into the backwater from upriver?"

"So, he was shot because he was fishing at someone's secret fishing hole?" Fritz said, then laughed.

"Well, we do take our fishing seriously, but not enough to kill anyone over it. We just beat the hell out of them, and send them on their way." Moses grinned, then smiled. "You know I'm just kidding, most people around here will tell you where the hot spots are. What if he was with a friend, and accidentally got shot? A lot of people carry guns around here. They take their guns fishing because you never know what you might run into in the woods. Lot's of critters roaming through here. "

"And then there's a possibility of a connection with what happened at Nick's place," Fritz said. "Don't you think it's too much of a coincidence, finding a body and those guys showing up at Nick's place and shooting at Carlo?"

"If we find Nick, we should have some answers," Moses said. "The body's right over there under that pile of branches and leaves."

"I see it," Fritz said.

They pulled off the branches uncovering the legs first. "I've got a pair shoes just like that," Fritz said. "Let's take the rest of the branches off. You didn't search the body when you were here before, did you? The forensic boys will want to check it out."

"Haven't touched it," Moses said. "Can't say what Nick did."

"That's a big hole in his chest," Fritz said. "I'd say a twelve-gauge. Don't see any other wounds. What do you think, Moses?"

"I'll go along with twelve-gauge," Moses said. "It's a pretty big hole, and it looks like he hit his head, too. Right there on the side."

"Yeah, I think you're right. Okay, I'll give my guy a call on the radio, and tell them we've found a body that might be connected to the fracas at Nick's place."

"Do you need me to stick around?" Moses asked. "I'd like to pick Michael up. He's worried about his grandfather."

"No, I don't need you to hang around anymore," Fritz said. "You can go. I'll wait here for the detectives, and we'll take care of everything, and if I have any questions, I'll come and find you."

"If you need me, I'll be at the shop. Got to check my schedule, and I'd like to get some things for Michael at Nick's place. Okay to go inside? I won't touch anything, just get Michael's things."

"You've got to ask the detectives about that," Fritz said. "They'll let you know if you can go in or not. I'm just working with them; they've got control of the case."

"Okay, then I'll head back and talk to them," Moses said, "and talk to you later."

"Thanks Moses," Fritz said. "I'll be in touch."

GAME OF CHESS

Detectives milled around going in and out of the cabin as Moses made his way up to the deck. He walked up to a baby-faced officer standing at the door. "Can I go inside and get some things for Michael. He's the kid who lives here with his grandfather."

"Not sure," the officer said. "Go in and ask the detective in charge."

"Who would that be?"

"His name is Brown," the officer said, and pointed. "That's him right over there, the guy who looks like Abraham Lincoln."

Moses turned, and watched as Detective Brown wrote something on the notepad he held, tore out the page, then said something, handing it to another officer.

"Okay, thanks," Moses said to the officer, and went inside to talk to the detective.

"Make sure that you check everything on that list," he said. "Let's find out whose blood this is on the floor," the detective said. "Get prints, pictures, and check all around the house and yard. Never know, might find something in the woods, so check there too."

When he saw he might have an opening and a chance to talk to Brown, he walked over. "Excuse me, I'm Moses London. I work with Nick Colt. He owns this place."

He stretched out his hand, and said, "Miller Brown. What can I do for you, Mr. London?"

"Well, until we find out what happened to Nick, his grandson is staying with me at my place. So, I was wondering, could I go inside, or bring him by later, to get some of his things? You know, clothes, books, those kinds of things."

"Later is better," Miller said, "after we go through place. Where's the kid now?"

"At Carlo Black's office," Moses said.

"He's the game warden? Yeah, I'd like to talk to the kid, too."

"Yes, that's right. If you hear anything about Nick, can you call me? I'd like to help if I can. We're all worried about what happened to him. Let me write down my number."

Miller took the paper with the number. "Sure, I'll contact you."

"I'll be back later to pick up the stuff."

"Okay, see you later," Miller Brown said, "Just tell an officer why you're here, and what you need. I'll let them know that you're coming."

After they shook hands Moses walked around to the back of the house into the woods and down the logging road to where he had parked his truck. He got in, waited a minute, and checked the rear-view. He watched the police walking around the cabin a minute, then drove to Hungry Point.

"How can a guy end up dead floating in a backwater? How can something like that happen? And what about, Nick? Where's Nick? How did he just disappear? Michael might know more than he thinks. I'll see what he can tell me."

After Moses arrived in Hungry Point, he parked in the Post Office lot. He sat in his truck a moment watching people walk by, waved at a few, then went inside. Michael and Carlo were at the desk playing chess. They had a local rock radio station playing, and the same DJ who was on every day was talking about the next song.

Moses knocked on the door frame and asked, "Who's winning the game?"

"Not me," Carlo said. "The kid's a pretty good chess player. You guys taught him well."

Then Michael picked up his knight, took Carlo's queen. "Checkmate!"

"You got me, kid," Carlo said. "Well, I'm going over to the restaurant and get something to eat. You guys hungry at all? Want to tag along?" Carlo asked. "Loser buys. Michael won fair and square."

"We'll head over there in a bit," Moses said. "I want to talk to Michael first. How about we meet up over there?"

"Sounds good," Carlo said. "You've got to give me another chance Michael, two out of three?" Carlo grabbed his cap. "See you in a bit."

"What about dessert, you paying for that?" Michael asked.

"I've got it covered," he said. "Just head over when you're done here."

"See you at the restaurant," Moses said, and pulled up a chair next to Michael. "I want you to tell me everything you can about what you did, saw, or remember about this morning."

"I'll try," Michael said.

"Okay," Moses said, "you're going to be a big help with this. Tell me, did you hear or see anyone else when you got to the river?"

"Well, I noticed Buster was barking more than usual," Michael said. "He was acting strange from the time we left the house, like he could smell something in the air."

"Good, anything else?" Moses asked.

"I remember hearing a motor boat, didn't see anything though. But it sounded like a fishing boat. Just like ours, you know, the same sputtering sound."

"See or find anything else?"

"A wallet, a picture of a girl, and there was a key and a notebook."

"Where is that stuff now?"

"Nick took it, and said to tell the police he found the body."

"So, where's that stuff now?"

"I don't know," Michael said. "I saw Poppi put the notebook in his pocket. I guess he could have taken the other things, too. As soon as we got back to the cabin Poppi said to wait at the tree line, and he walked up to the house."

"Nobody else knows about this except us?"

"Just us," Michael said.

"I asked the detective working the case if we could go back to the house and get some of your things, clothes and things."

"Okay, this all sounds just like the spy stories Nick's been telling me at night before bed."

"What kind of stories?"

"About the driver," Michael said, as his eyes lit up, and his grin got wide. "The driver always gets out of a tough spot."

"Yeah, Nick's got quite the imagination," Moses said. "Let's go over to the restaurant, see what Carlo's having, and get us some grub too. Then I'll head back to the house, and get your things."

"Can I go with you?" Michael asked.

"Maybe it's better if you stay with Carlo," Moses said. "We'll go back to the cabin together later after the police are done. When there won't be as many people there."

As they walked across the street to the restaurant where Carlo was waiting, Moses noticed old Mr. Vortich sitting in his truck who nodded and waved.

"That's the guy we're building a fireplace for, isn't it?" Michael asked. "And as Michael looked back at Mr.Vortich, a strange feeling connected them until he looked away, and up at Moses.

"Yeah, that's him," Moses said, and they walked into the restaurant.

MEAT WAGON

Moses left Michael with Carlo and drove back to the cabin. After he parked and made his way into Nick's cabin, he saw the ambulance pull into the yard and stop. Two paramedics got out. He watched as they took out a black vinyl bag.

"What you're looking for is down that way through the woods," an officer said. "Sheriff Fritz is waiting for you. Just stay on the trail, and you should run into him."

"Okay, thanks," one paramedic said, then grabbed another bag from the back of the ambulance.

Moses walked up to Miller Brown who was standing on the deck of the cabin. "I'm back to get some of Michael's things," Moses said. "Looks like more police and detectives are here. You guys calling in the National Guard next?"

"Well, when something like this happens we've got to take special care, investigate and go over everything carefully. We'll find out what's going on."

"Yeah, I understand," Moses said.

"I'd like to ask you and the kid some questions." Miller said. "Is he with you?"

"No, I left him at Carlo's office."

"I'm going with the paramedics to see what Sheriff Fritz has to say, and look at the body. After that we'll head to Hungry Point to see the kid."

"He's had a rough day, and with Nick gone, I'm not sure how he's holding up."

"Don't worry, we'll take it easy on him." Miller said. "See you in Hungry Point."

"Okay, at Carlo's then."

"See you later," Moses said. "I'm just going to get some clothes from the cabin for Michael."

Miller followed the paramedics down the path through the woods, and called to them. "Wait up, I'll go with you. I want to have a look at the body before you load it up."

"Yeah, sure, we're just here to haul it away, you can take all the time you need."

"You guys from around here?" Miller asked.

"Yeah, from Dodge," one paramedic said.

"You know the guy and kid who live in the cabin?"

"No, sorry, I don't."

"How about you?" he asked the other paramedic.

"No, don't know him."

Then Miller saw the backwater and Sheriff Fritz. "It looks pretty nice here. You must be Sheriff Fritz. I'm Detective Brown. So, let's see what we've got here."

"The body was found floating out there in the water, dragged out, and covered by some branches."

"And who did that?"

"Nick found the body according to what Moses said. We can't ask Nick because he's vanished into thin air. Maybe Michael knows something, he was out walking with his dog, and when he came back he heard a ruckus in the cabin. "

"What kind?"

"Said he heard glass breaking, and things being tipped over, then he ran into Hungry Point. He told Carlo what happened. Carlo said to stay in his office, and he came here to check the cabin alone. That's when all the shooting started."

"I just saw Moses, and he said the kid's with Carlo."

"Hope he's doing okay," Fritz said. "I guess after Carlo went into the cabin, then he heard some chimes or bells, and footsteps outside. He thought it was the backup he'd call for, but they started blasting, so he ran for cover in the woods. He returned fire, and said he got a couple of them."

"But there were no bodies at the cabin," Miller said.

"Whoever they were, they cleaned up, and took the two guys Carlo said he hit, and cleared out. Just left the cabin a mess, and must've taken Nick."

"Well, let's have a look at this guy who was floating in the river."

Brown and Fritz cleared off some leaves. "That's a big hole in his chest," Brown said.

"Shotgun at close range," Fritz said.

"I'd say shot this morning by the looks of it," Miller said.

"How do you know that," Fritz said.

"The body's cold from being in the water, so exact time might be difficult to nail down. Rigor mortis has started to set in, but I can move his joints a little. That might be from the water too. We'll leave it up to the experts."

"Okay we're done here. Let's load the body," Fritz said. "The photographs and evidence will be sent to all agencies local and federal to find out who this guy is. Maybe something'll lead us somewhere."

The paramedics picked up the corpse, put it in the body bag, zipped it up, and carried it to the meat wagon. Fritz, his deputies, and the detectives watched them disappear in the trees.

"You didn't find any identification or anything on him?"

"Nothing at all."

"Okay, we'll have an autopsy done as soon as possible," Miller said. "Have you guys got the facilities for that?"

"Sure, we can handle an autopsy," Fritz said. "They're taking the body to the hospital now. It's small, but we've done that kind of thing at the hospital before. I'll call ahead and have the doc standing by. Do you need anyone to stay here or are you guys finished?"

"No, we're done here, got everything we need, it's all yours."

"Okay, I'll have my guys look around Nick's place a little more, and if they find something I'll let you know."

"Great," Miller said. "Don't want any of this leaking to the papers, either, so keep it under wraps until you hear from us."

"Don't worry, my guys know what they're doing, they're pros," Fritz said.

"Well, let's go to Carlo's office and talk to the uncle and kid."

"Well he's not really an uncle, but Moses knows the kid well. He taught him, and worked with Nick. He asked me if he could go into the house and pick up some things for the kid. You know, some clothes and stuff. Is that good with you?"

"Sure, he asked me the same thing. We're finished at the house, he can go in anytime, and get whatever he wants."

"I want to talk to anyone else involved. Do you know this area pretty well?" Miller asked.

"Yeah, but I'm from Dodge," Fritz said. "Been fishing and camping all around here, but that was a while back. Moses is the guy you want to talk to about the area, he hunts and fishes around here—the kid too."

"Okay, thanks for all of your help, Fritz," Miller said.

"I'll keep my guys here as long as you need them," Fritz said.

"That would be a big help," Miller said, as they headed back to Nick's cabin.

Fritz walked over to his patrol car and got on the radio. "Fritz here, I want everyone to stay until Detective Brown gives us the green light to leave. Don't let any reporters into the area. And, good work by all. I'm heading into Hungry Point to see Carlo, so if you need anything, just give me a holler, Fritz out."

Fritz left the same time as the ambulance, and followed it until Hungry Point. The meat wagon went to the hospital in Dodge to take the body for an autopsy. Fritz wanted to talk to Moses to see how the kid was holding up. They'd never had a case like this in this area as far as he could remember; just some accidental farming and fishing deaths, car accidents, and old-timers kicking the bucket from old age.

He drove into Hungry Point and spotted Carlo's Ford Bronco in the Post Office parking lot. He pulled up next to it and parked. He's got a nice rig, he thought, and it looks new. Bet it cost a pretty penny. I wonder if I can ask for a rig like that.

As Fritz walked up to Carlo's office he thought about what he'd ask them, and give a heads-up about Miller Brown. When he stepped into the office, it was empty, not a soul in sight, just a chess board on the desk. "Wonder where they are? he said." He walked to the window, saw Moses get out of his truck, and walk into the restaurant. "I'm a little hungry, guess I'll join them."

Fritz saw Carlo, Moses, and Michael as he walked by the restaurant's window. They were sitting at a table in the back of the restaurant. The place was small and always busy it being the only restaurant around Hungry Point. The customers were fisherman, farmers, and kids.

Carlo stood when he saw Fritz and beckoned him to his table. Moses nodded, and Michael said hello.

"Hey, Carlo," Fritz said.

"So, what's the news?" Carlo asked.

"I can't pass on much because we don't really know anything concrete."

"What did you find out?"

"Well," Fritz said. "Not much as far as the guy who was floating in the river, or who the people were that shot at you. But I think we'll learn something after the autopsy."

"How long will that take?"

"Shouldn't be too long, they're taking the body to the hospital in Dodge City, and we've sent his fingerprints and picture to the FBI. I think we should know something fairly soon."

"Are you ordering some food?" Carlo asked.

"Sure, what do you recommend?"

"Here's a menu."

"How's the fish?"

"Really good,"

"Michael," Fritz said. "You've had quite an exciting day, young man. How are you holding up?"

"I'm fine," Michael said. "It all seems like a dream to me."

"Well, one reason for stopping by was to let you know that Detective Miller Brown was asking about you. He'd like to ask you some questions. Is that okay with you?"

"Sure, I'll talk to him."

"I think he's heading this way soon," Fritz said. "I just wanted to let you know."

"Okay," Michael said.

"I told him to go to Carlo's office. We can talk there, right, Carlo?"

"That's what it's for," Carlo said.

A BLACK DAY

The autopsy results Miller Brown was waiting for arrived. He opened the package, and flipped through the pages looking for the name of the John Doe. After he looked it over and sat down he threw the package on the desk, and that's where it sat, in the middle of his desk. He blinked, hoping that when he opened his eyes it wouldn't be there. Not only was it there, but as he looked at it through half closed eyes it seemed to be expanding, vibrating, and hovering.

He looked out the window, *It's up to me to break the news to him*, and looked back at the file, saying, "What am I going to tell him? And how do I say it?" He stood, walked over to the coffee pot and poured himself another cup. After he took a sip of coffee, the phone rang. He looked at the phone, waiting for it to ring again, then set the coffee cup down. *Showtime*. He grabbed the phone, hesitated a moment, then said, "Miller Brown here."

"Hi, Carlo Black here, just got your message that you wanted to talk. By the sound of your voice it seemed serious. What's on your mind? What can I do for you?"

"It's better if we meet, and I tell you in person," Miller said. "Are you free today?"

"Yeah, I can make time this afternoon," Carlo said. "Can't tell me what's going on now?"

"I'd rather not talk about it over the phone."

"Does it have something to do with the ruckus at Nick's place?"

"Yes, it does, and that's all I want say over the phone. If it's okay with you, I'll drive up to Hungry Point and stop by your office around one this afternoon. That okay?"

"Fine. I'll hook up with you later today then."

"Bye," Miller said. He put the phone down, grabbed a piece of paper and scribbled some notes. He had to think of something to say, anything to make it easier to break the news.

***

"I wonder what he wants to see me about." Carlo checked his watch. It was time to meet Moses at the restaurant to talk, and find out if he remembered anything else about Nick and that day. As he walked out of his office Moses drove by and pulled into the parking lot. When they saw each other, Carlo pointed at the restaurant. "See you inside."

"Hey," Carlo said to Steve, the owner and head cook, and walked to his usual table. Moses followed a few minutes later, and sat down at the table. A waitress brought two cups and a pot of coffee to the table. "What's the news about the commotion at Nick Colt's place? Everyone that comes in is talking about the body."

"You know as much us," Carlo said. "They're doing an autopsy on the guy who was floating in the backwater, but no clue about the guys who were shooting at me. It's spooky the way they vanished."

"It's all people are talking about around here," the waitress said. "How's Michael doing, Moses? Holding up okay?"

"He's fine, and staying at my place until we can go back to Nick's."

"Yeah, pretty wild stuff going on in Hungry Point. So, what'll it be today?"

"Same as usual for me, a couple of eggs over easy," Moses said.

"Yeah, same here," Carlo said.

"Okay, be right up," the waitress said.

Moses leaned over the table, and in a quiet voice said, "Any news about Nick?"

Carlo took a sip of coffee, then put down the cup. "Got a call from Miller Brown this morning, but he wouldn't tell me anything, just asked if we could meet today. Said he couldn't say why over the phone. I think he knows something, so I guess I'll find out this afternoon."

"Think it's about Nick?" Moses asked.

"I don't know," Carlo said. "Miller is acting a little mysterious, and I don't get why he wouldn't say anything on the phone."

"Yeah, you're right, does seem to be a little bit odd, but there must be some reason for wanting to talk to you. It has to be about the shootout at Nick's. Maybe they've got some leads."

"Well, when I find out later, then I'll fill you in."

The waitress brought the food to the table carrying two plates. "So, here we go, eggs over easy," she said. "Let me know if you guys want anything else."

"Thanks," Carlo said, "looks delicious."

"I've got a job to finish on a farm a few miles out of town. I'm repairing the block wall of a guy's old barn" Moses said. "Why don't we meet up later, and you can tell me about what Miller Brown had to say, I'm anxious to hear."

"Sounds good, when will you be back from your job?"

"Be there till five or six. It's a big job, can't finish today. It'll take at least a couple weeks. You want to meet back here or at your office?"

"I've got some paperwork to clean up, so I'll be at my office. Drop by when you finish."

Moses nodded, and finished eating his food. He picked up the check, left a tip on the table, and drove to the job site.

Carlo sat at his desk, his Colt .45 taken apart, the pieces cleaned and lined up neatly across the table. As he started putting it together there was a knock on the door, and he looked up. Miller Brown was standing in the doorway, no smile, reserved, like a man who had something to get off his chest.

"Hello, Carlo, and thanks for meeting with me today."

"Come in and have a seat." They shook hands, then Carlo said, "Like a cup of coffee? Can't say it's good, but promise it's hot."

"Coffee sounds good, thanks."

"You know if there's anything I can do to help, just ask. Whatever you need, I'll do my best to help. I realize I'm not a detective, but I know the people around here, and got involved in this when I was almost killed at Nick's place, so I am part of this case for better or worse."

"Well, thanks for the offer. First, I'm going to share some news that might knock you off your feet. You are part of this case for that reason, and linked to it as well."

"Okay, you've got my attention. What news is so important that you had to make a special trip down here to see me?"

"Okay, I'll get right into it, but first let me ask you a question. When was the last time you saw your father?"

"Saw my dad? What's he got to do with this?"

"Has it been a while?"

"Yeah, quite a few years. Since moving away from Hungry Point he's only been back a few times. We don't talk, and I haven't seen him for some time."

"What did he do?"

"He worked for the F.B.I. in Chicago until he retired."

"Chicago? And retired?"

"Yeah, he lives in Deerfield, but now he spends most of his time at his place in Florida, on Key West. He likes fishing. When I was young he'd go off for days at a time, work I guess, but never really said why, where or what. We didn't press him for information because he said his work was sensitive and confidential."

"So he never mentioned anything about his work?"

"No, nothing really. We grew further apart after we got into an argument. He was angry because I dropped out of law school. I just couldn't stand the thought of being stuck inside behind a desk all day. We didn't say much to each other after that."

"Sorry to hear that."

"I think he was set on me being a lawyer because he studied law, and wanted me to follow in his footsteps. It wasn't to be. Why all of the questions about my dad? Where's this going?"

"Carlo, damn-it, how do I say this?"

"Just go ahead and say it, and stop leaving me in suspense!"

"Carlo," Miller Brown paused, the guy floating in the backwater," he paused again. "We cross checked records, fingerprints, and a name came up."

"Who's name?"

"Your dad."

Carlo, stone faced at first, closed his eyes, and was silent. "How can that be? Are you sure?"

"There's no doubt," Miller said. "We double checked everything. It's definitely him."

"All this time I never called or got in touch with him when I could have, and now it's too late. I just don't understand. What was he doing by the river? And who shot him, and why?"

"We're looking into it," Miller said. "We'll find him, and bring you justice."

"I still can't understand what he was doing."

"If you need anything let me know."

"Where is he?"

"At the hospital in Dodge."

"Dodge . . . he never liked Dodge, or Hungry Point for that matter."

"We checked the records after the autopsy, fingerprints, teeth, and it's definitely your dad. There's no mistake."

"We didn't get along, like I said before, after I quit law school, and didn't talk much. I always thought someday we'd sit down, mull everything over, go fishing or something."

"Really sorry, Carlo. If there's anything I can do?"

"When can I see him?"

"Today if you like. I'll call and set it up. Is your mother alive?"

"No, she passed away years ago. It's just me now."

"We'll find out who did it, I promise."

"Can I help you with that, and could you let me know if any information turns up, keep me updated?"

"Well, I don't think that it's a good idea for you to work directly on the case, but we'll keep you informed on what's happening, and let you know of any new information. And if you come up with anything, pass it on to me."

"Thanks, I'd like to know what's happening."

"We can head over to Dodge today if you like. I'll drive you there and back."

"This is not going to soak in for a while."

"You want me to drive you there?"

"Okay, I'd like to see him, but I'll drive myself. It'll give me time to think"

"Let me know when, and I'll meet you there."

"Okay, I'll give you a call when I head out. Got to think this through a bit."

"Of course, and remember if there's anything that you need just let me know. See you later."

"I'll have to make burial plans," Carlo said.

SAYING GOODBYE

Carlo decided to have the funeral in Hungry Point, and Singleton Black's ashes were spread over the Mississippi during a ceremony held at a vista overlooking the river. At this point there was a sign with words carved on it that read, **THE LAND BEYOND THE RIVER IS CALLED THE SWEET FOREVER**.

Michael remembered one time he walked by the sign to go fishing with Poppi, and asked him what it meant. Nick said he had carved it and it meant just what it said. Michael asked once more because he wasn't sure he understood. Nick pointed to a place across the river. 'Over there beyond the river, see how it blends with the horizon? The sweet forever is where earth and sky meet.' He looked at Michael a moment, then touched the amulet that hung around his neck. 'It's the door to everywhere, anywhere you want to go, and you can go through it anytime,' then winked, and smiled.

The morning air was fresh, it was sunny, and a breeze brushed the leaves while waves of the river washed the rocks of the shore. Carlo, Moses, Michael, friends and relatives gathered to give their respects. The spot they chose was near a popular hiking trail, so a lot of hikers stopped to check what was going on. Some asked, they were told, and their curiosity was quenched after realizing they'd crashed a funeral service. One person stood away from the group, he was an older man who just watched the ceremony quietly. Moses recognized him, but when Michael asked who he was, Moses said, "Just a guy we did work for." Michael watched the old man leave after the ashes were thrown over the Mississippi, and spread into the air.

Everybody slowly made their way to the parking lot, and cleared out. Only Moses and Carlo were left.

"Sorry about your dad," Moses said as he walked with Carlo to their trucks.

"Thanks, Moses. We weren't close toward the end, but you know, I miss him. I should have talked to him or called more."

"Are you going to be okay?" Moses said, "If you need anything just let me know."

"Thanks, Moses, I'll be fine; it'll just take some time to get over."

"Have you heard anything else from Miller Brown?"

"Not really, nothing yet, but he said he'd contact me as soon as they get any information. You heard anything on your end?"

As they walked Carlo felt Moses had something to say and was just trying to figure out how to say it. They didn't say a word until they reached the parking area, then Moses put his hand on Carlo's shoulder as he opened the door to his truck.

"Carlo, I don't know if I should tell you this, and after I finish you can ask me all the questions you like."

"What is it? What do you need to tell me?"

"It's about your dad."

"What about him?"

"There are some things about your dad that you don't know."

"We were never close," Carlo said. "He was always busy. What is it you want to tell me?"

"I guess I'll just get right into it, so here it is. Singleton worked with Nick after they were discharged from the service. It's why they stayed in Europe, to handle some special operations. You've heard of INTERPOL?"

"Yeah, they're the international police."

"Did you know it was founded in 1923, and later controlled by the Nazi Party? Well, there was a mission to infiltrate and find who was still working for the Nazis."

"Maybe that's why he never talked about his work."

"He couldn't," Moses said. "If he had, his family would have been in danger."

"How do you know this stuff?"

"I know because I was there toward the end. I don't know what operations they had before I got there. But it was a government services group called the Strategic Services Unit, or SSU, and our project was called MKUltra."

"What kind of project was it? What did you do?"

"Intelligence, counter espionage, and jobs like relocation of an inside ear, occasionally close the deal on someone."

"What's an inside ear?"

"An agent that flipped over, and our job was to close the deal, to terminate. Later it became a mind control program."

"Why tell me all of this now?"

"I joined SSU just as your dad and Nick left. Michael's dad was part of it too. It's why Nick left.

Michael's dad was secretly given mind altering drugs because someone wanted information from him. He jumped out of a fifteen story hotel window. Nick was getting older, got fed up with it all, and just called it quits. Singleton stayed on, and took over MKUltra. I don't know what else he worked on, but all that's happened the past few weeks, to you and Nick; it might have to do with what they did back then."

"Why did you come to Hungry Point, and start working for Nick?"

"Because he asked me too," Moses said. Said he wanted to make sure Michael would be taken care of if anything happened to him. Guess he was right about that."

"Who started this program?"

"I don't want to get into that, but it was started in Europe after the war was over. The United States, and other allies wanted to decide what, and how, to do everything. I think you should watch your back. Let me know if you notice anything unusual."

"Okay," Carlo said. "I'll let you know if anything happens or if I hear anything."

"And I'll look into it a little bit more, too. I'm out of the loop with most of this now, and these people, but I'll try to find out what I can."

"What if something happens to you?" Carlo asked.

"Then you'll know there's something going on, and you'll have to handle it."

***

After the ceremony Carlo packed his things and drove to Chicago. On the way he stopped at Frank Lloyd Wright's architectural school near Spring Green, and the Harley Davidson Museum in Milwaukee, Wisconsin. Then he headed south to Chicago to meet with the lawyer

Singleton had hired to handle his estate. During the meeting he read his father's will. From what it said, Singleton had houses in Chicago and Key West. Carlo remembered the house in Chicago. He had grown up there, but never went back after he left for school, and the Key West house was where Singleton went alone.

"Do you have any questions about the will?" the lawyer asked after Carlo read the last page.

"No, everything looks pretty clear. Do I need to sign anything?"

"Yes, could you sign this here?" he asked. "This amount is for my fee, and signing it means that you've acknowledged and understand that."

"Do I sign here, too?"

"Yes, right there, very good. I'm sorry for your loss, and if you have any questions, you've got my number. Call anytime."

"Thank you."

Carlo drove back to the house, and after looking through some things, memories of growing up in the house were fresh in his mind. There were lots of pictures of Carlo growing up, riding a bike, swimming and camping. The camping trips were the most fun, and maybe the reason for liking the outdoors so much. *Ironic, he took me horseback riding, fishing, hunting, then we argued about it, and split because that's what I wanted to do.* "He said I was wasting my life."

Carlo boxed up everything he wanted to keep, contacted a real-estate agent and put the house up for sale. Next he drove to the airport and got on a plane for Florida to see a house he'd never been to. After landing in Miami, he rented a car and got on Highway One South, driving across the Overseas Highway to Key West. It was his first time to Florida and he thought the scenery was breathtaking. *Why didn't he ever bring me here?*

He headed down Duval Street where he saw once beautiful homes that had been built long ago that now had been converted into hotels, bars, and restaurants. Many of them had flags flying in front or from the second floor instead of a sign. He drove to Mallory Square where he saw crowds of people watching fire eaters, jugglers, and other entertainers, and got out to check out the view and watch the show. On the way back to the car he noticed The Hard Rock Cafe, a place called Fogodies, The Coyote Ugly, and the Shipwreck Museum. His dad's house was near a canal that flowed into the ocean, and according to legend at one time was used by pirates to smuggle and hide stolen treasure. Carlo had written down the address, and pinned it to the visor, glancing at it and the street signs as he drove.

"Some of these places are really nice, so I understand why he wanted to come down here. I wonder what the house looks like." He drove up and down the same streets once, twice, and finally a third time until he finally stopped the car. "Is that it?" he said and looked at the address. "Got to be it!" He pulled over to double check the address. "That's definitely it," he said, and pulled into a car park that had just enough space for one car. After looking over the place, he mapped the area in his mind, then got out of the car and walked down a narrow path that was covered with a canopy of tropical plants.

"So, this is dad's secret hiding place," he said, then grabbed the key for the front door from his pocket and opened the door. He stood quietly for a time examining the entrance, then stepped inside. "That's an interesting odor," he said as a flowery humid smell hit him in the nose like a right cross. "Let's get some windows open and let in some air to make this place breathable." The old place was run down, and the paint was peeling off in clumps inside and out. Loose stones on the path sat off kilter, some in the overgrown weeds, and the interior didn't fair much better. Inside was empty except for Carlo's footsteps echoing from the hardwood floor.

Singleton had rented it out on occasion, but now no one lived there. Carlo decided to keep the house in Florida because it was a charming place, and he wanted to know more about his dad. He would head back to Hungry Point for now, and decide later whether to stay, or move to Key West.

NICK'S ANNIVERSARY

Since Nick was a perfectionist, he treated all of his work like art. The stone fire places he built *were* a work of art, and had become the talk of the area and out to parts unknown. Word of mouth spread about his work even though they were no longer built by him. Having one built by his apprentice grandson or journeyman partner was the next best thing, and that kept Moses and Michael busy. The one Nick built in the Outsiders Inn was a masterpiece just like the one at his cabin. People would go there just to take pictures of it. Michael was trying to write his story as he did with a stone foundation in a house or fireplace. *Will I be known as the mason's grandson all of my life or the writer?* He hadn't let anyone close read anything he'd written up to now, only agents who had rejected it over and over. He had been working on this book for so long now, and it was time to do something with it. *I'll have Sue read it for me*, he thought as he drove up to Outsider's Inn and parked. *I trust her judgment.*

"I wonder if I should keep trying to find a publisher or do it myself. Should I send some letters to agents again, and hope to find one that might be interested? Maybe all this writing is a waste of time, and I should just stick to building things out of stone instead."

Michael sat in his truck watching the people who were there to celebrate Nick's anniversary. Every year a ceremony was held for Nick at Outsiders Inn. It started the year after the incident at his cabin. Nick had not been a religious man, but all of his friends wanted to celebrate Nick's life and keep his memory alive because there really wasn't a funeral after he disappeared. The turnout was always big. Of course Sue was there planning most of the event, and she basically ran the bar now. People in and around Hungry Point all knew Nick Colt from the chimneys, stone, and brick work. His name would be talked about for years to come.

Nick's anniversary party was originally for friends he'd done work for, but people from around the area showed up just to enjoy the food, beer, and games. It became an annual all-day event with local bands playing, and a pool tournament held in Nick's name since he was an excellent player himself. It was a day of games, horseshoes, volleyball, and food donated by farmers and people who Nick had done work for. One guy brought horses for kids to ride.

"Sue, you did it again, great party," Michael said. "Nick would be pleased, so many people show up every year."

"Your granddad was a great guy, and I hear lot's of stories about him," Sue said. "That German guy over there comes every year. You know him, right?"

"We did some work for them," Michael said. "Don't talk to the old man much, just his son. They usually stick close to home. What are you doing later?"

"Just cleaning up after, I guess," she said. "You can stick around and help."

"If I can get Moses and some guys to help clean this up, want to go to my place? We can relax."

"They'll do that?" she said.

"I'll talk to him, then meet you at my truck. We'll sneak away without anyone knowing."

Michael and Sue were on their way to the cabin in no time.

"Another year gone," Michael said. "Sometimes I feel strange having these parties because Poppi's never been declared dead. Down deep I know I'll never see him again, but there's that slight glimmer of hope that I'll see him again."

"Will they ever find out what happened?"

"You'd think they would have. It's a mystery, just to vanish without a trace."

"Why don't we investigate on our own?"

"I wouldn't have a clue of where to start."

"When do I get to read your book?" Sue asked. "You've been working on it forever."

"Sometimes I want nothing more than to make it as a writer, but there's the business Poppi started. I couldn't just leave it all up to Moses. He's getting older now, and we're busier than ever."

"Let's not think about it anymore and just go the cabin," Sue said. "I've got a surprise for you."

Michael looked at Sue. "A surprise? Well, well, well, can't wait for that," he said, and stepped on the accelerator. "What is this surprise?"

"Can't tell you," she said. "It's a surprise."

"What is it?"

"No, you'll have to wait until we get to the cabin."

"We're almost there," he said. "Give me a hint."

"Okay" she said, opening her bag taking out a bottle. "Here it is!"

"Wine! I remember you used to sneak a bottle out when we were kids, and go to the shack we built on the river."

"Yeah, I've got this one, too," she said, and showed him a bottle of Chardonnay.

"And I thought I was doing all of the planning," he said. "It looks you've been doing some planning too. This is going to be a wonderful night. Just the two of us!"

THE MEETING

Ten years after the incident, Nick was officially declared deceased. Michael had inherited Nick's estate, including the business, and moved to the cabin. He thought about making some changes to modernize and spruce up the cabin, but ended up leaving things as they were. Moses had taken care of the place and stayed there occasionally, but now Michael had Sue. As it turned out, Nick owned a big chunk of land around the cabin, and being that he was a good business man, his bank account had a sizable chunk of money parked in it. Michael was set. Now he could hire a few people to help do the masonry work so he could concentrate more on writing, and spend time with Sue. Using the stories and characters Nick had told him at bedtime, Michael's story took shape, but when he sent it to agents they still rejected it.

Michael stood on the deck facing a tree line that completely surrounded the cabin. Even the road leading to the cabin had tall trees running along side. The only lights bearing any afterglow hung from above the deck casting ghostly shadows that moved as living creatures. On the deck was a long wooden table surrounded by chairs that he and Nick had made with trees from the forest. Together they drew up the plans, measured, cut, and built tables and chairs that would last one-hundred years. There was a stone grill in yard that they had also worked on together. It had some wear and tear, but still as good as ever. Michael wanted to be as self-sufficient as possible, so he installed solar panels and a wind-mill tower that produced more than enough power. He rigged an antenna for a short-wave radio and monitored radio transmissions from around the world, and he studied Morse Code because some of the transmissions were only in code. For back-up there were a couple of gas generators that he also used on job sites.

It was after midnight. Stars filled the sky like a radiant patchwork quilt, and the air was fresh with night-time sounds in the distance as he glanced again at the brilliance above.

Sue walked out on the deck. "Lonely out here by yourself?"

"I never get tired of looking at those stars," he said. "It's one reason I stay here."

"I like it here, too," she said.

The moon floated like a lost, lonely pearl as he watched what was left of the cigar he was smoking drop from his hand. After hitting the deck, he stamped it out, and kicked it into the yard.

He grabbed a glass from the railing, then drank what was left of the wine. After a clean swallow he let out a sound of satisfaction.

The house was secluded, and there was a feeling of belonging. He was connected, attached, and it would always be that way. From his earliest memories he knew this place, every tree, rock, and path. When he thought of a place nearby like the backwater, or a spot on the river, he could transport himself there. Those moments were relived in his mind along with the stories Nick had told him. He remembered and knew them word for word, how he wrote them down. They seemed like real events that had actually happened. Sometimes he felt it was as if his life had been programmed like a computer, all the information input into his mind, waiting to be used for some specific reason or time.

"Let's go inside, Michael, and finish off that bottle of wine."

Michael opened the front door of the old rustic cabin, the place where he had grown up, and the place his Grandpa Nick had built. He paused a moment before closing the door, turned, and scanned the darkness—there was only darkness, and a soft breeze. He closed the door, and turned the deadbolt lock until it clicked into place. He grabbed the wine, and poured what was left into their glasses. After watching the last few drops fall they sipped it slowly. It went down smooth, like feathers floating in a breeze dancing to a waltz.

With glasses in hand they walked the stairs, and passed the room where he had slept as a kid. Every night while growing up, that was the room where Nick had told him stories. They were tales about the driver: the guy who could get out of any situation. He remembered all of them, and all of the details, and now he was using the stories in his book. He sat at his desk and turned on the computer, and Sue was on his lap.

"Let's see. Here it is! The chapter about the professor. I want to show you one of the stories Poppi told me, and after, you tell me what you think. I've written it down, but basically just repeating what Poppi told to me when I was a kid."

"Okay, I'll look at it," Sue said.

Michael sat down and recalled what he'd written as Sue read it.

Bedtime Stories and Dreams—Memories of Michael Colt—The Professor

The driver had heard of a professor who had studied and taught logical science, and used a system that he invented to predict future outcomes. Companies, the military, and some private operators were his clients. From time to time he would bet on sports, or maybe the stock market, with a pretty high success rate, and this afforded him a comfortable lifestyle. His cosmopolitan accent gave him an air of sophistication; he usually left his audience clapping, spellbound, asking questions, and clamoring for more. He even had groupies who waited around to have a book autographed or a picture taken with him. That's where the driver saw the professor the very first time, at a conference where he heard him give a presentation on logic.

Something the driver read and heard during the program and presentation struck him, something he couldn't get out of his mind, and it went something like this: There is a thing called Sidereal Time based on the constellations. It mirrors our own twenty-four hour system, but in a celestial way. So, using this as a starting point, we take a body of raw information and make presumptions with a subject matter and a quality. Then we change the quality with a logical formula, and perhaps with intuitive skills we can predict outcomes to forecast the unknown. For example, we can say, all men are mortal, some men are mortal, no men are mortal. This reads as non-logical except for the one logical concept that we believe. And from simple deductive reasoning we conclude that all men are mortal. This model can be used with any idea as long as we have some negatives and one positive. This is a simple explanation of the concept, and illustrates it visually. Using other formulas, which are much more complex, the future can be predicted to the highest degree of success.

Building a logical model would include some other program components: factors like resources or barriers, activities along the lines of processes, techniques, relationships, outputs, outcomes, and impact. A checklist would be made covering everything that has been done, is being done, can be done, can't be done, hasn't been done, and on and on. We have to ask who, what, where, when, how, which, why, and make a case for or against. Using the raw data as a premise, reflecting rationally, making inferences, and finding what's plausible allows us to systematically make judgments. A body of knowledge, intuition, and refined arguments help us navigate unknown territory, and leads us to a systematic theory.

Discipline and valid logic keep us on the path to reach our goal, and give answers as we construct a pattern that in turn becomes a shape, and finally an idea. Now, how do we do this? Well, we could use words like the sentence given as an example previously, or propositional connectives. What are they? Basically just symbols, for example, let's say M stands for a proposition of movable change and negation. M = a man is sitting on a chair. So, we have M. What next? Well, this can change to a man standing on a chair, a disjunction=M^N; a man is standing next to the chair, conditional=M&N; a man holding a chair, biconditionan= M#N; a man under the chair=M>N, on and on we make all the possibilities and decide if they are true or false. Then we throw in the quantifiers, universal and existential, necessity and possibility. Our solution comes from symbolic logic. How can any of this help anyone you may ask? That's a good question, but simple and logical.

Negatives and one positive, is it as simple as that? the driver thought. *Could I predict the outcome of anything? I've got to talk to this man, and find out how he does it. This could be helpful to me.*

After the conference the driver got the chance to speak with the professor, and after some interesting banter, set up a meeting at a hole-in-the-wall coffee shop in a nearby town the next week. When the driver arrived at the restaurant, the professor was already there sitting at the table drinking coffee. He waved as he came through the door and introduced himself again when the professor stood.

"Hello, Professor, nice of you to meet with me. I can't thank you enough for taking the time. I know you're busy. I'm John Ray"

"Mr. Ray?" The professor repeated. "Is that your real name?"

"Why would I tell you that's my name if it wasn't?"

"I don't know, would you? Have you got a business card?" the professor asked.

"No, sorry I don't."

"Join me, have a seat. What can I do for you, Mr. Ray?" the professor asked, and with a smile as he sat down.

The driver had an ordinary looking black cloth bag that he put on the floor, then he sat down. "What can you do for me?" he said almost parroting word for word what Professor had said. "I'm hoping a lot. It involves your system for predicting outcomes."

"Tell me what you need."

"My work can sometimes be dangerous, so if the outcome could be predicted to some degree, I could choose whether or not to take on projects that might otherwise seem so."

"I'm not sure I can help you unless you tell me more. What do you want?"

"A system to lower my risk as much as possible while still being able to complete my task is what I'm looking for. So after hearing your presentation, I was impressed with the simplicity of your system."

"There are ways, logical ways, to predict anything, but my technique is more complex than what I speak about, and most people would never understand how it works."

"Yes, your presentation last night interested me immensely, and I know there's more to it, but I was very impressed with what I heard. So, a scenario for example, if I gave you random information about a project, would it be possible to predict the outcome?"

"It could be done," the professor said, "but I'd need to know everything, all the variables, nothing left out. If just one part is missing it throws everything off."

"How long does your process take once you start working on something?"

"Of course it depends on the content, but I should finish in a day or two."

"What if I gave you a situation now, could you get back to me in a couple of days?"

"Sure, don't see why not."

The driver handed an envelope to the professor. "I need to know all I can, and whether or not this plan will work."

The professor opened it, took out the documents, then after a few minutes, said, "Yes, I think a day or two will be fine. How do I contact you?"

"I'll get in touch with you," the driver said. "Is that okay?"

"No problem. I can work that way."

"I'll give you the meeting place tomorrow night," the driver said. "I'll leave a notice in your mailbox."

"How will you do that, I didn't tell you where I live?"

"I know where you live."

"Secretive, and a careful guy you are, Mr. Ray. Don't know if I like that or not."

"It has to be that way; the nature of the work dictates every move. That's why I'm interested in your system, to raise the percentages in my favor. So, the bigger the risk, the more I make, and that's a larger piece for you."

"I understand," the professor said. "So, let's talk about my piece."

"Have you got an amount in mind?"

"Well, if my formula has the potential to save . . . or give you a higher means of success, it could be very valuable to you."

"Yes, it could," the driver said, "but un-tested. We don't know if it'll really work yet, do we?"

"I can give you a guarantee that what I tell you, after looking over your information, will have a success rate of at least 90 percent."

"That's very high. How can you be so sure?"

"I know my work, and how it works. I understand that you need a guarantee, so let's just say the first report is on the house."

"And after that?"

"And after that it'll be expensive, but guaranteed success is priceless."

"Can you give me a ballpark figure?"

The professor took a napkin, wrote a number on it, and handed it to him. "Think you'll be able to afford that?"

The driver smiled. "Okay, I'll contact you tomorrow, and let you know the meeting place."

"Until then," the professor said, and held his cup up in a toast celebrating their bargain. The driver walked out of the coffee shop and vanished after turning the corner.

As it turned out, the professor had a spot-on assessment that seemed to show that the job would succeed. From then on the driver would provide a problem, one similar to the task, and the professor would measure the probability of success. If the percentage was high enough, the driver would take the job.

***

"Well, what do think of it?"

"It sounds interesting, Michael," Sue said. "How did your Grandfather come up with this idea? Or are you making it up?"

"I remember every story he told me, and that's my book. I'm dedicating it to Poppi."

"I think he'd like it!" Sue said and kissed Michael.

"Here read this next part."

"Okay, I will, but then that's all for tonight."

Bedtime Stories and Dreams—Memories of Michael Colt—The Last Job

"Tell me about the SSU," Michael said. "How does someone get into it?"

"The driver worked with some guys he served with in the Army before joining the SSU."

"Can I join the SSU when I grow up, Poppi?"

"I don't see why not, Michael, but it's dangerous work." Nick said, knowing that it was impossible for that to ever happen. "You're not afraid?"

"The driver always gets away, doesn't he, Poppi?"

Nick hesitated a moment. "Yes, Michael, he always gets away. Okay, let's get back to the story. On this particular operation in the mountains of Austria the target was the great grandson of a prominent family dynasty founded years before. The family had built a large multinational business, and had their tentacles in everything."

"What's a dynasty, Poppi?"

"A very big and important family distinguished for their success, wealth, and power."

"Rich people," Michael whispered.

"That's right, super-rich," Nick said. "It's a story of control like the trilogy written by Frank Norris. His first book was called, *The Octopus*, the second, *The Pit*, and the third, which he didn't finish because he died, was supposed to be called, *The Wolf*."

"What are those stories about?"

"Well, *The Octopus* is about the control of wheat production in the United States; *The Pit,* is control of the wheat trade in Chicago; the third was going to be about how Europe takes over all of the markets completely."

"Can that be done by someone?"

"Sure, Michael," Nick said. "People with lots of money control the world."

"How do they do that?"

"They make, and change the rules to benefit themselves."

"Tell me more about the family in Austria."

"Well, the grandson spent most of his time at the family château, and apparently the family didn't like how he was moving to take over the business, and they wanted him out. Otto, the grandson, was to be taken to a special meeting place and handed over to a group, who he was told would protect him, but if the plan had worked they would have been accused of kidnapping and killing him. As it turned out, the driver and team were duped."

"What's duped?"

"Tricked, fooled, and deceived by both sides."

"I thought the driver used the professor's formula to avoid that kind of thing."

"He did use the professor's formula, but this time it didn't work."

"Why not?"

"The plan changed."

"Why?"

"Otto was supposed to be taken out of the picture completely. The team first found out about the plan to kill Otto when they heard the plan was to hand Otto over to the family's goons. The driver knew them from previous missions, and what the real purpose was, so he decided to help Otto. He felt sorry for him."

"That's why the formula didn't work?"

"It was the one time the professor's logic formula would be tested. During their meeting he explained what he needed from him. The driver gave the information to the professor to sort out whether it was feasible. After a couple of days he got the answer. The information from the professor was correct, but like I said, the plan changed. The driver decided to rescue Otto from the killers, and Otto was hunted from then on by the family who had arranged the whole caper from the start."

"Caper? What's that?" Michael asked.

"The job they were hired to do for SSU."

"What happened after that, Poppi?"

"The team broke up, the driver retired to a life in the country."

"Where did he go?"

"Sorry, Michael, can't tell you that because it would put the driver in a perilous situation. That information would be valuable to the family who hired SSU, and be the end of the driver."

"Perilous means dangerous?"

"Yes, grave danger."

"Wow!" Michael said. "What happened to the professor, and the formula?"

"The professor disappeared, and the driver hid the formula in a place so no one could find use it."

"But you said it didn't work the last time. Why would anyone want it?"

"Yes, that's right, but the professor worked on it, and came up with a formula that could not only predict, but change the future, and it was infallible."

"What does infallible mean?"

"Faultless and full-proof."

"What happened to the professor?"

"Let's put that on the back burner for now. I'll tell you that story another time. Better go to bed now, it's late."

***

"Well?" Michael said."

Sue looked at Michael. "I want to read more."

"Not tonight," Michael said. "Let me work on it a little more first."

Sue kissed Michael. "I think it's good start for a story, and can't wait till I read all of it."

Michael looked at Sue. "Let's go to bed."

SSU

The office for the publishing house was on the top floor of a modern Art Deco building located in Chicago. Agents from around the world held monthly meetings there. No one really knew what was done there, but it was registered as a publishing company, and they represented a number of authors. They chose various books from authors, some famous, others unknown, and published them as a cover. On this day he had to tell his associates about a manuscript, and writer, that he had been in contact with. R. Lee sat in a taxi on his way from the airport thinking about the manuscript he had in his possession. He had just flown in from New York, and there were a few other manuscripts he'd read, but one in particular made his face go pale. It contained confidential information that only a handful people knew about. There was only one way that could have happened; the writer knew an agent who had retired.

For the most part, after an agent retired, all of the secrets stayed and died with him when that time came.

What they knew would never be shared with anyone. This had been the policy since SSU had begun. It was a private organization that would hire out to the highest bidder. Agents would receive assignments from governments, companies, and individuals. On occasion agents would compete with each other to complete a contract. Now some of this information had the possibility of leaking out through a book from an unknown writer.

R. Lee placed his hand on the identity reader, then walked through the secure entrance. He got into the elevator, pushed the button for the top floor, and when it stopped to pick someone up, he greeted them with a nod. Some agents were not known to each other because levels of security had been put in place to keep them in the dark about what was really going on. One could be in the elevator with another agent at any moment and not know it.

His first stop was the men's room to put on a tie and freshen up after his flight. He opened his bag, took out an electric razor, and began shaving. Then turned on the tap, tossed water on his face, and did it again after looking at himself in the mirror. R. Lee was getting old, and gray. This job had taken a toll on him, and he was ready to call it quits. His blues eyes couldn't see as sharply anymore, there was a ringing in his ears, and his voice was weak. There was a stack of towels on the side, he grabbed one and dried his face. His hair was short, so there was no need to comb it. After taking a deep breath, he left and walked down the hall with the sound of each footstep clicking, and counted them in his mind. He turned left and right as he made his way to the end of the corridor where his office was located.

He sat down behind his desk, and dialed the phone. "Good morning."

"So, what do you have for me today?" A voice with a hint of a European accent replied.

"I'd like you to have a look at a manuscript," R. Lee said.

"Is it good?"

"It's an interesting book," R. Lee said. "A book written by a guy whose name is Michael Colt. Does the name Colt ring with you?"

"Colt?" the man asked. "How did that happen?"

"He's Colt's grandson."

"I thought you took care of this problem years ago?" the man said.

"Yes, I've been working on it, and thought it was under control, but somehow the grandson knows about some major operations from the past when Nick Colt was active," R. Lee said.

"This is unacceptable," the man said.

"Fortunately, I was able to intercept the manuscript before anyone got their hands on it. I've been in contact with Michael Colt, telling him that his book isn't very good, and he should forget about being a writer, but, he's persistent, and says he may self-publish it."

"Are there any copies of this book out in the public?"

"We're not sure."

"Why has this been going on for so long?"

"Like I said, I thought I had it under control."

"Does he know about the professor, and the formula?" the man asked.

"Singleton Black may have had some information about him, but he didn't have the formula on him, he didn't talk to anyone as far as we know. Nick Colt disappeared; we don't know where he is. He's been missing for years."

"What about Moses?" the man said. "What does he know?"

"We haven't contacted Moses," R. Lee said, "but he's becoming curious. He did work for us."

"So, what's your next move?" the man asked.

"I think I should arrange a meeting with Colt, and perhaps help publish it with a ghost writer. If we do that I can edit out what we don't want known. I think I can make it work."

"Even with a ghost writer some information is going be leaking to the public," the man said.

"I think I can fix it so nothing leaks out."

"Yes, it's your responsibility, see to it!"

THE BOOK AGENT

The cell alarm clock howled like there was a disaster approaching, and his computer screen was dark. "What time did I go to sleep?" Groggy and tired, Michael closed his eyes a minute trying to remember what time he had fallen asleep. "Looks like I wrote some last night," he said, looking at the computer monitor, "but don't have time to read it now. I'll save the file and read it later." He turned off the computer, went into the kitchen and made coffee. He opened his schedule book and checked what was on for today. There were two jobs: give an estimate on a stone fireplace, and finish up some masonry work on a barn foundation.

Buster was playing with his old baseball glove from high school. The dog would bite into it, and shake it trying to rip it apart, but the glove was resilient, and would take many more years of abuse. The dog liked the glove so much that Michael let him have it, and bought a new one when he finally destroyed it. *If you could put it on your paw, we could play catch.* "Hey, boy, come here," he said, then whistled. Buster looked up, dropped the glove, charged the bed, then jumped on Michael. "Okay," he said, "take it easy." Michael put up his hands to block Buster from licking his face. "Okay, okay," then the dog jumped off the bed, let out a couple of hearty barks, ran down the stairs, and stood by the door waiting. "You want to go?" Michael said, then opened the door and Buster charged outside.

Michael filled the coffee maker with two cups of water, ground some coffee, then took out two eggs, and dropped them in a fry pan. He put a piece of toast in the toaster, and flipped the eggs as he looked at some notes tacked on a bulletin board next to the refrigerator. Michael had received so many rejection letters from editors, agents, and publishers they were piling up. He resolved not to give up, and occasionally he'd send a letter out to find an agent interested in his book. R. Lee always sent the most negative replies, and for a guy he'd never met, the replies about his book from him sure were negative. Michael couldn't help but write back. In the letter Michael asked R. Lee for some references, titles of books that he'd published, and names of writers he represented. R. Lee wrote back saying that Michael's book would never be published.

"This is crazy, so why do I keep doing this?" Then the phone rang, and knocked him out of the trance of negativity he was in after looking at the rejection letters.

"Hey, how are you doing?" Sue said.

"Good, good," Michael said. "Just having something to eat. How about you?"

"Walking to the bar."

"I'm going for a walk after I eat. Buster's already waiting for me. I'll stop by the bar later on my way into town."

"You okay?" Sue said because she thought Michael didn't sound the same.

"Yeah, fine," he said, "just reading some rejection letters."

"Don't worry about what they say," she said, "your book is good! Come by the bar and I'll make lunch for you."

"Okay," he said as Buster barked. "The dog's getting impatient. I've got to go."

"I hear him," Sue said. "See you later."

"Bye."

Michael took his time walking along the river this morning. He was on a well-worn path in the woods, playing fetch with Buster, listening to all the sounds of the woods come to life. It usually took thirty minutes to walk to his favorite spot. Once out of the woods, the river shimmered, reflecting the brilliant light off the water and leaving a spectacular view at sunrise as it flowed south. This was his world, his playground, and the only life he knew. Hungry Point, a general store, restaurant, and the best bait & tackle shop around. Hungry Point was the place that made him feel good. He had Sue, the woods, the river, fishing, hunting, infinite stars at night. Why wasn't he happy? It was because of the book he was writing, and the letters from R. Lee.

As he walked after the dog the day felt eerily similar to a morning years ago: the day he found the body floating in the backwater. He brushed off the feelings of worry and continued down the path like he always did. Buster began barking and took off running to the edge of the tree line. Michael followed at a quick but leisurely pace. Buster stood near the water barking. "What's he barking at," Michael said, then saw a bulky object floating out in the middle of the backwater. It was a repeat of the morning so long ago when he was a kid, and that morning flashed through his mind.

"How could this happen twice?" he whispered. "I'm not going out there this time. I'll let the police handle it," he said, and took out his phone and dialed 9-1-1.

"Emergency operator, what's the nature of you call?"

"Hi, this Michael Colt out on Double X Road, and want to report finding a body floating in a backwater near my place. I think you should contact the police. I'll wait here until they come." After a few more questions and filling in some details, he hung up the phone and put it back in his pocket, then looked at Buster. "I guess now we just wait," he said, and looked for a comfortable place to sit.

Soon sirens blared, and police and first responders descended on the scene.

Michael stood, waved at the officers walking out of the tree line, and recognized Carlo Black. He was still a game warden, and leading the sheriff.

Michael smiled, and said, "Can you believe this, it's almost a repeat of what happened years ago, remember?"

"I'll never forget that day," Carlo said. "Didn't go out this time? Can't blame you."

"I sometimes dream about it," Michael said, "and don't need any more sleepless nights."

"Well, we'll take care of it from here," Carlo said, "but I think you should wait a bit in case the sheriff wants to ask you some questions."

"I understand," Michael said. "I'll be right here."

"Okay, I'll go see what we've got," Carlo said, and walked over and joined the officers standing at the edge of the water.

Michael sat on a stump next to Buster watching the action. He noticed Carlo point over in his direction a few times as he spoke to the sheriff, then two officers got into a flat bottom boat, and made their way out to the floating hulk. When they got back to shore two other officers put on waders, and helped retrieve the body. After they dragged the body to shore, they examined it, looking in pockets and through the clothes. The sheriff had a camera and began taking pictures from every angle possible. Finally, the paramedics arrived; they put the body in a bag and into the ambulance, then drove away.

Carlo walked over to Michael. "They'd like you to come to my office and answer some questions. Just routine. They're taking the body to the morgue to confirm the identity."

"What do they want to know from me?" Michael asked. "I told them everything. I really don't think I've got any other information that'll help solve this."

"Yeah, I know, but they've got to follow up and tie up all the loose ends. You can ride with me if you like. I'll give you a ride back."

"No, that's okay, I'll get my rig and meet you at your office, Michael said. "I've got to meet Sue, and a job to finish today. How long do you think it'll take?"

"Not more than an hour, I guess. So, I'll see you at the office then."

"I'll head there right after I stop by the house."

POLICE INTERVIEW

Michael pulled into the parking lot of the post office. Carlo's rig was parked in front, so he pulled in next to it the sheriff's car and another police car.

Michael sat in the truck thinking about the morning. *Why is this happening all over again?* "Well, guess I'll go in and get this over with," he whispered. He looked at Buster, "Stay here boy, I'll be right back." Michael rolled up the windows a little, so Buster couldn't get out, and got out of his truck. Just before he closed the door, Buster's ears stood up, "I'll be right back," he told the dog. "You stay and guard the truck."

Michael walked into the building wondering what he'd be asked. He climbed the stairs to the second floor and stood in the doorway a moment. Carlo sat behind his desk, two officers and Miller Brown were in front of it, and they both turned his way. He stopped inside the doorway waiting for some instructions from them.

"Thanks for coming Michael," Carlo said. "We'd like to ask you some questions about how you found the body."

"Sure, whatever I can do to help," Michael said. "What do you want to know?"

"First, I have to tell you that we're going to record this interview," one officer said. "Is that okay with you?"

"Yeah, go ahead."

The officer pulled the chair from the desk. "Please have a seat right here," he said, and moved the recorder to the center of the desk. He switched it on and put the mic in front of Michael. "Just speak toward the mic; it should pick up your voice. For the record could you state your name please?"

"Michael Colt."

"And where do you live?"

"On Double X Road, next to the river."

"How long have you lived in Hungry Point?"

"All my life," Michael said.

"Do you live there alone?"

"Yes, I do."

"Is your place near where the body was found?"

"Well, it's not near, but in the vicinity."

"How far would you say it is on foot from your place? How long would it take to walk there?"

"About twenty or thirty minutes, I guess."

"So, it is near your place?"

"Yeah, I guess."

"Do you walk around there a lot?"

"Almost every morning."

"How did you find the body this morning?"

"I usually take a different trail to make it more interesting. And I always end up at the backwater. Sometimes I go fishing there."

"What time did you find the body this morning?"

"About six-thirty."

"And you called 911 as soon as you found it?"

"Yes, that's right."

"You don't know the man we took out of the water?"

"No, no I don't. I didn't go into the water. I have no idea what he even looks like," Michael said. "Who is he? Do you know?"

"We're in the process of finding out," the officer said. "Okay, if we need to talk to you again we'll be in touch. Thanks for coming in."

"Sure, if you need anything else, give me a call."

"Oh, one more thing, it's quite a coincidence that you found another body in the same place when you were young. I remember working on that case."

Michael looked at Carlo. "Yeah, that's right," Michael said. "I was young, and with my Grandfather after he found the body."

"And what happened after is still a mystery," the officer said. "The shootout Carlo had, and how Nick Colt vanished without a trace."

"I was a kid when that happened," Michael said. "I don't know what happened to my grandfather. No one does!"

"What about the guy who works with you," Miller asked. "Moses, right? He know anything about this?"

"You'll have to ask Moses if he knows anything about it."

"Okay, thanks for coming in Mr. Colt."

Michael left Carlo's office, and headed for Outsider Inn. *Wait till Sue hears about this.*

***

"So, Carlo, how long have you known Michael Colt?" Miller Brown asked.

"Oh, known him since he was a kid. Was good friends with his grandfather, Nick, and Moses."

"What else do you know about, him? Has he ever been in trouble?"

"Michael in trouble? No, he's a great guy."

"What does he do?"

"He's a stone mason, builds fireplaces, construction, does some carpentry work. He's lived here all his life. His grandfather raised him, and he lives in the same house that his grandfather Nick built, out on Double X Road."

"Okay, when we find out more about our dead man we'll be in touch. Michael sure has grown up. He's pretty big. I guess lifting and building fireplaces all these years had something to do with that."

"Yeah, I guess so," Carlo said. "Let me know when you find out who the guy we found is."

***

No one was at the bar yet, but he saw Sue's car, and pulled up next to it.

She walked out and waved. She was dressed in jeans and a white shirt, and getting ready to open the bar. When Michael got to the top of the deck she gave him a hug. "That put a smile on your face?"

Michael hugged her back, and wouldn't let go.

"Wow!" Sue said. "Don't know where that came from, but I like it."

Michael looked around, then said, "Let's go inside; I've got something to tell you."

"What is it?"

"I'll tell you inside."

"What is it?' Sue asked as they entered the bar.

"Right after I talked to you on the phone, I went for a walk with Buster to the river. Everything seemed normal until I heard him barking. When we got to the backwater I saw something floating out it the water."

"What was it?"

"A body!"

"What?" Sue said. "Isn't that where you found the other body when you were a kid?"

"Yeah, almost the same place. I called 9-1-1 and they came to collect the body. After that I had a strange talk with Miller Brown. He was the detective that handled the other case."

"What did they ask you?"

"Typical stuff about finding the body," Michael said. "And they mentioned the other time too. Carlo brought it up I think." Sue brought a plate with a hamburger and fries, and put it on the bar. Michael took a bite. "Nice!"

Sue grabbed some fries. "What do you think will happen?"

"I don't know, but I got some bad vibes from the cops, and Carlo."

"It'll be fine; you have nothing to do with him."

"I found him near my place," Michael said. "Other than that theres's no connection as far as I know."

Sue put her hand under Michael's chin, and bit her lip as a cold chill went through her body. She kissed Michael. "It's going to be okay, don't worry."

"Thanks for the lunch," he said, and held her close. "I'll see you tonight," Michael said. "I've got a fireplace to build."

Michael left the bar, Sue watched him drive away, to where they were putting up a large stone fireplace for a guy and his son who had bought land outside Hungry Point. This family was building a grand log cabin as well as buying and accumulating land, so he was obviously well off. Peter Voritch was a thin older man in his mid-seventies who spoke with a slight German accent. Michael had only met the older Voritch a few times, but whenever he did, he felt they'd met before. He bought a herd of cattle and told everyone he intended to raise them and crop farm the land. Most of the work was done by his son Max who spoke with no accent, but in an educated tone. The word was they were avid hunters planning to keep their place private for his family and friends.

The log cabin was being built by Michael's classmate who was somewhat of a local celebrity after building a replica of Laura Ingles home. A Japanese tourist visiting the area liked the cabin so much he hunted down his friend. Soon his buddy was hired by this same Japanese person to build log houses in Japan at a place called Utsunomiya, just north of Tokyo.

One summer Michael went along, and stayed there to build stone fireplaces in a few log cabins. They stayed in the countryside at a chicken ranch surrounded by a Nashi orchard; it was their temporary home away from home. At night they relaxed soaking in a hot tub, ate, drank, and while talking with one of the Japanese carpenters Michael heard how this Japanese guy had traveled extensively all over the world, living in a kibbutz in Israel, and playing guitar in a rock band. But going to such a far off place like Japan had become difficult, so Michael never went there again, and just did work around Hungry Point. Instead he sent Moses to Japan who enjoyed it immensely.

CONNECTION

Michael's phone rang while he sat on the deck of the cabin. He turned toward the open door and listened, then his recorded message started. *Hi, you've reached Michael Colt, please leave your name and number, and I'll get back to you.*

"Hey, Michael, Carlo here, pick up if you're there. Call me back right away. " Michael finished his drink, then went into the house.

He hesitated a moment, then dialed Carlo's number.

The phone rang once. "Carlo Black speaking."

"It's Michael. What's going on?"

"They know who he is."

"Okay, so, who is he?"

"His name is R. Lee, a literary agent from New York."

"New York?"

"Yeah, he publishes books, well . . . used to anyway, and is pretty well known among people in that field. Have you heard of the name?" There was a long pause. "Michael, do you know anyone by that name?"

After another long pause he said, "Well, not really."

"Not really? What does that mean?"

"I've never met him in person."

"You do know him?"

"I sent copies of a story I've been working on to some agents, and one guy's name was R. Lee."

"You're writing a book?"

"Yeah," Michael said. "Does that sound strange?"

"Never thought of you as a writer," Carlo said. "What's it about?"

"Some stories Nick told me at night when I was a kid."

"You don't know anything about how this guy ended up floating in the river?"

"I didn't know the man," Michael said. "We emailed. I don't know how he ended up floating in the backwater by my place."

"Well, I think Miller Brown will be paying you a visit to connect some dots."

"Fine with me; I don't have anything to hide. I sent the guy some emails, that's all."

"What did you say in the emails?"

"The guy was an asshole, so I just told him what I thought, said what was on my mind."

"Okay, I'll give you a heads-up if I hear anything, and you let me know if anyone contacts you about this."

"Okay, be in touch."

"Bye."

Michael stepped out on the deck and looked over the landscape. *I wonder what R. Lee was doing here. I can't imagine him coming to see me, so maybe he came to see someone else. But who could that be?*

Then he heard Buster barking out front, and a car door slam. "Now who's that?" There was a knock on the door. "Buster, quiet. Sit!"

A voice from outside said, "It's Miller Brown."

"Come on in, wasn't expecting a visit from you so soon. How's the investigation progressing? Any news?"

"We know who the guy you found is."

"Who is he?"

"His name is R. Lee? I've got to ask you if you knew or ever met him before him."

"No, never met him," Michael said, "but I know the name, and saw his picture online."

"How do you know the name?"

"I sent him a copy of my story, and he wrote back telling me it was crap. We've been emailing each other, but never met. Unfortunately he's dead, so I can't tell him he's an ass, and now I should speak kindly of the dead."

"Michael, I've got to say this looks a little peculiar."

"Why's that?"

"Finding a guy you've been in contact with, who was found dead near your place, doesn't it seem strange to you?"

"I swear I had nothing to do with it other than finding him."

"Can I see some of the emails you sent?"

"I'm not sure I should do that."

"Well, I think you'd better get yourself a lawyer because we'll want to see those emails, and maybe search your place."

"This is crazy, there are lots of agents that I sent my book to. He wasn't the only one."

"The only one found dead floating in a backwater near your house. Are there any other dead book agents we should know about?"

"Are you kidding me? Go get your warrant and we'll talk after that."

"Sorry it has to be like this, Michael," Miller said. "I'll give you a call to let you know when to come to Dodge for questioning."

THE QUESTIONS

Michael sat at a small square table in the center of the room. There was something like a window on the side, but it was dark, and probably a one-way mirror where he was being watched by someone. Cameras stared down from every corner capturing the view of the table from different angles. He was surrounded by silence except for the spinning fan above the table. As he looked up at the fan, footsteps clicked down the hallway, but no one came into the room. He sat and waited with passing glances at his watch. He took a drink of water from the bottle that sat on the table, and listened to it trickle down his throat as he swallowed. When he stopped drinking and eyed the bottle, he saw that he'd drunk half of it.

He watched the doorknob turn and the door open, and Miller Brown walked in followed by a man he'd never seen before. After they sat at the table, they fixed their eyes on Michael and grinned.

"Hi, Michael," Miller Brown said in a friendly sort of way.

"Hi," Michael said.

"This is Detective Tom Class. He's going to ask you some questions as well."

"Hi, Michael," Detective Class said. "Sorry we've got to meet under these circumstances. I've heard a little about your situation from Detective Brown."

"So, what can I do for you? I know I'm here to answer questions, so ask me anything. I want to help in any way I can."

"Okay, Michael, let's start then," Miller said. "For the record, we need you to state your name, and just answer the questions. Just speak in a normal voice. Your name is Michael Colt?" Miller asked.

"Yes, Michael Colt. I told you this already."

"Again please? Where do you live?"

"Hungry Point."

"Have you lived in Hungry Point your whole life?"

"Yes I have."

"And what do you do?"

"I'm a mason. I build things with stone, and write a little when I have time."

"Next we're going ask you some questions about R. Lee, the man you found in the backwater."

"Go ahead."

"Did you know R. Lee?"

"We never met, but I sent him a copy of my book. I was looking for an agent who could help me find a publisher. I got his name and some others from a publishing magazine."

"What kind of book is it?"

"Do you really want to know that?"

"Yes, we do," Detective Class said.

"About life in a small town, intertwined with bedtime stories my grandfather told me. His stories were about undercover agents. It's like a spy story, especially about one character who Nick, my grandfather, called the driver. My grandfather never gave him a name, so I didn't either, I just call him 'The Driver'."

"How did you communicate with R. Lee?"

"Email, never met or talked to him in person."

"What did he say in the correspondence you had?"

"Basically he told me my book was crap, and that it would never sell. I sent an email back. I don't know why it continued as long as it did, the back and forth, taking turns bad-mouthing each other."

"Did you ever threaten him in any of the emails?"

"What do you mean?"

"Threaten to kill him," Detective Class said.

"Those are your words, not mine," Michael said. "I never said I'd kill him, but said some other things about his skill as an agent and his taste. Do you really think I had something to do with what happened to R. Lee?"

"We've got to ask some tough questions. We're not accusing you of anything. Just trying to put together a picture of what happened to R. Lee."

"Okay, sorry, ask away."

"How often do you walk to the backwater?"

"I go there just about every day, and have since I was a kid."

"Did you meet or see him before that morning?"

"I told you that I've never met him, and don't know what he looks like."

"I mean without knowing," Detective Class said. "Maybe he was tailing you without you knowing. From what you've said he sounds like kind of a fanatic."

"Tailing me in Hungry Point?" Michael said, and just shook his head in disbelief. "I think I'd know if he was following me. There aren't too many strangers walking around here."

"There are tourists that go to Hungry Point, aren't there?" Detective Class said. "He could have looked like one of them and blended in."

"You think he confronted me and I killed him because he didn't like my book?"

"We didn't say that, Michael," Miller said. "We want to get the truth, that's all."

"I don't know, I don't remember. It's possible, I guess. But why would he come after me? He could have called or emailed, there's really no reason for him to come to Hungry Point. "

It was silent a moment as they wrote on their legal pads. "Okay, Michael that's all we have for now," Miller said. "You can go, and we'll contact you if we need to talk to you." Miller Brown and Tom Class watched as Michael stood and left the room.

As the door closed, Detective Class turned to Miller. "What do you think?"

"I think he's telling the truth," Miller said.

Then Tom Class took out a file from his briefcase. "We just need to find out about this," and handed the file to Miller Brown.

"What's this?" Miller said.

"Read it," Tom Class said.

THE WITNESS

After Michael finished working for the day he stopped at the bar for a drink, and to say hi to Sue, then headed home. As he walked into the cabin the phone was ringing.

"Michael," Carlo said. "I just heard there's a witness to R. Lee's murder."

"A witness? Who?"

"Why don't you come to my office and we'll go over it again."

"I just got home," Michael said.

"They'll come to your place and get you if you don't come in," Carlo said.

"Is this witness saying that I had something to do with killing R. Lee?"

"An eye witness, that's all Miller Brown said. He didn't give me any details."

"Well, whatever this witness is saying to them, they're lying. I wasn't there, and I didn't do it!"

"They've got to check out the story, and if it turns out not to be true, we'll know. A person can't lie about a thing like that and expect to get away with it."

"Hey, I can tell you it's not true. Isn't my word good for anything? Why am I under the microscope for this? Why are they focusing on me? Aren't there any other suspects?"

"No one else's name has come up as far as I know. If there are other suspects they could be keeping it under wraps."

"Is this all happening because I found the body?" Michael said. He was getting frustrated, but agreed to go in again. "What time do you want me there?"

"Come as soon as you can," Carlo said. "Miller Brown and Tom Class will be here too. They have more questions to ask."

"More questions about what?" Michael said. "What questions? My name and where I live?"

"I don't really know what they'll ask."

"I'll head out now, see you soon."

I've got to call Sue, he thought, and dialed her number.

"Sue, they want to ask me more questions about the book agent."

"What do they think?" Sue said. "Do they know what happened?"

"Carlo said there's a witness."

"Really, then it's over."

"No, the witness said they saw me there."

"How can that be? Michael?"

"I don't know what to think anymore. I'll call you after I meet with them."

"Should I go with you?"

"Better not, I don't want you involved in this, I'll call you later."

"I'll be at the bar," Sue said. "Call me back when you know more."

"I will. So long, Sue."

"Bye, Michael."

Michael pulled into the Post Office parking lot. *I've been coming here a lot lately. What haven't they asked me? Hell, I don't know anything about this. Just go in and get this over with and go home.* Michael opened Carlo's door and saw Miller Brown sitting in front of the desk and Tom Class standing next to a book shelf in the corner. They all turned and looked at Michael as he walked in.

"Okay, I see we've got the whole crew together again," Michael said. "What are we going to talk about now, the St Valentines Day Massacre? I wasn't in Chicago on that day because I wasn't born yet."

"Michael, this is serious," Miller said. "There's a witness that'll testify that they saw you shoot R. Lee."

"Who is it?" Michael said. "Because they're lying. I didn't do it."

"Well, Michael I'm afraid we've got to take you in for questioning, and formally arrest you for the murder of R. Lee."

"Arrest me? Really? I just found the guy, I didn't shoot him."

"If the evidence shows that you had nothing to do with it, you'll be free to go."

"So I have to stay in jail? How long?"

"Well, if the judge allows bail, maybe tomorrow. If not, until the case is over."

"I can't believe this," Michael said, then closed his eyes and took a deep breath.

"Hold out your hands," Tom Class said.

"Handcuffs? You're actually going to handcuff me? Why? What do you think I'll do, run away?"

"It's standard operating procedure," Tom Class said. "We have to do it."

"So this is what it feels like to be a criminal." *I've never been arrested in my life. What would Poppi say? What would he do?*

Tom Class locked the cuffs. "Let's go, Michael."

"Do you want me to ride along?" Miller asked.

"I think I'll be okay," Class said. "Michael's not going to do anything crazy, are you?"

"I don't see how it could get any crazier than it already has. Where are we going?"

"First we'll drive to Dodge," Miller said," then process you, ask a few more questions, and find out about this witness."

"I want to call a lawyer," Michael said.

THE PLAN

This is where he was in his life, and it was a deep dark place, alone with limited options. Is this a test? he thought. Am I a guinea pig? I've got to get out tonight.

Jarred by a clanging key in the cell door lock, Michael looked up and watched the guard open the cell door. The lawyer walked in, set a briefcase on the table, unsnapped it, then reached in and took out a pile of files. He placed them on the table and sat down. For a moment they just stared, silent, measuring each other.

The lawyer pushed the stack of files over to Michael. "That's what they have. Their whole case is right there in that stack of files, and it doesn't look good," the lawyer said. "We should plead guilty. There's really no other choice because you're going to lose. Pleading for mercy, and asking the judge for leniency is the only course to avoid a death penalty."

"And I stay locked in the can forever, staring at concrete walls and bars."

"You'll be alive."

"Alive? Being locked up eternally isn't living. I should be out," Michael said, then raised his arm, and pointed to the door, "out there. You're my lawyer, do something to help me get out of here. Why are you giving up so easily?"

"Maybe you think you should be out, but what about the evidence?" the lawyer said. "It's there written down in black and white, pictures, testimony. Is all of it a lie? A frame-up?"

"Yes, it's a lie! All of this is some kind of stupid or weird misunderstanding," Michael said. "And, if I have the chance, I'll prove it! I know I will. I can prove it."

"How? Look at the evidence," the lawyer said, and pointed the files on the table. "There's a stack of documents here, and that information proves you're guilty."

"I know what the documents say, and I could disprove it," Michael said. "I just need more time to sort it all out. I still can. It'll just take a little time, that's all. I still have some time left. "

"Well, you'll have plenty of time if we take the offer and plead guilty. Why not sort it out after?"

"I didn't do it," Michael said. "More time is what I need."

"What is there to sort out? What can you change? How can you change any of it? What's done is done, so accept it and move on."

"I can't tell you now because, if I do, I'll rot in here forever, and they'll never let me out."

"Well, if you plead innocent, but found guilty, you'll be in here waiting for your last meal, and on that day your life will end. They'll walk in here, say it's time, and life as you know it will be over. It'll be your last walk, and your last sunrise."

"I need time," Michael said.

The lawyer looked at the Michael and knew he wasn't going to change his mind. "Okay, he said, "we'll go to court and plead innocent. You can get up in front of a judge and jury, tell your side of the story, and let them decide the outcome. I'll see you in court tomorrow." The lawyer put the files back in, grabbed his briefcase. "Oh, I almost forgot, this is for you; it was delivered to the office yesterday." The lawyer handed Michael a large manila envelope similar to what he used for his manuscript.

"A package for me?" Michael whispered. "What is it?"

"I don't know," the lawyer said. "It was dropped off by courier. Have a good night, and see you in court tomorrow."

The lawyer left the cell, and Michael sat on the bunk holding the package. It wasn't heavy, and he wondered what was inside. One by one the lights went out like electric light bulb dominos, then sounds of footsteps tapped on the concrete floor, and groans of sleepiness floated through the air. There was a metallic clanging; the whole cell block seemed like a huge musical instrument, an orchestra playing a mysterious tune. A cough here and there sent echoes out to what seemed to be an endless night. Michael opened the package, and as he took out a letter, an object fell into his hand. "Where did this come from? How did this happen?" Michael whispered, then took the amulet and draped it around his neck. When he held it in his fist his hand became warmer.

He unfolded the letter, and began to read.

Michael,

Prison is a junkyard filled with scrap metal, and it can be torn, ripped, and crushed. In this world of the cosmos, space, and existence, do you ever wonder who, or what, controls what we do, think, and imagine? Some people believe there is a God, others believe in something, but not sure what, while another percentage believe in nothing. Consider this from a basic level, not from any testimonial or historical background, start with the fact that you are, I am, we all are, somewhere. The question now is how did we get here? We really don't remember anything from an early age, so we rely on what we're told. We can see pictures of ourselves, and perhaps they hold a secret. If we examine them closely, what do we see?

We grow up following the crowd; some take a different path and go their own way, just like in the poem, by Robert Frost. People want to change the outcome of their lives. As all this happens the world around us continuously sheds information. We're re-loading our minds; tempting our spirit, and it tears at our soul. Someone is always trying to teach, preach or reach us. Maybe they have no idea what they're talking about, or maybe they know everything, the list of philosophers is endless. Think of how they learned what they know, and what principles are kept by them. Have they gone to or seen a different world? Know that through dreams we can go anywhere.

Are we born and bred to live with beliefs inherited, to follow a trail for their life? Some lay the track and set their own goals. Most plod along day by day lost in a fog, hidden in a shadow, living in light half of the time, and darkness the other half. Parents, grandparents, friends, and people celebrating life to its fullest, or condemning themselves all the time releasing an overflow of emotion that fertilizes humankind for good or bad.

So, where does God come in, and how does it affect the mind when we're told there is a God? People always look up to the sky to give thanks, and ask for forgiveness or help. We look forward when we want to escape, and down when we run from death and sadness. Is that because the body ends up in the ground as the spirit floats to Heaven as we leave our memories behind for others to share, or eventually forget? But, memories are not forgotten. People who have seen the future in dreams never forget.

The plan, your plan, my plan, so many plans, and each person finds the one that's right for them. Sometimes they make a mistake and go the wrong way. They've got to search for a way to use their talent to its full potential, try to do their best, try things until we feel it's right.

And where are you? What path did you choose? You're in a small room, it's cold, and the concrete walls are guarded with bars. There's no escape as

far as you can tell. No way out! But
there is a way to escape this place if
you remember where you came from. Your
first memories seem vague, like a dream,
but feel them down deep. Is it destiny
that didn't turn out the way it was
supposed to? I know that you don't want
to be in this cold damp place. You want
to escape, so escape!

The Professor

Michael stretched out on the bunk, closed his eyes, and gripped the amulet firmly. Poppi's voice spoke to him like the times when he was a kid, and told him bedtime stories.

Bedtime Stories and Dreams—Memories of Michael Colt—The Flight

Poppi's laconic voice delivered information about places and people, and painted a picture that could be imagined. I would fall asleep and dream of the stories again and again, and they were endless.

"An airplane flew through bulging white clouds, then it was dark, so dark he couldn't see. The driver heard the wind flapping outside while inside the passengers were asleep in their seats. He glanced out the window and looked down."

"What did he see?" Michael asked.

"He saw water, and said," 'We're flying low.'

"He was over the ocean?"

"Maybe, but then he saw a man in a black suit in the front of the plane, but the man paid him no notice."

"Why not?"

"He wondered if the man could see him, and whispered, 'Am I invisible?' then blinked."

"Was he?" Michael asked.

"No, he wasn't. Then he saw the man's hand, he was gripping something. A pistol syringe device with his finger on the trigger. The man walked down the aisle injecting the passengers in the neck with some kind of concoction. And a few minutes later they began waking up, moving their heads, bobbing, moaning, and stretching out their arms. One after another the passengers were injected, and one by one they woke out of their slumber, rolling their heads, and groaning."

"They were waking up?" Michael asked.

"Yes, and in the front of the plane another man in a dark suit appeared. He took a handheld microphone from the wall and he began to speak. He told them to stay calm."

"What did the passengers do?"

"The passengers sat still with their eyes locked on the man talking. He told them they were given a choice to board the plane or not, that they had all accepted, and now it was time to tell them why they were here."

"Why were they there?" Michael asked, then listened.

"After a moment the man disappeared, then reappeared, and said they would be landing soon. And, after landing, they would be given a file to read, so they would know their task. He said handlers would be waiting on the ground to assist them."

"What was in the files?"

"Their mission!

"What was the mission?"

"Nobody spoke to the driver, and just ignored him as if he wasn't there. The driver said, 'Who are these people? How did I get here?' then blinked."

"How did he get there?" Michael asked.

"We'll find that out later because they landed, then the passengers stood and began leaving the plane through the front hatch. They filed out in quick order, and lined up outside to get on silver vehicles that looked like oversized buses. After the passengers loaded onto the silver truck-like buses they drove away. The driver stood alone at the door of the plane. No one was there to meet him. When he turned back a man with the syringe device was standing there."

"Did he use it on the driver?" Michael asked.

"The man smiled, held the syringe up, and told him that he had two choices, this, meaning the syringe, or that, and pointed down the runway. The driver looked down the runway at a car coming closer. A black limo stopped, and the back door opened by itself. He walked closer, looked into the front seat, but could only see the shape of a person behind the wheel, then the door closed after he got into the back seat. Dark tinted windows and a divider prevented him from seeing anything outside clearly. The car drove off as he knocked on the glass trying to get the driver's attention."

"Where were they taking him?"

"Good question, kid. He pressed his face against the glass and saw a long empty road, and a barren landscape. He tried again to communicate with the person driving the car, but the guy said nothing, and never turned around. He opened a small cabinet that sat in the middle of the limo, and took out a bottle of mineral water. He wondered if anything was put in this water."

"Did he drink it?"

"Yes, and after that asked where they were they going."

"He heard an electronically modified voice say, 'Sit back and relax. I'll let you know when we arrive.'

"Why couldn't he tell him where they were going?"

"He'd dozed off by then, and a while later the car stopped, and he woke up. After a few moments, he rubbed his eyes and looked in the front seat, but saw nothing."

"What happened to the guy driving the car?"

"He wondered the same thing, and pushed the handle down and opened the door. He got out and stood, whirling, dizzy, then walked down the road a bit, then turned, and looked back at the car. It was gone. He wondered why he felt like he knew where he was. With only the clothes on his back he wandered down the road not knowing where he was going.

"What happened to the passengers from the plane?"

"We don't know yet, that'll come later. We do know they drove off in buses and trucks."

"What were all of those people doing on the plane? Why was he on the plane?"

"They were all going to a foundry."

"Why were they going there?"

"To get the bell amulets that were made at the foundry."

"He walked and walked to what looked like the end of road, but there was no end only more road and dust, then a fountain."

Bedtime Stories and Dreams—Memories of Michael Colt—Place of Iron

"In Dodge the main intersection somehow aligned perfectly with the compass. It was a trading settlement with a small business on each corner; a tavern, grocery store, gas station, and restaurant. The intersection was always busy and gradually changed into a village, then a town, finally a small city. It had a few nice parks, a pool, and a Country Club with an eighteen-hole golf course."

"Tell me more," Michael said. "What else was there in Dodge?"

"A foundry, a family owned blast furnace and the largest employer in town located on the north side near the old railroad turn-around with a workforce of 1,500. Freight trains came in one end, parked on the rotating platform, then a switch was thrown sending them out in another direction. After the round-house closed it was used by the foundry in town to stockpile scrap-iron. They built a new addition, so it was abandoned, and left to crumble. Over the years it became a club house for teenagers, home for transients, and finally where wildlife lived."

"Why did they let it fall apart?" Michael asked.

"Too expensive to keep up," Nick said. "There was a picture of the old brick round-house hanging in Dodge's river museum with an blue and yellow Stearman flying above it, and next to that another aerial photo of a huge bridge spanning the river. The photo had been taken in dead winter, and the frozen river reflecting an orange cast from an early sunset on the iron from the foundry. The museum was the place where visitors bought tickets for summer river cruises, read the history of the area, and had lunch in the café that overlooked the wide and fast flowing channel."

"You ever fly in a plane like that?" Michael asked.

"Sure did! Now, the foundry was a big place with machines and castings piled high and wide at one end inside the new addition. Outside virgin iron waited to be turned into liquid metal. It was stored in a huge bin made of old railroad ties stacked like Lincoln logs waiting to be burned. It was a mountain of external scrap that never shrunk. All day long small end-loaders slammed into this heap, scooped up and carried the mixture of scrap metal odds and ends inside. After the smelting process all this material became massive electric motors, machines, and other fantastic devices. These heavy forged castings moved from station to station on forklifts and carts where men removed runners, gates, and risers with torches and sledge hammers. At the final stage men holding grinding machines looked like dragons spitting fire as they systematically peeled off any leftover excess metal as they milled slag from the surfaces leaving the castings gleaming. The castings were put on oak pallets, secured with tight black metal banding, and marked to be sent to places around the world, then loaded on trucks."

"What did it smell like in the foundry?" Michael asked.

"Like molten metal. From the foundry the smell floated on the wind along with surplus ash that was carried over the town descending on anything and everything: houses, cars, streets and people. The foundry tang was the essence of Dodge; it was in the air, in the food, and traces of it even lingered after each breath in conversations. And that's why it was called Iron Town: a dirty, dark, exciting, horrible place all rolled into one leaving a permanent tarnish, and nothing in close proximity escaped the iron clutch."

"It got on everything? Even the people?"

"Yes, even the people. So, the men who worked in the foundry varied in age from the early twenties to the sixties. They were a lively and rough bunch of characters joking about everything; not serious about anything, or anyone. Many were outdoorsmen: fisherman, hunters; some liked cars, and had pretty nice rides because a foundry worker was paid well to work with the iron. A few were farmer's sons who didn't care to stay or work the family farm; others came from nearby towns, and some were life-long residents of Dodge. They worked three shifts on weekdays, and when it got busy, on Saturday for double-over-time pay. The president, a third generation grandson of the founder, learned from his father that the foundry men must be paid well for their hard labor."

"So, it was there for a long time?"

"A long time, and it was a hot, smelly, noisy, non-stop, constantly-crashing-clanging, metal-banging place. A twenty-four hour bell ringing church tower, shrill buzzers that hummed deep in the brain, and machines that vibrated through concrete foundations. A breeze blew through the open windows and doors carrying the kindred blood, sweat, and tears of the workers all through Iron Town. The company slogan said it all, ***Our product is iron; like the people who work here***, and after a day's work the employees were covered with a fine black metal mixture of dust that oxidized on their skin. Everyone would gradually turn orange, and be in need of a shower before leaving the company, so the slogan fit, the employees looked like iron—rusty iron statues."

"Really, they looked like statues?"

"Just like statues. Inside molds held dry black powdery sand was compressed into unusual shapes in dump boxes, or split boxes that moved down steel conveyers, then they were filled with hot liquefied orange iron poured from a copula that hung on a gigantic rail system from above. The cupola was controlled by a Furnace master who wore a silver heat reflective suit that covered his entire body. With a switch box connected to a long thick electrical cord about the diameter of a water hose that wiggled like a long black snake, he controlled the contraption. He opened a tap hole, and watched the iron flow and fall in orange cascades disappearing into the molds splashing like wild lava flow. These red-hot molds rattled their way cooling and shaking on conveyer belts; standing there felt like teams of jackhammers busting out the roots of your teeth, and you could feel them beating against the back of your eyeballs. At the end of the ride the cooled molds dropped into huge metal bins, then the hunks of iron moved onto bigger and noisier conveyers that shook the building with a daily dose of what an earthquake felt like. The castings were fished out and hooked by workers with hand-held cranes, put into huge metal baskets, then dropped at work stations around the plant."

"It sounds like a dangerous place to work."

"It was dangerous, and at the foundry there was always a job for a guy who worked hard. They never ran any ads for hire in the paper unless it was for an engineer, sales, or executive position. People who lived in the surrounding towns knew about the foundry, and that a job there paid well, a lot more than any other work in the area. But they also knew the work was hard, and only the tough and determined need apply. If you couldn't hold up your end, you'd be gone in a week or two, but if you followed through, and had staying power, were rewarded with money, and the status of being a man of metal."

"Did a lot of people quit?"

"Many quit. 'This place feels like hell,' a son told his father on the first visit to the foundry. 'Pretty damn close to it,' the father said, 'pretty damn close, but there's money in iron.'

"The kid described the foundry to his friends this way; 'Working all day in there's like being in one long nonstop car wreck! Sparks fly from the grinders, burn through the air, and land on everything, like walking through fire.'

"But the knowledge picked up from the men who toiled at the foundry would be valuable to a worker later, and serve him well for upcoming special moments in time and life."

Bedtime Stories and Dreams—Memories of Michael Colt—The Room

"There was a room in the foundry that had limited access known by only a hand-full of people. It was behind a bookshelf in the president's office. There was a statue of Atlas holding the world on his shoulders. All one had to do was push it to the side and the door would open. It was specially built in a space for the owner."

"Who built it?"

"I did of course," Nick said, and laughed. "This is where custom-made devices and weapons were made by skilled people who owned the foundry. The president of the foundry had served along side the driver, and when he returned to civilian life opened the foundry. He was an engineer who could design and build almost anything."

"How did he know what to make?" Michael asked.

"An order would come delivered by special courier, usually exactly what was needed for the operation. A design would be made, after that a prototype, testing and finally delivery, done by a courier or the driver would pick up the device."

"What did the room look like?" Michael asked.

"When you walked in the room there was a bench on the far side with tools and equipment hanging on the wall, file cabinets on the left, and drawing tables on the right. In the ceiling bright lights bathe the room in light, so there were no shadows. Pull-down lights were hanging as well for close up work. Hands drew and sketched all of the parts and pieces needed for the devices. The sketches were made real, assembled and tested, a prototype built, finally a phone call made to say it was done."

"Sounds like a smooth operation," Michael said.

"Yes, except for one night," Nick said.

"What happened?" Michael asked.

"A car pulled into the parking lot of the foundry; the driver got out, and went into the president's office. The president said to follow him, and they walked to a bookshelf in the office. He pushed the Atlas statue, and it opened, revealing the secret room."

"What was in the room," Michael asked.

"Let's just say the driver was always amazed by the work that was done there, and asked to see what he'd built for him. The president handed a device to the driver, and asked if it would suit his needs."

"What did it do?" Michael asked.

"He held the device in his hand, and poured in a chemical that was made by the professor, then watched how it began to glow."

"What kind of chemical?"

"It was a special one of a kind chemical made by the professor who assured the driver would do the job."

"What job?" Michael asked. "What happened next?"

"The president asked what the purpose of the device was, and the driver said, 'To travel.' The president said it was difficult to make the crystal device, and he had only finished a few of them, and needed more time to duplicate it."

"The driver agreed to give him as much time as he needed, and gave him the payment. He handed the president a briefcase, which he opened. Gazing at bundles arranged neatly, ran his hand over the bills."

"Was it a lot of money?"

"Yes, it was."

"The president of the foundry thanked the driver, closed the briefcase, and asked if he'd be staying in town tonight."

"Was he staying in town?" Michael asked.

"The driver said yes, but he would leave in the morning, and grabbed the case with the crystals."

"Then what happened?"

"The president invited the driver to dinner. He accepted and they decided to meet at the restaurant in town at seven."

"Did they meet?" Michael asked.

"The driver left the foundry, checked into the hotel, and arrived at the restaurant at seven p.m. A waiter came over, gave him a menu, and asked if he'd like a drink? He ordered a beer, then told the waiter he was expecting a guest, and to show him to the table when he arrived. A few minutes later the waiter brought the beer, and asked if he was ready to order. He said he'd wait until his guest arrived."

"Did the president show up?" Michael asked.

"After a time the waiter returned, asked if the driver would like another beer. The driver looked at his watch and said, yes."

"Why was the president late?"

"The driver was thinking the same thing because a number of people had come and gone. It was strange for him to be late. He checked his watch again, and thought something must have happened. So, when the waiter returned the driver asked for the bill, and said, 'Looks like my guest won't be joining me.'"

"What did the driver do next?"

"He left the restaurant and drove back to the foundry. It was dark and quiet as he parked. He went into the office just like he'd done earlier, but as he opened the bookshelf to the secret room, he fell to the floor after being hit on the back of the head."

"Was the driver dead?" Michael asked.

"No, he wasn't," Nick said, "but after he cleared his head he found the president dead on the floor, the money and plans gone. He closed the secret room and left."

"Who hit the driver, and who killed the president?"

"Well, a while later a security guard walked in, and wondered why the light was on. The secret bookshelf door had been closed, and there was no sign that it had been open. The guard turned off the light and went about his business. In the morning foundry workers came to work, but the president's car wasn't in its parking space. He had always shown up for work at the same time every day and was never late. There were times when he went on a business trip, so no one thought it unusual, and work went on as usual at the foundry. But the next day, and the day after that, it was the same, no president. The workers began to talk."

"Did they find the president?"

"No, but one week later a new man with a German accent arrived at the factory, and went into the president's office. An announcement was made that there would be a meeting after the lunch break. When the workers gathered in the shipping area of the plant, they were worried about the foundry closing."

"Was the news about the president?"

"Well, a man they'd never seen walked out on the floor, holding a microphone. He raised it to his mouth, said hello and thanked everyone for their hard work. He said the foundry had been acquired, but things would go on as usual, then asked if anyone had a question. A hand in back went up, and a worker asked why this change had happened so fast."

"What did the man say?" Michael asked.

"The worker asked why the foundry was being taken over. The man with the German accent said that it had been in the works for some time, and takeovers must be kept under wraps because leaks would affect the stock price. He said that not only would things continue as usual, and all employees would see a substantial increase in wages."

"Then what?"

"The man thanked them for their service to the company and left."

"That's all! What happened next?"

"Let's save that story for tomorrow," Nick said. "Good night, kid."

Michael went to school the next day thinking about the story Poppi had told him the night before about the secret room, and the special device that became warm when held tightly. He was excited to know what happened next.

Bedtime Stories and Dreams—Memories of Michael Colt—The Next Night

"You're telling me a story tonight, aren't you, Poppi?"

"Sure," Nick said. "It was a foggy morning as two trucks pulled into the parking lot of the foundry and parked next to each other. The truck's brakes released a blast of air, and the engines were cut. It was silent, then a minute later the garage doors in the shipping area of the foundry rose. Standing in the frame of the middle door was a group of men. The side doors of the trucks opened, men stepped off the trucks and were guided to the foundry. The usual workers had a day off; these men were brought in from outside. They were led into the plant's secret room."

"What was in the secret room?" Michael asked.

"It's a secret," Nick said and laughed. "Anyway, the next morning the usual workers were back and the machinery began to whirl, grind, and scrape before long the noise was deafening. Chains rattled, forklifts growled, conveyor belts squeaked on a long journey and back round again, bells rang and buzzed. The new owner and a few executives walked through the plant nodding in approval, pointing to moving objects being carried on overhead cranes, observing the workers who were unaware they were all part of a cover-up."

"So, nobody knew what had happened?" Michael asked.

"Right," Nick said. "Then, later that night inside the plant a bright light flashed, everything outside the place vibrated, then something extraordinary happened. Complete silence was followed by an explosion which sent a shock wave that bent the trees, shook the earth, and gathered dirt into plumes of clouds. Sirens roared in the air from around the city, a steady stream of fire trucks, ambulances, and patrol cars covered the streets. From the plant came the screams and moans of metal melting and crashing down."

"The place blew up?" Michael asked.

"Yes, there was a huge explosion. A firefighter yelled, 'Okay, let's move those trucks around the plant,' the fire chief shouted. 'Connect the hoses! Get some water on the fire! This'll take forever to put out!'

"Did they put out the fire?"

"Eventually they did, but they knew it would be a miracle if anyone working there survived the blast let alone the fire. More trucks roared on site, dizzying red lights twirled in time with the sirens. The firefighters jumped to the ground, attacking the truck, unscrewing hoses, clamps, and ladders. The fire was a living breathing animal that had to be exterminated. More trucks pulled into the parking lot and around to the back of the plant as workers, some on fire, ran out though an opening in the blown out wall."

"They were on fire?" Michael said.

"Yes, and then a fire truck turned to avoid hitting the workers, but could not, and they were run over, and crushed under the tires. The bodies continued to burn into charcoaled lumps of flesh. Another explosion shook the air, another, and another, then a plume of smoke, dust, and debris rose over the plant, reached a high point, then fell back to earth. Some fire fighters collapsed to their knees, others continued to fight the fire."

"The truck ran over the workers?" Michael asked.

"Yes, it did, and all of them were dead."

"What happened next?"

"In the morning the Police and more Firefighters arrived on the scene to control and confine the situation, and to clean up the smoldering remains. The sun rose the next day to a devastation never seen in this town before. People from the area walked around with jaws dropped, staggered steps, and tears for the loss of life. No one understood what or why this had happened to their town. In the paper and TV the story went out describing the event as an accident."

"Was it an accident, Poppi?"

"No, it was planned."

AWAKE

Michael woke, his eyes blinded by the sun, and his body warmed by it. He looked around, "Where the hell am I?" he said, then looked up into the sky above at some bulging clouds that floated away and a few birds navigating to somewhere. *The last I remember I was in a jail cell, and I know this place,* he thought, looking around at the architecture. Stone structures that seemed from another time rose all around, and these buildings would be of interest especially for a stone mason. *For some reason this place is familiar,* he thought, *but why?* "Have I been here before? Don't think so. Did I see this place in a magazine or did Poppi tell me about it in one of his old bedtime stories? He was good at describing people and places; must be because I remember from one of Poppi's stories because I've definitely never been here."

He had no bag, nothing other than the clothes on his back, the shoes on his feet, and absolutely no idea where he was. He reached in his pocket and felt it was empty. All of his pockets were. *I'm awake, so this isn't a dream,* he thought. "What should I do? Don't know where

I am, and don't know anyone. I'll look for a phone. Don't see one, but there's a water fountain over there. I'll have a drink."

Michael lowered his face into the fountain and let the water run over his eyes, then drank as much as he could. He watched men and women walking down the street dressed in old worn out clothes. Some were dressed in gray overhauls, and soldiers in uniform scurried about. Some kids on bikes, small children with mothers strolled along after.

"It all looks like a foregone time," Michael said. "A place from the past, but when or where though, I haven't a clue."

He listened and heard different languages, German, English, French, and others he couldn't identify. "The people in this place look worn out and tired," he said, "wherever this place is. Are they going to work, shopping?"

Then he watched others walking the streets that seemed to have no particular destination or goal in mind.

What time is it? he wondered. *Is it morning or early afternoon?*

"Looks like late morning to me according to where the sun's hanging in the sky. What year is it, forties, early fifties? This has to be a dream, a dream that I can't wake up from. Why don't I know?" *Think, where were you before being in this place?* "Can I remember? Yes, in a prison cell. I was in a jail cell, but where am I now? This place seems so real, but it can't be. How can it be?"

He looked down at his feet, then examined his hands. "I look the same as far as I can tell. Now I've just got to find out where I am, the name of this city, and what I'm doing here."

Michael walked through the park, followed a path that wound through a garden of flowers and weeping willows to what looked like a gate that led out of the park. Outside of the park he proceeded over a bridge along a river where he saw birds fly in formation. They landed on the banks on the other side for a minute or so, then some bounced back into the sky and disappeared. *I wish I had a camera,* he thought, *that's a nice shot.* He watched the birds picking at the ground eating their lunch, then a siren screamed in the distance, and they all flew away, scattering in different directions. "I wonder what the siren is for," he said. "Is it noon?"

The city spread beyond the park, the river flowed to no end, and the mixture of smells floated back and forth in the air. After walking a short time he noticed an older man up ahead on the right. He was standing on the steps that led to an official looking building. In his hands were tools Michael recognized immediately because he had used similar ones.

"He's a mason," Michael said. "Maybe he'll help me."

A feeling of longing came over him as he approached the man. Michael froze in his tracks, his face stone as the old man turned. Michael knew him immediately.

"Poppi?" Michael said, then raised his arms. Embracing each other, emotion flowed, exploded not wanting to let go of each other because they felt like one.

"Hey, kid," Nick said, "I knew you'd come," and stepped back. "Let me look at you kid. You've grown. Sure good to see you!"

"Poppi, what are you doing here? What am I doing here? And where are we?"

"You're in Salzburg, kid."

"What year? It looks like we're in the past. How can that be?"

"It's 1950. The war's over, but forces are still here controlling displacement camps and helping refugees from all over. The allies are in control of the city, they're cleaning up the mess."

"Why are you fixing the steps? I thought you were in the Army back then?"

"I am in the Army, well a branch of the government. I'm under-cover. Remember all of the stories I told you at bedtime?"

"I'll never forget them, not as long as I live."

"Well, they were more than just stories. The things I told at bedtime really happened."

"All of the stories really happened? There's a driver?"

"Yes, there's a driver, Michael, and it's me."

"You were the driver?"

"Well, there were others," Nick said, "that worked together."

"How did you get here?" Michael asked. "Hell, how did I get here?"

"The amulet," Nick said, "the professor's formula, remember?"

"I remember something," Michael said, "a key for some kind of locker. And I remember there was a notebook."

"We need the key and the notebook, Michael. Do you remember the last place you were, or the last thing you were doing before waking up in this dimension?"

"The last thing I remember was a jail cell. I was talking to a lawyer. He told me to plead guilty because there was no chance of me being found innocent. What he said, and showed me, made my future look pretty grim. He had a stack of files explaining how guilty I was of killing R. Lee, and that there was a witness who saw me do it."

"You're talking about the book agent?"

"Yes, the book agent. Who was he? Do you know?"

"He was a book agent, but he was working for Otto Voritch, and Otto wants the missing pages from the notebook."

"Otto Voritch?"

"You know those people who have the log home on Double X Road, the one your friend built? They bought a lot of land. Remember?"

"The guy I built the fireplace for? The old guy?"

"That's him, the same family, but here and now he was the target. The family wanted to get rid of him because he was taking over the business. They had connections in the military, INTERPOL, and other groups that destabilize the world."

"What exactly is this formula, and how does it work?"

"The professor developed a way to predict what might happen in the future."

"Did it work?"

"No, not at first, there were problems. We did save Otto, though, which turned out to be a mistake."

"He wants the formula?" Michael asked.

"The professor was able to not only predict the future, but to travel through time, forward or backward. It's how I got here, and how you did too. Otto wants it, so he can control the world. He might be holding the professor somewhere."

"Why do you think he's got the professor?"

"The day those men showed up at my cabin, you remember, don't you?"

"I remember waiting at the edge of the woods with Buster, and after I heard the noise from the cabin I ran to get Carlo."

"That's right, and they all vanished, and so did I. maybe Otto has some variation of the formula, but he's missing some pages from the notebook. That's what the key is for! The missing pages of the formula are locked away in a locker, in another dimension, and we've got to get them before Otto does."

"How does it work? It's just a formula, numbers and letters on paper."

"It's more than a formula, kid. It's time traveling in your mind, and that makes it real."

"How does it work? I didn't do anything, just held it, and had a dream."

"That's how it works, through our dreams. The formula's the gate that leads to inner and outer realms of time. I had the key for the locker, the notebook and the picture of the girl, remember? Remember that morning when you found the body, and came back to tell me?"

"I do," Michael said.

"When I walked into the cabin, Otto was waiting there," Nick said. "I'm certain the professor had something to do with all that stuff disappearing. I think he's the one who put the missing pages in the locker for Singleton to retrieve, and to lure Otto in, and end this. But it didn't work for some reason. No one really knows how the mind works; it's a mystery. Anyway, the professor's plan failed."

"Why me? Why am I involved in this?"

"Can't tell you now, only thought you might need that," and Nick pointed to the amulet around Michael's neck, "in the future because of the work I did, and what your father did. I had a hunch Otto would come after you."

"Are there only a few people who know, and are connected with the formula?" Michael asked.

"It's a powerful thing, and can't be just given away to just anyone," Nick said.

"I still don't understand. Exactly how does it work?"

"Even I don't know that, kid. Only the professor does because he's the one who developed, refined, and made it do what it does."

"Is the professor still alive?"

"I think so, but I haven't seen him in years. I think Otto's trying to get the rest of the formula from him. There are an array of persuasion techniques with ethics be damned. For all I know he's dead unless he used the formula to escape to a different time like we did, and Otto's looking for him."

"Is there any way we could find out if he escaped?"

"I don't know, kid. Like I said, the professor is the one who came up with the formula."

"Where are my parents, Poppi? Any idea about where they are?"

"Sorry, kid, don't know, but maybe they got out, and escaped to another time. I wish I knew to where, and if they're safe."

"Why is the book agent, R. Lee, involved in this," Michael asked, and who is he?"

"R. Lee turned and was my agent," Nick said. "His job was to protect you, that's why Otto got rid of him, and framed you for it."

"Who's the witness they have that says they saw me kill R. Lee?"

"Otto," Nick said, "Otto Vortrich, the old man."

"And the girl in the picture," Michael asked. "Who is she?"

"She was my wife," Nick said.

"What happened to her?" Michael asked.

"I don't know, one day she just vanished."

"Can we choose the time and place? Can we decide where we want to go?"

"Yes, we can," Nick said. "I chose this place because everything started here. This is where I joined the SSU, and I'm going to change that if I can. Then there's a slight chance the future will be different."

"How can things change? You were younger then, and now you're old."

"Being here is the same as a dream, Michael. We're like ghosts watching the action, and generally go unnoticed.

"Unnoticed?"

"That's right, but maybe by being here can change the future to have a better outcome. My younger self is here, and I've watched him. Maybe together we can have some influence."

"What are you going to change?"

"This time I'll get rid of Otto . . . I won't help him get away. I'll end it here!"

CHANGE IS COMING

"I'm staying in a small place a few blocks from here. We'll have more privacy, and talk more about this. I'll tell you what I know about being in this time or dimension, and you can ask me questions. I know you'll have some."

"Okay Poppi, lead the way."

"Follow me."

"Is this place you're staying at nice?"

"It's a vacant house, and the same place I lived in when I was here way back when. It's just over there."

"So, is your younger self living in the house?"

"No, he moved before I got here. Funny saying that about myself, that way. Come on, it's just over there."

"How can I help you change what happens to Otto?"

"I need you to nudge him, make him show what he really is to my younger self. I can't take a chance on getting too close or involved because it might change other things we don't want to change."

"And he won't know who I am?"

"Shouldn't because it was an older Otto at the cabin that day when they came for me, and don't think he saw you there either."

"What do you want me to do?"

"Well, Otto lives in the château, and I'm sure you've seen it because can be noticed from every vantage point in town. You're going there at the precise time before my younger self and other team members get there. You've got to try to get Otto to say something that will change my mind."

"How?"

"We'll figure out something, kid. Let me ponder it for a bit. I'll come up with something."

"How old is Otto?"

"Just busting pimples, twenty, but he's a wily one."

"Why did you help him?"

"I remembered how afraid he was, and thought his life was over, and how he'd never see another day if we followed through with the plan. I felt sorry for him, that's why I let him go."

"What if I give him a letter describing the plot, and how it would happen? If he knew about it beforehand I'll bet he'd plan how to get revenge. Then he'd say something or act a certain way that might change your younger self's mind."

"It's worth a try. He's got a short fuse."

THE HOUSE

"There it is kid, home sweet home."

It was a two story brick structure that had some wear and tear, but looked pretty solid over all. At least all of the windows were intact. The trim and shutters needed painting, but it gave the place character. One set of steps led up one flight to a wooden door with a brass handle. There was a mail slot in the door, and lights hanging from cast iron holders attached to the wall on either side at the same height as the top of the door.

"Why has it been vacant?" Michael said. "It seems like a livable place."

"I wondered about that myself because it's a pretty nice house, and big enough for a family. Maybe people think there's something wrong with it."

"Maybe they think it's haunted," Michael said.

Nick laughed, and said, "Never thought of that, kid, maybe you've got something there. Let's go in and see if we can find some ghosts."

They stepped into the entry-way onto hard oak floors. "Nice floor," Michael said as their shoes clicked across the floor.

"It'll last a hundred years if not longer," Nick said.

The walls were covered in dark green paper, and that was a good match for the oak floors. Ahead a long hallway with doors and openings to the left and right stretched through to the back of the house. "The kitchen's down at the end of the hall. This way, kid, down here. I have some food I got from the Army. They're always stocked pretty well, everyone else has to scrounge for a meal. Have a seat, and I'll rustle up something to eat."

"How long have you been here, Poppi?"

"Since the thing at the cabin . . . when Otto found me."

"Seems so long ago."

"It was come here, or be killed."

"No choice I guess, Poppi."

Nick opened the cabinet and checked what there was to eat. "We've got pasta, and there are some tomatoes over there on the window sill."

"I'm so hungry I could eat anything," Michael said, "but pasta, that's a meal for a king the way I see it."

"Okay, kid, I'll get the water a boiling, and put some bread in the oven. I might even be able to dig up something for dessert."

"Dessert? Definitely a meal for royalty."

"Just sit back and relax, and leave it all up to me."

"Mind if I look around the place?" Michael said.

"Go ahead, kid, my house is your house. Just like old times, Michael."

"Thanks Poppi."

The smell of oregano mixed with tomato sauce permeated the house. Nick opened the oven and took out the bread. He put both slices on a big plate, dripped olive oil on, then sprinkled some garlic, pepper, and topped it all off with a few drops of vinegar. *The kids going to like this!*

"This house is pretty nice, Poppi," Michael said when he came back into the kitchen. "And the aroma reminds me of when you cooked at the cabin."

"Sit down, I'll dish up. How about a drink? I've got some bottles of red wine. Been saving them for a while, and waiting to drink it for something special. I think today's the day for that."

"I've missed you, Poppi, and your cooking."

Nick put the plate on the table, "Here you go, kid, enjoy," and poured the wine.

Michael twisted some pasta on his fork. "Delicious, you still have the touch, Poppi."

"Yeah, it's pretty good grub for a stone mason."

"You mentioned getting your younger self to deciding not to save Otto, but to get rid of him. How?"

"My younger self, is meeting Otto at the château in two days. I've been going over in my mind how to do it, but getting Otto riled seems to be the best way. Then he'll show his true colors."

"So, you think we should get the information to him about the family plot to kill him? Why can't we just go in, and get it over with? Just do it ourselves?"

"There are things I can't explain, or understand," Nick said. "I've tried that and it didn't work. I believe it has to be done by my younger self, and you're the only one who can help."

"So, what do I do," Michael asked.

"I think he's hot-headed, and will want to blow off some steam about it. If we time it right, and get you to the château at the same time as my younger self, it might work."

"But how can I get the information to Otto about his family planning to kill him?"

"We could write something in a letter and give it to him. It would say what the family has planned. I think he'd snap, and my younger self would take care of him."

"And how would we do this?"

"We need some time beforehand, before my younger self and the team go there. The letter could say, your family is sending a team not to help, but to kill you. After he reads it, hopefully he'll feel angry enough to blow up and talk about revenge. Then my younger self will see what a sadistic asshole he is, and forget bout saving him."

"You want me to deliver this letter?"

"It has to be you," Nick said, and raised his glass of red wine. "I'll tell you why someday. Cheers Michael! It'll all work out. We'll talk about it tomorrow."

"We'll make it work, Poppi," Michael said. "There's no road we can't go down."

The sun set as they finished dinner and another bottle of wine.

THE LETTER

Michael woke after hearing the traffic clanging and rattling. He took a deep breath, covered his face and sat up. "I had too much wine last night. Feels like someone hit me in the head with a baseball bat. I need a cup of that coffee I smell." The smell of morning brew lingered as Michael stood, then he meandered his way downstairs. He bounce off the wall and grabbed the railing to stay balanced. "I think I'm still drunk," he said. "I wonder how Poppi feels."

"Hey kid," Nick said when he saw Michael standing in the doorway, his arms outstretched in the frame to keep from falling. "You okay? Coffee's on, and you look like you could use a cup. Get in here and sit yourself down. I'll make you some grub. Eggs okay? How many bottles of wine did we drink last night?

"I think we drank a lot. How many empty bottles are there?" Michael asked.

"They're on the back porch, go count'em," Nick said and laughed. "You'll feel better after eating. Have a seat."

"A cup of coffee ought to wake me up and get me going."

Michael watched Nick flip the eggs, then listened to them fry. He filled his cup to the brim with black coffee and sipped it. Once he knew how hot it was, he timed his sips, then took larger ones. Finally he drank the whole cup, then filled it again.

"Here you are, kid, chow down, plenty more where that came from."

"Poppi, you can make a top-notch breakfast in any dimension."

"Let's go over what you'll say to Otto to rile him up enough to get my younger self to change his mind about him."

"He'll read the letter, and that should be enough, but I'll do my best to time it as your younger self shows up. Did you write a letter?"

"Got it right here," Nick said and placed it on the table in front of Michael. "Want more to eat, kid?"

"I'm full, but I'll have another cup of coffee."

Michael opened, and read the phony letter Nick had written from Otto's family to the SSU.

```
Mr. Colt,


We're pleased you have accepted
our request regarding Otto. This
decision was a difficult one for us,
but there was no other course that could
be taken. Because of Otto's actions
considerable wealth has been lost, and
our family name has been severely
tarnished. We have contacted Otto and
told him he must leave the château,
also about the team meeting him there.
So he'll feel safe, ready and waiting
as he thinks the team will be escorting
```

```
him to our house in the country. He'll
go along peacefully. And per our
agreement his body will never be found.
His disappearance will remain a mystery.
The funds you've requested have been
transferred to the numbered account you
gave us.


                  Vortrich
```

"Oh yeah, this letter will rile him," Michael said. "What kind of family does that to one of their own? Are these people heartless?"

"Their kind care about money," Nick said. "Money is what they live for, and they've got carloads of cash. They get it any way they can, and getting more is priority number one. Otto was blowing it too fast."

"All he did to call for this kind of action from his family," Michael asked, "was spend money?"

"Besides losing and spending a lot of money, he was trying to take over the family business. He wanted to get rid of them. But that's we're going to do. We're going to make him vanish. And his older brother did die in a hunting accident. Otto claimed his brother shot himself, but the family had some suspicions. Since we did some things for the family in the past, they asked us to check into it. After our report, the family decided to get rid of Otto."

"Man, that family's screwed up," Michael said.

"Put the letter in your pocket," Nick said. "After we finish eating we'll head to the Château, and get this show rolling."

They left the house and walked. "I'll wait at the turn at the bottom of the road for you. You okay, Michael?"

"I'll be fine," Michael said. "Where will it be done? Up there or another place?"

"We're changing history, so it's got to be done at the château."

"I don't need to be there do I?"

"No, just leave after you give the letter to Otto and the team will take care of everything."

"What happens then?"

"I'll meet you back here, we'll walk to the house, and you'll go to the same place you were before you showed up here. You'll wake up, and remember all of this like a dream. Then get the missing pages of the formula."

"You're not coming back with me?"

"I've been here a long time, and might not be able to, but you have a few more trips. It seems that if you stay too long in one dimension, leaving becomes difficult. The complete formula is timeless and endless. That's why Otto wants the missing pages, so he can travel from dimension to dimension at will, raising havoc, killing off his family and my team. If he gets his hands on it, he'll be able to change the world, and history. He's a contemptible asshole now, with the hybrid formula he'll be a massive one. We've got to stop him!"

"What should I do after I get back and find the missing pages?"

"After you get the missing pages, destroy them. Anyone who has them is bound to be tempted to use the formula."

"What's going to happen to you, Sue, and me, and all the people we know?"

"I don't know, Michael, and you'll have to figure that all that out on your own. You'll know what to do because all of this is connected in some way. You'll have a dream, or meet someone who'll give you a clue. I can't tell you what to do because I don't know."

"Okay, Poppi, I'll worry about that later."

"Remember to get out of the château right away; don't stick around to see what happens. We'll have to hope it goes the way we've planned. Remember the timing of when you arrive and leave must be spot on!"

"Okay, meet you at the bottom of the road after I leave."

Michael and Nick walked closer to the Vortrich Château.

THE ESTATE

"All of these old structures are lessons in building with stone if you know how and where to look," Nick said.

They both turned their focus to the château as they walked, their eyes dancing back and forth studying the place. It was architecture a stone mason would be interested in examining, spotting techniques from the past when some things seemed impossible to accomplish.

"I was astonished about these techniques when I was young," Nick said. "How people built these structures with no modern tools is still a mystery. And now we wonder why it's a mystery."

"Why don't we know?" Michael asked.

"Maybe we're not supposed to know."

"Do you think we'll ever know?"

"These buildings are old, but imagine how they moved some of the enormous stones of the pyramids, and at Baalbeck, or the Easter Island Statues, all a mystery," Nick said. "Today large cranes are used, but how was it done long ago?"

"I remember you telling me those stories when I was a kid, and how you told me about building with stone, and the process."

"It all starts with the first step, and that's choosing the right stone for the job; granite, marble, slate, pumice, sandstone, limestone paving for building roads, walls, or monuments. Quarrymen split veins to supply large blocks of stone, then Sawyers cut them into smaller sizes, and finally Masons shape them to fit, dressing the stone with a hammer chisel."

"A lot of people are involved in big projects," Michael said, "a very organized operation. I can't imagine how they did it years ago with the pyramids."

"Right," Nick said, "very well planned. Walls and window moldings are done by Carvers to make stone into art. Dry laying was used in the past, and is still used today, but to add cosmetic features or structure, and for strength, mortar is applied between joints."

"Those guys were real builders . . . artists."

"And it's basically still done the same way as they did in the past," Nick said.

"You taught me these same methods."

"It's the only way these structures have lasted as long as they have" Nick said. "The château's been there for a while, and built to be around, to last."

"Some of your fireplaces have been around a long time," Michael said. "And your foundations are still holding up a lot of buildings."

"Stone and brick always leave some ruins, a trace of some kind even after thousands of years. In Japan they built castles out of wood, and most are gone, but the rubble from the foundation is always left, and we can see what the masons did."

"Have you been to Japan?"

"Been everywhere, kid, seen all kinds of structures, old and new, and if you examine the methods, they're very similar to present day."

"I wonder how old the copper roof of the château was made," Michael said.

"Copper, what can I say; it's been around for years, and goes back to the Egyptians. All kinds of things have been covered or made from it. It's durable, easy to work, lightweight, and esthetically very nice to look at."

"That roof sure is a piece of art." Michael said.

"One more thing about copper," Nick said. "It's a shield for unauthorized surveillance, and has intrinsic properties that protect from mold, bacteria, and some viruses. It's sometimes used for handrails, countertops, in hospitals and public places."

"Maybe that's why it's on the roof, to block signals?"

"Could be," Nick said. "Okay, kid, this is as far as I go, and where you're on your own. If you run into any trouble or think it's not working, just get out. Leave and meet me here. I'll be waiting for you."

"I should be fine. I'm not planning to hang around too long after giving Otto the letter." Michael gave Nick a hug, and started walking up the narrow cobble stone road to the Château.

Michael headed up the cobblestone road, turned a few times watching Nick nodding, and giving a thumbs-up. The buildings on either side of the road were homes and small shops. There was a bakery with bread and pastries, a butcher shop with sausage and hunks of meat on display, a barber shop, and book store. Michael wanted to go into each shop and look more closely to get a feeling of what it was like to live at that time, talk to the shopkeepers. He moved forward slowly, methodically going over the plan in his mind, and how and what he would say to Otto Vortrich. He took the letter he was to give to Otto from his pocket. Michael looked ahead at the château as it grew in size, surprising him how big it was, nervousness running through his veins.

He stopped and took a deep breath. "Well, here we go."

Then he took the final steps at a regular pace so he wouldn't draw attention from people or soldiers that he passed. The château stood overlooking the town hovering like some powerful master. The dark windows hid the family who lived there, along with their plans to control and drive wedges between rival groups.

"After I pass the letter to Otto the future's going to change. The dead men I found, and Poppi disappearing never happening. Yes, the future will change, and my own life will be different. I wonder what I'll remember from this?"

Michael saw some cars parked in front of the château. *Is that the team,* he thought. "They're here early," he whispered, "or I'm late. Should I still go into the château? What if they go in to soon, or before Otto reads the letter? What will happen then?"

Michael stood in front of two large wooden doors leading into to the château. His heart was pounding; his left hand moved over the side of his head and wiped the sweat away. He took deep breaths and exhaled while closing his eyes. Then he heard car doors squeak open and slam shut. *They're getting out,* he thought, *do I have time to give Otto the letter?* "I've got to try."

He reached up, lifted the ring on the door, and hammered it three times into the wood. He heard footsteps approaching, and drummed the ring into the door again.

The door opened. "Yes, sir," a man dressed in a suit said. "What can I do for you?"

"I have a very important letter for Otto Voritch."

He put out his hand as to accept it, and said, "Very well, I'll make sure he gets it. May I have it?"

"Sorry, you don't understand," Michael said. "I have to give it to him in person, directly, to see he has it in hand."

"Oh, very well," the man said like he'd bitten into a lemon. "Come with me."

This is going to be close, he thought, and walked inside following the man.

"Please wait here," the man said. "I'll get Mr. Voritch."

Michael stepped into a library filled with books in shelves that reached to the ceiling. There was a step ladder in the corner to reach the top. He gazed at the knowledge waiting on the shelf, walked to the middle of the room and stood in awe, then the door opened and a young man walked into the room. *He looks like the guy who owns the log cabin and land in Hungry Point,* Michael thought. *Well, he won't after I give him this letter because the future will change.*

He walked in like a soldier marching across the room, a newspaper in his right hand; the other in his pocket. He wore his suit well, and looked very fit. A thin well cropped moustache graced his upper lip. "Hello," he said in a German accent. "May I know why you are here? I was told by my man that you've got some kind of letter for me."

Michael swallowed, cleared his throat, and said, "Yes, sir, here it is."

Otto reached out taking it from Michael, looking at it a moment, then like a fan waving it to cool himself. "And where are you from, definitely not from around here judging by your accent."

"I'm from the States. I'm a courier for the Army, and was told to deliver that letter to you personally."

"Personally, well, isn't that interesting. But I see you're not in uniform?" Otto said, and tossed the letter on the desk. He grabbed a bottle from a cabinet. "Care for a drink?"

"No, no thank you." *He's got to open and read the letter soon. I've got to do something to get him to open it.* "I think it's urgent, and you should read the letter now. In case you have a reply."

"Urgent? So, you know the contents?"

"No, sir, I don't, but why else would I have been sent here to give it to you in person if it wasn't?"

"Oh, very well," Otto said. "Sure you don't want that drink?"

"Well, if you insist, okay."

"Help yourself."

Michael walked to the liquor cabinet, and poured a glass of scotch as he watched Otto read the letter. Otto's eyes opened wide, his face red, he looked at Michael. "You haven't seen the contents of the letter?"

"No, I haven't, and I have to go if there's no reply."

"No, I don't think I'll be responding right at this moment."

"Okay, then, and thanks for the drink." Michael raised the glass in toast, forced the whisky down, and turned to leave the room.

"Nice seeing you, Mr. Colt, and do pop in again."

He knows my name. He knows what's going to happen. "Thank you again for the drink," Michael said, and left the room. He made his way to the front door where the man who greeted him was waiting at the door, and opened it for him.

"Have a nice day, sir," he said.

Michael walked down the hill to where Poppi was waiting. He heard no shots fired, so they were probably taking Otto to a safe house.

"How did it go kid?"

"He knew! He knew me, and that I'd be there. And probably about the team," Michael said. "Shit!"

"Let's get out of here," Nick said. "You've got to go back now. We don't have any time to waste. You've got to find those missing pages of the formula before he does. Otto must have the professor; it's the only way he could have known about you and the team. Somehow he could be forcing the professor to help him time travel. Let's go back to the park where you first woke, and get you back to your time. Do you remember the place?"

"At the park there was a fountain, and a pool of water around it."

"You can go back from there. We have to find the exact same spot where you came in, and line it up like it's your shadow. That place at the park is the way back for you."

MORNING AT THE RIVER

Michael heard the rush of water flowing and opened his eyes. "The river," he said, then sat up looking at a place he remembered and knew well. Sounds coming from the surrounding forest jarred memories of growing up there, exploring, and running the trails with his dog Buster. "I'm back, back home! My favorite fishing spot is right over there. Home," he repeated, and looked out across the backwater to the river. "That's where I first saw Singleton Black's body when I was a kid, floating and bobbing like an old log. Am I back in that time? This place looks the same; it's absolutely amazing to be able to travel like this." The sound of a boat engine and voices up river startled and grabbed his attention. As it became louder and closer he said, "It's coming this way." He looked toward the forest and ran to the trees, ducked down, and was still. He watched a flat bottom fishing boat in the distance cruise at slow speed toward the shore. "It's Singleton Black, and he's wearing the same clothes as on the day I found him dead. I'm back at the morning when I found his body floating in the water, and this must be what happened before he was shot." *Who's the guy with him?* he thought, and watched the boat hit the shore, listening to what they were saying.

"This is where he wants to meet, so we'll wait here," Singleton said.

"So, he agreed to my terms?"

"Yes, he did."

"He didn't think the amount was too high?"

"He'd pay any amount to get your formula; especially the one that you say will let him move through time and dimension again and again. What do you call it?"

"Who is that guy?" Michael whispered.

"The Bell," the man said.

"Has a nice ring to it, pardon the pun, but why call it that?"

"Anyone using my formula cuts through time, like breaking the sound barrier. A bell echoes when it works, but without knowing the code it won't."

"So, only some people can use the formula?"

"Everyone can, but imagine what would happen if it was available for anyone to use."

"What would happen?"

"No one knows the answer to that, so I limited it to the ones who have a lot of money."

"How do you think Otto will use it?" Singleton said. "He's an opportunist. I wouldn't trust him completely."

"I don't, and plan to feed it to him bit by bit until I feel the time is right. And that may never happen."

"It's the professor," Michael whispered, and moved farther back in the trees.

"I'll pull the boat on shore," Singleton said, "and we'll wait over there next to those trees. Otto should be here soon."

"Sounds like a boat coming now," Singleton said. "That must him."

A boat with a lone passenger floated to the shore. It was another flat bottom boat like the kind many fishermen use, but the man in the boat didn't look like a fisherman.

"Funny, he doesn't look much different from when I saw him at the château, Michael said. "He's aged well."

Singleton waved and said, "Hello, Otto, glad you could make it. Have any trouble finding this place?"

"No trouble at all. Your directions were very precise," he said in a German accent. The clothes he wore didn't seem to fit. He looked uncomfortable and seemed nervous. You could just tell he was a person who probably wore a suit every day, and was raised by servants with a silver spoon up his ass. Otto was definitely a man used to the finer things in life.

"That's good to hear," Singleton said. "Here's the man you've been waiting to see. Let me introduce the Professor. He's been anxious to meet and talk to you."

"And I too have looked forward to this moment." Otto reached out his hand, but the Professor didn't raise his, and it seemed to be an awkward moment for Otto. "Finally we meet Professor. I'm Otto Voritch. This certainly is a day that I will remember."

"And for me as well," the professor said.

"Singleton has told me about your formula, and device," Otto said. "I've used the Prediction Formula, and am very pleased with the results. He's told me the new formula can do much more."

"That's right, Otto, much more," the professor said. "It goes beyond predicting, and actually can be used to change what will happen even after it's happened."

"How does it work?" Otto asked.

"I think we have to talk about the payment before I get into any of the details," the professor said.

"Name your price," Otto said. "Whatever it is, I'll pay you."

"Gold," the professor said. "I want to be paid in gold, and want it transferred to a place of my choosing," he said.

"What place," Otto said, "where?"

"This is the place," Singleton said, and handed Otto a piece of paper with the name, address, and amount of gold to be sent.

Otto took the paper, looked at it, and said, "I know this place, and I can do that. Yes, it's doable. Now, tell me, how does the formula work?"

"If I tell you now, how can I trust that you'll send the gold?"

"The gold will be sent, and I think you know that."

"There's a key to a locker," the professor said. "I'll give it you, and the formula will be yours."

"Okay, I see," Otto said. "How does it work?"

"I call the method I used a numeric pulse," the professor said. "Thoughts are input into the wearable device that I've designed, and that allows the wearer to transfer to another time, a different dimension, like a copy of yourself living in another time."

"Have you tried it?" Otto asked.

"Yes," the professor said. "After the gold is transferred the formula is yours, and you can take over and control the world."

"Where's the formula?" Otto asked.

"Close by."

"Here in Hungry Point?" Otto, asked.

"I'll tell you when I know I have the gold," the professor said.

"The gold is yours," Otto said. "Where is it?"

The professor looked at Otto. "In a locker at the post office."

"Fantastic! Thank you for setting up this meeting. I'll have your gold shipped. Let me get my phone, and make the arrangements." Otto stood next to the boat, moved a bag, smiled, then lifted a shotgun and blew a hole in Singleton's chest. "Well, Professor, I think I'll have the key now." Otto aimed the gun at the professor. "Since I have what I need, I'll be saying goodbye."

"That may be true Otto, but then again it might not be."

"Enough of this foolishness," Otto said. He held the gun up, aimed at the professor, and said, "Auf Wiedersehen!"

The professor said nothing, he turned, and started to walk away. "Going to shoot a man in the back?" he said.

"Front, back, sideways, it doesn't matter to me," Otto laughed, then pulled the trigger.

"The professor turned, and smile at Otto. He waved as the blast went through him, and stood there as if nothing had happened.

Otto's face went red, then white. "He was using the formula all along," Otto said as the professor's body fell away, and melted into the ground like raindrops.

Then Otto heard the professor's last words echo. "I'll be seeing you in your dreams!"

THE LOCKER

Michael stayed in the trees watching to see what Otto would do next. "He's some kind of sadistic maniac," Michael said. "He blew Singleton away without a thought. Michael moved closer. "What's he up to now? And what happened to the professor? It looked like he turned into a shadow, and just vanished into space." He maneuvered closer, and watched Otto look around scanning the tree line where Michael was, then watched him go to the boat and set the gun down. Michael stayed there, quiet, quivering, the hair on his skin standing up. Otto walked over to Singleton, grabbed him under the arms and dragged him in an awkward way, lumbering along to his boat. He sat Singleton upright on the side of the boat, then Otto put his hand under Singleton's chin, looked the dead man in the face, and Michael heard him say, "Afraid this will be your last ride, my friend. And your cohort the professor is very clever and lucky for now, but his day will come— I guarantee it."

He let Singleton fall back and drop into the boat, the body landed flat, and his head bounced once. Otto watched the boat rock back and forth, then he put his foot on it to stop it, and said, "These people don't know who they are dealing with."

Otto checked Singleton's pockets looking for the key, but found nothing. Then he looked over the ground, walking over the area searching for the key. Carefully policing debris, and removing any clues that he'd been there, then he towed Singleton's boat out to the main channel. After getting far from shore, he rolled Singleton out of his boat into the river, and set it afloat down stream. Michael watched Otto cruise away, the boat's engine roaring at high rev, leaving a fresh wake behind with Singleton's body floating and bobbing on it. "The Colts have something to do with this; I feel it."

"Looks like he's out far enough, and can't see me now," Michael said, then stepped out of the woods keeping an eye on Otto's boat. He waited at the edge of the trees, then stepped on the shore watching Otto's boat vanish down stream, the sound of the boat's engine fading and blending into the sounds of nature.

"I've got to get those missing pages before Otto gets his hands on them." Michael got on a trail that led to the cabin where he'd grown up. He looked around at the forest, reminiscing, then a bell echoed in the air. "It feels exactly like the day I found Singleton's body when I was a kid," then he heard a dog barking. "That's Buster running to the river."

Then he heard a voice, a boy's voice say, "Buster! Hey boy, what's wrong?"

"That sounds like me as a kid," Michael whispered, and headed off double-time on another path. First the barking grew louder, but after a time it faded in the distance. "Buster's going for the river, just like before, and he'll, I mean I'll, find Singleton's body floating in the backwater." Michael stopped and said, "Should I stop him from finding it? Don't know what that might do, or affect what happens later. Better just find the missing pages of the formula."

Michael heard the footsteps walking behind him and turned.

Standing there was a young Michael. "Hi," the kid said.

He was looking at himself as a kid. "Yeah, hi. You live around here?"

"Just over there on the other side of that pocket of trees. You just move here," the kid said. "I haven't seen you before."

"I'm visiting from out of town, staying with some friends."

"Who's that?" the kid asked.

"Not from Hungry Point, they're from Dodge. They said I should check out the river because it's really beautiful."

"It sure is," the kid said. "I walk to the river with my dog every morning. I'm Michael."

"I see." *Should I tell him my name?*

"Well enjoy the day. I've got to find my dog. He's barking like crazy. Guess he's chasing down something. See ya."

"Yeah, see you, kid," he said, and waved as the kid turned. "That felt like looking at an old picture, or watching an old video of myself. He'll find the body soon. I better get moving."

Michael stayed on the path, "I wonder where the professor is now." he said, and walked down a path through the woods. "He must be jumping between dimensions and time. Why doesn't he just get the formula himself? He knows where it is." *It must have something to do with Otto. Maybe he's setting a trap for Otto.* Michael stood in front of the cabin. *What if I warned Poppi about Otto,* he thought. He took one last look, turned, and walked toward the road that headed into Hungry Point. He walked through the lumber mill, past Poppi's shop, and down a trail into town.

"The Post Office, that's where it is. All I have to do is walk in and check the lockers. Hopefully no one will recognize me." He walked in. *There they are! I wonder if the formula is in one of these lockers.* He looked to the right where a lady stood behind the counter. "Hello," he said, and walked to the lockers. *What's her name,* he thought. *I know her name.*

"Morning," she said, and picked up a container filled with envelopes, and began sorting them.

Michael remembered back as a kid, when he first found Singleton, there was a key. "The key," he whispered. "I don't have the key. It was in his pocket. Should I go back to the river and get it? Too late; the kid's probably found the body by now. It was locker number eleven. There it is, and I don't have the key." Michael left the Post Office.

"Have a nice day," the woman working there said.

"You, too," Michael said, as he raised his hand and waved to her, then stopped after stepping out of the Post Office. He heard footsteps going up the stairs, and turned to see Carlo walking to his office in the Post Office. *He looked happy, but that'll all change after he goes to the cabin, and checks on Poppi.*

THE FORMULA

Michael left Hungry Point and walked down a trail to the river where he could be alone, to take his time thinking about how to get the missing pages from the locker. "I'll go to the place on the river I fixed up with Sue when we were kids. No one will bother me there. I don't know what'll happen to me if I stay in this dimension too long. Maybe after thinking about it a little I'll know what to do."

He walked back on to the river on a different trail. "There it is," he said, "and it looks pretty good, too." Michael made his way into the hut. "All the stuff we brought here is still in the same place." He stood at the entrance thinking about the time he spent there with Sue when they were kids. "I wonder how she's doing, and if she'd recognize me if we ran into each other in this dimension? Maybe I should look for her?"

"There's the chair I made of branches," Michael said, and sat down, and scanned the makeshift hideaway he and Sue had made. *Is that a boat coming?* He stood, and looked through an opening in the wall. "Otto! How did he know where to find me?"

The flat bottom fishing boat cut through the river, and was making for the hut. Otto ran the boat onto shore until it stopped, then looked over the hut. "Well, it's not the château," he said, "but that's not important because it is what's inside that I want." He sat in the boat looking around, assessing the situation, then focused on the hut. "There's no use trying to run, Mr. Colt. I know you're here. Let's make a deal."

Michael hesitated, and thought how he could get away or end this now. *He wants the formula. That's the only deal he wants to make.* "And after he gets it he won't need me," Michael said. "The notebook must be pretty important for you to follow me here. How did you find me?"

Otto sat in the boat scanning the landscape. "Well, you see," he said, "there's a girl, her name is Sue," Otto said. "Remember her, Mr. Colt? She's very nice, and pretty."

Michael took a deep breath, that seemed drained of life. "What did you do to her?"

"Oh, Mr. Colt, I don't want to bore you with the details. You can take her with you to anywhere you like, or stay here living in your Shangri-La on the river."

"Where is Sue now?"

"In due time, in due time, that's why I'm here Mr. Colt. Why don't you tell me what you'd like for the information you have. I think we can come to an arrangement. Will money satisfy you? Land, property, fame? I know you're writing a book about this adventure you're having. Why not let me help you make your story a success. Along with that you'll have all the money you need to do anything you like. Name your price, and it's yours. Money is one thing I have in abundance."

"Why do you want the missing pages," Michael shouted from inside the hut. "Don't you already have the formula?"

"Oh, I've got some big plans," Otto said in his German accent, "and need what you've got to make them work. You're right, I already have a part of the formula the professor developed, but it's limited to a few short trips. I need the pages that are missing to do things right. I think you are holding onto them. The Professor was going to sell them to me. He said they were nearby."

"Big plans?" Michael said. "I've got some big plans of my own."

Otto climbed out of the boat, and stood on the shore. "Why do you want to ruin such a nice day? The sun is shining, the sky is clear," He reached into the boat, opened a cooler, and said, "I've got a six-pack," he said and raised the beer. "Let's talk it over."

"Where's the Professor?"

"I'm afraid he got away, and has hidden the pages I need. People don't understand how this all works my boy. Things don't happen by chance. There's no good or bad luck. Things happen because of what is going on in other dimensions. These micro changes create an effect forward and backward in time."

Michael moved to another spot and looked out at Otto. "I've seen some of the changes you've made. I was there when you shot Singleton. How did that change the past and future?"

Otto's voice changed, and became more aggressive. "In order to progress we need to change," he said, then drank a beer, and tossed the can into the river."

"Are you sure you haven't been drinking a little too much, because it sounds like you're drunk."

"Are you armed Mr. Colt?"

"Armed?

"Yes, I'm going to give you to the count of three before I begin shooting." He turned again, walked to the boat, and picked up the same shotgun he used on Singleton. He opened the breach, loaded two shells in the chamber, and snapped it shut. "I'm going to count to ten. If I don't hear from you before that it'll be over for you, and dear Sue. One!"

"I have to get out of here and help Sue. I should be able to leave this dimension like before," Michael said. "What do I do? Go, stay?" He grabbed, and clenched the glass amulet from around his neck in his fist. Just think of where I want to be, that's what Poppi said. Think of the place; and I'll go there."

He heard Otto count, "Two!"

"Nothing to lose. Here goes!"

"Three-four- five!"

Michael squeezed his eyes shut, and thought of the place he wanted to go."

"Six, seven, eight, nine, ten! Say goodbye, Mr. Colt."

Otto aimed the gun at the side of the shack, and pulled the trigger. The corner of the hut splintered and broke into pieces. "Why don't you make this easy on yourself, and give me what I want. You can't win." He loaded the shotgun again, fired both shells, and the blast ripped through the roof. "I'm coming in to see you, Mr. Colt."

It didn't take much effort to kick in the door down. The cabin was small, so there was no hiding place, but Michael was nowhere to be found.

THE CHURCH

When Michael opened his eyes he was sitting in a pew in the back rows of St. Aloysius Catholic Church. The 8:00 a.m. service had ended a few minutes before, so the last of the kids were filing out and heading to the elementary school. It was a vampire red brick rectangle building covered with uniformly arranged square windows in shouting distance of the church. Between the church and school was the nun's house, and two priests lived on the other side of the church in another brick dwelling that had a porch surrounding fifty percent of the house. There was a table and bench with plants hanging from the eves.

Michael watched as two alter boys put out the candles. "Why am I here?" he whispered, and that echoed around his head for a moment. He turned back to see the large wooden doors at the entrance slam shut with an echo that vibrated up to the ceiling. Soon the altar boys were gone, and he was all alone in the cavernous dark structure. *I can't stay here*, he thought.

Then Father Miller walked out of the rectory, genuflected in front of the altar, made the sign of the cross, and walked down the aisle toward Michael. "Hello, my son. Can I be of any assistance? Would you like me to hear your confession?"

"Yes, Father, I would," then wondered why he'd said that.

"Come this way," Father Miller said, then gestured for Michael to go into the confessional before him. Michael hesitated a minute, then entered the small box through a wooden door. It was dark and hard to tell the time of day as light began to leak through the stained glass windows. With every breath he could smell the wood of the old church. It creaked, the sounds amplified and echoed to the point of lingering on the dust floating in the air. Once inside, a small door slid open, and he saw the silhouette of Father Miller's face through a screen made of a mesh-like material.

"Tell me your sins, my son, and don't worry, anything you say is kept in my confidence."

"Actually, Father, I don't know why I'm here."

"You're not here to confess your sins, my son?"

"It's tough for me to logically tell you my situation because I don't know where to start."

"Start at the beginning, or whatever time comes to mind."

"You're going to think I'm crazy."

"I've heard many confessions, and many stories. Go ahead and just start."

"Okay, here goes. My father, grandfather, and Moses were spies. My grandfather received a formula based on logic from a professor that enabled him to predict outcomes of his missions. The professor improved the formula to the degree that allows a person to travel through dimensions, forward and backward in time. Now I'm being chased by a guy called Otto Voritch, who wants the formula. I was accused and arrested for killing a book agent who worked at an organization similar to the one that my grandfather worked for, but I didn't do it."

"That's a pretty good story, my son, but you haven't committed any sins. Is there anything else you'd like to tell me?"

"There's more, but I'm running, and trying to get away from Otto, and worried about Sue"

"Who is Sue, and this man, Otto?"

"Sue's my girlfriend, and it sounded like he had Sue, but now that I'm in this dimension, I don't know what's happened to her, if anything. Otto's family tried to have him killed because he was planning to do the same to them, then take over the family business. They're extremely wealthy and powerful people. My grandfather's team was given the mission from the Voritch family to kill Otto. At the last moment my grandfather felt sorry for him, and couldn't do it, and let Otto go. After that Otto proceeded to eliminate his entire family. Using the formula, my grandfather and I went back in time to do the mission over, and this time get rid of Otto for good. Don't know how, but he was on to us, and now he's after me trying to get the missing pages of the notebook. And I think my grandfather is still back in another dimension."

"If this man Otto can do these things, then he must already have this formula you're talking about."

"He has a part of it, and needs the missing pages of a notebook, but they're hidden away."

"How can I help you?" Father Miller asked. "Remember, killing is not something I can do."

"I am here for some reason, and I have to find out why. I know how Singleton Black was killed."

"Singleton Black?" Father Miller said. "That name is familiar. Who is he?"

"I found his body floating in a backwater, and now I know who killed him."

"I remember the name," Father Miller said. "A funeral is being held for him in the church tomorrow."

"Tomorrow? Then Carlo will be here," Michael said. "If I can figure out a way to contact him without freaking him out, maybe he can help me."

"You know Carlo?" Father Miller asked.

"Yes, he's the game warden in Hungry Point, and I think he'd be happy to hear who killed his father. Otto might show up if he knows I'm there. What time is the funeral?"

"It starts at ten tomorrow morning."

"Ten? Maybe I could talk to him beforehand, but I need transportation."

"I can let you use my car, or I could drive you. Where do you need to go?"

"Hungry Point, to Carlo's office. When can you let me use your car?"

Father Miller took out the car keys, opened the mesh curtain, and handed them to Michael. "I don't need it, so anytime."

"Thank you, Father," Michael said. "Be careful tomorrow at the funeral. Otto's capable of anything."

"We have to look to God for answers. Only he knows what will happen."

"You haven't been listening, Father. Otto knows the future. How much I'm not sure, so be careful. I'll see you at the funeral."

Michael walked out of the church, and around to the back of priest's house. Father Miller followed Michael, and stood on the steps of the church. As he watched Michael get into the car he looked up at the sky. "Keep him safe, Lord."

Michael got into Father Miller's jeep, backed out into the street, and stopped a moment when he saw Father Miller wave, then drove away. Now he had to think of a way to convince Carlo to help him stop Otto, and thought about what he'd say to him. *Will he believe who I am? He just knew me as a kid a few days ago. Will he think I'm crazy.* "Hell, I'm not sure the priest believed my story."

Michael parked on the street across from the Post Office where Carlo worked, and noticed his truck in the parking lot. *He's in his office*, Michael thought, *it's time to go.* "What should I say to him?" Michael walked through the parking lot, hesitated, stood in front of the door, and looked at the stairs that led to Carlo's office. *I was here before to tell him about Poppi*, he thought. He took a few deep breaths and climbed the stairs, counting each step. When he got to the top, he stopped at thirteen. "Never counted them before," he said. "Lucky thirteen." He moved slowly toward the door to where Carlo worked. *Should I knock?* he thought, then tapped the door three times, didn't hear anything, so he knocked three more times a little louder. No sound. "He must be here," Michael whispered, and turned the door knob, then opened the door.

"Carlo!" he said, and froze. He was slouched over the desk with a pool of blood under his head. Michael watched the blood slowing drip onto the floor. Bloody papers were scattered around the desk and office. Michael moved closer, and looked at how his neck had been sliced revealing the raw flesh. Michael stood wondering if anyone had seen him go into the office, then walked down the stairs at a normal pace, across the street, and got into the jeep. *Is there a way to bring him back?*

TIME TO TALK

Michael sat in Father Miller's Jeep. "I should call or do something, he was my friend, and just leaving him like that seems cruel. Someone will find him, and contact the police. I can't get caught up in this now. They'd ask me all kinds of questions that I can't answer. So, where do I go from here? Poppi's cabin would be a good place because no one's there, or is there?"

Michael drove with dozens of images rolling around in his head. Carlo's father had been killed by Otto, and now him. "I'm always a step behind. Why? Is this planned? Am I supposed to go to the cabin? Maybe Otto's waiting there for me? He turned onto the road leading to the cabin and stopped. Maybe it's better to go to the shop and wait. Moses will be there, and he'd know what to do." He drove out of the parking spot and headed to the shop.

He stopped and parked to check the shop. "That's his truck, he's here."

Moses came out of the shop, and Michael got out of the car. "What took you so long?" Moses said. "I've been waiting all morning."

"Waiting all morning? How did you know I'd come here?"

"Just had a feeling, and yes, we have to plan for tomorrow. Otto will be at the funeral, there's no doubt about that. We've got to be ready. Carlo is dead."

"How do you know that?" Michael said.

"I watched Otto leave Carlo's office when I was at the restaurant."

"Otto left him bleeding on his desk. He's always a step ahead."

"Why do you think that is?" Moses said.

"Don't know. We should be a step ahead of him."

"We'll be a step ahead tomorrow," Moses said. "We'll bury Otto tomorrow along with Singleton. Help me unload these stones."

"I remembered doing this when I was a kid."

"What?" Moses said.

"Where is the younger me?"

"The kids at the cabin."

"Is it safe there?"

"He'll be fine."

"I met him," Michael said, "walking down a path to the river, just before he found Singleton Black. He was running with Buster."

"Don't think about that now, let's load the stones, and go for a ride to the job. We'll unload them, work a little at the job, then go to the cabin."

"Where's is this job?" Michael asked.

"It's on Double X," Moses said. "Some guy, and his son, bought a farm out there. The barn needs some work, and he wants a fireplace built for the log cabin he's building."

"When did you start working on it?"

"Last week."

"What's he like?"

"Only met him once," Moses said. "I always talk with the guy's son."

"We should find out where he's from."

"Why?" Moses asked.

"I think I know who he is."

"So do I," Moses said. "There's the place over there." He drove into the driveway and backed up to the house where the fireplace was to be built.

"Doesn't look like anyone's here," Michael said.

"No, it doesn't." Moses said. "Let's unload the stones."

"Where do you think the guy who bought this place is from?" Michael asked.

"He's got an accent," Moses said, "sounds German, so maybe they're from Germany. Let's head back to the shop after we unload, then head over to the cabin. We can talk, and plan for tomorrow."

"I think you know more than you're telling me Moses."

Moses looked at Michael. "Maybe I do, kid."

Michael wanted Moses to say more, but that's all he said as they drove. "What should I say to young Mike?"

"It should be fine," Moses said. "I've got an idea."

"Can I hear it?" Michael asked.

"I'll tell you while we're driving."

Moses turned on the radio looking for a good station. "Okay tell me your idea," Michael said.

"It's simple; you tell him that you're his father."

"I'm supposed to tell myself that I'm my father?"

"It'll be fine, you look like each other, act the same way. He'll believe you."

"Are you sure that's the best thing to do?"

"You can't say anything about being an older version of yourself."

"Why not?"

"You can't do that because it'll cause a lot of problems later. Just say you were held prisoner in Europe by a group of fanatics and escaped."

"You do know more than you're saying, Moses. What's going on?"

"Just tell the young Mike you're his dad, and you'll find out later what this is all about."

"You think he's going to believe that?"

"He'll believe it if you sound real. Remember those stories Nick told you?" Moses drove into the driveway to the cabin, stopped, and turned off the engine. "Well, we're here."

Nick was sitting on the porch when he saw the truck and who was inside. He stood, Michael waved, and Nick nodded. Moses got out of the truck. Young Mike stepped out from the cabin, and waited on the deck. Nick made his way off the deck to Michael. They shook hands and hugged. "Good to see you," Michael said. "How did you get back?"

"Good to see you," Nick said, "long story. I was wondering when you were going to show up, and what to say."

"You were expecting us?" Michael said. "None of this is making any sense."

"Not a hundred percent sure, but pretty certain you'd come. It'll make sense later."

"I don't know how this is going to be with me and the kid, so we thought I'd let him think I was his dad, pretend to be his father."

"As good a plan as any," Nick said. "Does Moses know?"

"My idea," Moses said.

Nick turned to young Mike, waved, and said, "Come on over here. I want you to meet someone."

For a moment young Mike wondered what was happening, and didn't go closer, and stayed on the deck.

"Come on, kid, there's someone here who wants to meet you," Nick said. "Now that we're all together, kid. This is your dad!"

Michael seemed to know him, but didn't know what to say, so he raised his arm, and extended his hand. After they shook hands, and hugged, young Mike said, "I never thought this would happen. I never thought I'd ever meet you. Where's mom?"

"That's going to take some time to explain," Michael said.

"What should I call you?"

"You can call me dad."

THE FUNERAL

Michael opened his eyes to a view of the ceiling. He didn't move a muscle for a time, then stretched. He felt at home after sleeping the night on the black leather sofa in the living room of the cabin. It was the one he'd slept on many times and was like an old long lost friend. He stood and went into the kitchen. "That smells pretty good, Poppi."

"Sit down, and I'll fry you a couple of eggs. How do you want them this morning?"

"Anything's fine."

"Moses and young Mike have had their grub, and are getting ready before we head into town for the funeral."

"I had a dream about the professor last night," Michael said. "At least I think it was a dream about him; seemed so real like he spoke to me. All I remember is a silhouette walking down a street. Is he going to help us?"

"I don't know where he is," Nick said, "he pops in and out dimensions. But I bet a dollar to your dime he'll be at the funeral today."

"Will Otto be there alone?"

"I don't know," Nick said. "Remember what happened when you were a kid? After finding Singleton we went back to the cabin, and I told you to wait in the tree line until I checked out the house."

"Yeah, I remember noise coming from the cabin."

"Otto was in the cabin waiting for me. I used the formula to travel to Austria, back in time to an older dimension. That's where we met again, on the steps, and I wanted to change what happened by getting rid of Otto once and for all."

"Yeah, I gave him the letter from his father about hiring your team to kill him, but he knew," Michael said. "Somehow he knew everything."

"Remember when you ran to get Carlo? He was almost killed when Otto showed up again with his goons. They shot the place up, then disappeared. That didn't happen this time. Instead he killed Carlo at his office."

"It's my fault that Carlo's dead," Michael said.

"Don't blame yourself. Otto's changing events. We've got to figure out his next step. We've got to get ahead of him, then he'll be on the run, and we'll be controlling the outcome. The amulet he has isn't working as well anymore , and he's running out of time to get those missing pages."

"I hope you're right," Michael said.

"It'll turn to our favor," Nick said. "Here, have something to eat."

"Thanks," Michael said as Moses came into the kitchen.

"Well, I think we'll be ready for Otto if he's at the funeral," Moses said.

"After Michael's done eating we'll head out."

"I'm done," Michael said. "Let's go."

"You go with Moses, Michael," Nick said. "I'll follow in my rig with young Mike, and we'll meet at the church. Keep an eye out for Otto; he could be anywhere."

They headed down the narrow driveway, and turned onto Double X. "Just what are we going to do when we run into Otto?" Michael asked. "You guys have some kind of plan, right? We can't just shoot him at the funeral. He's too clever for that."

"Everything will change after we take care of Otto," Moses said. "When we show up, and he sees you, he'll come out because he wants the formula, and believes you've got it."

"And we're going to give it to him?"

"Yeah, we're going to give it to him, and more," Moses said.

"There's the church," Michael said. "I don't see Poppi's truck."

"He's here somewhere," Moses said. "This looks like a good spot to park. You head in first and find a seat. I'll follow. It's better if we stay separated."

"What should I do if I see him?"

"Don't do anything. Just wait, you're the bait," Moses said. "We'll back you up, and I think the professor will come too. I reckon he's got a surprise for Otto."

Moses put out his hand, and grabbed Michael in a tight grip, and said, "It's time."

Michael made his way to the church. He turned once to wave, but Moses was not in the truck. *Where did he go?* Michael thought as he stood in front of the wooden doors, then took a few deep breaths. "Here goes."

Inside, the church looked like a huge cavern. People sat in front talking to each other in whispers that echoed off the walls. He sat down next to young Mike and waited like he was told to do as the pipe organ began playing hymns, then Father Miller stepped out straddled by two alter boys. They stood waiting, then heads turned as the rear doors opened letting the light stream inside. A casket and six pallbearers rolled down the aisle. When they got to the front, Father Miller and the altar boys met it, and waited while the pallbearers went to their seats. Father Miller took a Single-Chain-Thurible, opened the top, and lit the incense. He walked around the coffin swinging it low, high, and over the top while saying prayers. The smoke rose, then heads turned to the back when the church doors squeaked opened, and slammed shut. Otto had arrived.

"Where's Poppi," Michael said. "And the professor, where's he?

"I know where Poppi is," young Mike said.

"What? Where is he"?

"He told me not to say anything."

"Great, I haven't got a clue as to what's happening," Michael said as he looked around, watching as Otto ignored the ceremony, strolling down the aisle straight for Michael, eyes glowing, like a man in charge.

The church members were silent. "Where are they?" Otto said.

"I'm sorry, sir, are you a member of the family?" Father Miller asked.

Otto looked at Father Miller and said, "Oh, yes, Father, of course I am. Why else would I be here?"

"Please have a seat. We've just started the ceremony."

"I'd rather stand," Otto said. "I may have to move quickly. There are people here who mean to cause me harm."

"What people?" Father Miller asked. "This is a house of God, no harm will come to you here."

Otto turned slowly with his arms raised. "Good people of this community, please join me in saying goodbye to our friend. Don't be afraid, come, and we'll wish our friend a happy journey. And if any of you'd like to join him I can be of assistance in that area."

"I'm sorry, sir," Father Miller said, "but who are you?"

"Who am I?" Otto said, and snapped his fingers. A few men appeared in the balcony with guns raised. More in black uniforms appeared from what seemed to be out of nowhere. "I'm afraid the only person here who doesn't have a worry or care is this man," Otto said, then he put his hand on the casket tapping gently. "This man had a secret. Unfortunately some pieces, or should I say pages, are missing. And you, Mr. Colt over there," Otto raised his hand and pointed at Michael. "You, Mr. Colt, have something I desire. So, unless you intend to end up like this man here, I'd like you to hand it over, now!"

The silence inflated every muffled sound, squeak, and shuffling shoe in the church. Then voices of fear and puzzlement could be heard throughout the congregation.

Otto walked to the top of the altar. "Please Father," Otto said motioning to Father Miller to move aside, so he could stand at the podium.

"Now see here," Father Miller said. "I think you've overstayed your welcome. I may have to call the authorities. Please have a seat or leave. This is a funeral for a man of the community."

"Call the authorities?" Otto said. "I'm afraid the authorities are otherwise engaged.
So, Father, please have seat, and young man, would you join me here at the altar?"

"Excuse me," Michael said. All heads watched as he stood, and made his way to the front of the church.

"Yes," Otto said. "Come up, Mr. Colt, and show these fine people what you can do." He opened his arms as if he were welcoming his son home from a war. "There's plenty of room up here for the both of us."

"I don't know what you want," Michael said as he stood in front of Otto.

"Oh, please, don't start that routine again. I know you, or that boy there, has what I want. It's of no use to you. You've never wanted it, never sought real power, power to change everything."

"You're right about that," Michael said. "I've been through enough change to last me a lifetime."

"Just what I wanted to hear," Otto said. "So, you'll give me what I want, and these fine people can go on and live their boring lives." Otto held out his hand. "You're running out of time, Mr. Colt."

"We're all running out of time," Michael said, and reached into his pocket.

Otto's face lit up, and a grin of victory appeared. "See, now that wasn't so hard," he said, reaching out his hand, ready walk over and snatch what Michael had. Then he jumped backward when the coffin lid popped open. "You again!"

Nick jumped out, aimed the rifle he held and fired, but the shots ricocheted off the altar sending chunks of marble pieces flying. Otto grabbed Michael to use as a buffer, and fought with him while blocking Nick's view. Then he pushed Michael forward. "Well, this has been fun, so until next time." He turned around becoming a shadow for a moment, then faded and disappeared.

Nick turned around toward the back of the church and aimed at the balcony, but no one was there. "Damn!" he said. "Almost had him this time."

"You okay, Poppi?" Michael said.

"Yeah, I'm fine. We had him. So, close."

"Where's Moses?" Michael asked.

"He's keeping an eye out in the parking lot," Nick said.

"Better go check on him," Nick said. "I'll stay here and talk to the congregaton, hopefully calm them down."

"I'll go see where he is, and be right back." *It's a miracle that no one was killed. This is like a dream.*

"Okay, Michael," Nick said, and walked up to the altar. "Everyone listen. Most of you know me as the stone mason who lives out on Double X Road, but there's more of the story to tell. It's too difficult to go into detail. Just know we're here to help." Nick stood there waiting to hear if anyone had any questions, and tried to listen over the din to what they were saying.

THE BURIAL

Father Miller walked to the edge of the stairs. "We should continue the service of our dearly departed friend."

"You're right, Father, please go ahead with the service," Nick said. "I'll be right outside if you need anything."

Father Miller looked into the empty coffin. "Where's Singleton? We need him to continue the service."

"He's outside in the hearse, I'll go and get him," Nick said, then walked through the people standing in the aisle. They had blank stares, and some had questions on their faces, but for some reason were silent. Nick watched the young, middle-aged, and old as they slowly milled around or returned to their seats and sat down. He knew them, had done work for some, and known their relatives.

Then a man asked, "What's this all about? What the hell is going on?"

Nick stopped. "We're all living on the edge, flowing in waves of time, remembering the past, and looking for a future filled with hope. But there are greedy people who want to run and control the show, and we're going to do our best to make sure they don't."

"What the hell are you talking about?" a man asked.

"What are we supposed to do?" another voice in the crowd said.

Nick saw the vacant gaze on their faces. "Don't worry, everything will be fine," he said, and walked out to the parking lot to find Michael and Moses. He saw them standing at the bottom of the steps at the end of the sidewalk that led to the parking lot. They turned when they saw Nick, and gave him a nod.

"Well, that was close," Nick said, getting closer. He's a slippery one."

"What's next?" Michael asked. "Who are the guys with him, and what happened to them?"

"Not only can he break time dimensions," Nick said, "but he knows enough to bring a crew along for the ride. He's done it a few times now, but can't keep it up"

"He's gathered quite an entourage," Moses said. "How many guys did you see in the church?"

"A few in the choir, and some at the doors," Nick said.

"What are we going to do, Poppi?" Michael asked. "Have you got a plan?"

"We've got to draw him out again," Nick said.

"What's the next move?" Michael asked.

"We've got to take Singleton back into the church, so Father Miller can finish the service. Give me a hand."

They lifted Singleton out of the hearse and carried him down the aisle. "Don't know what Otto's planning, but we could chase him down," Moses said, "if we knew where he was."

"Maybe we don't know where he is now, but can guess where he'll be next," Nick said.

"Where's that?" Moses asked.

"I think at the cemetery or the cabin," Nick said. "Could be he'll show up. Michael, you want to be the bait again?"

"As long as we can get him," Michael said. "I'll do my part,"

They dropped Singleton into the casket, and Father Miller continued the service. Later they carried the casket back down the aisle. They looked up when they heard the church bells ring, then they focused on the double doors of the church opening as the casket was pushed through the doors and down the walkway to the waiting hearse. Despite the sober feeling of the day, it was sunny with white clouds floating above, and there was a hint of jasmine in the air. They stood to the side watching Singleton being loaded back in the hearse.

"Moses, why don't you go ahead, stay out in front of the procession, and we'll follow up," Nick said. "I'll ride with Michael this time, and you go with young Mike."

"Okay, see you at the Calvary Cemetery."

A convoy of cars led by the hearse headed about a mile out of town to the cemetery where Singleton would be laid to rest. And in a few days his son Carlo would join him, father and son together, something that didn't happen too often while they were alive.

"Why don't you drive, Michael, and I'll keep an eye out. Let's stay back a little bit, so we don't look like we're part of the caravan."

"Okay, got it," Michael said, and waited until the cars were just in site.

"What if Otto shows up at the cemetery?"

"If it happens, it happens, but if he doesn't show up he might send someone to watch us," Nick said. "There will be people there, but maybe we can spot him or them.

"Almost there, let's park on the road if we need to leave in a hurry."

"Looks like the ceremony started. There's Moses over there," Michael said, and nodded.

"We say goodbye to our friend Singleton one last time," Father Miller said. "He's gone to a place where love abides. Today we think of the memories of those who are no more. Months and years will pass, but we'll remember always that when the link of life is broken, our love for them never stops. Thank you Lord for letting Singleton in our lives, and remember we will be united with him in paradise. Amen." Father Miller took the Aspergillum and sprinkled holy water on the casket. "Would anyone like to join in the blessing?" Father Miller asked, and held out his hand.

The mourners took turns sprinkling the water. After the last person finished they returned it to Father Miller. "Go in peace, children of God."

People began to leave as a truck pulled up, and a man lowered the box into the ground, disassembled the carriage, and loaded everything onto the truck. Later someone would cover the box with dirt, then raise a gravestone to mark his grave. Moses joined Nick and Michael.

"Let's drive back to the cabin, and figure out how to get Otto out on the river," Nick said. "He'll be back with his crew unless we maneuver him away from them."

"Why the river?" Michael asked.

"It all started there, and I've got a feeling that's where it will end."

"Where's young Mike?" Moses asked.

"He was walking around looking at the names on the tombstones," Nick said.

"I don't see him," Moses said.

"Maybe he went back to the truck," Nick said. "Let's check." Nick walked quickly to the truck, opened the driver's side door of the truck's cab, but it was empty. "He's not here."

"Otto's got him," Michael said. "I feel it. I can feel it as if I'm there."

"In a way you are there," Nick said. "He's you! Where are they? Do you know?"

Michael closed his eyes and concentrated. "It's dark, can't see a thing, just dark. Wait, I can see them, and it looks like they're at the cabin, standing outside just looking at the cabin."

"What are we waiting for," Moses said. "Let's get moving."

"We have to get there before he hurts the kid," Nick said. "I'm getting a strange feeling about this."

Michael looked at Nick. "What kind of feeling? And if anything happens to him, what happens to me?"

"Let's try not to think about that," Nick said.

They jumped into their trucks and headed out of town down a country road, then along the river. Moses followed Nick's truck. "When we get there I think we should park on the road and approach the cabin from different angles," Nick said. "How do you feel, Michael, anything happening?"

Michael closed his eyes and focused on young Mike. "Nothing's happening. I think they're still standing in front of the cabin."

Nick closed his eyes as if in pain. "Let me know if anything changes," Nick said. "If they move, go in the cabin, or anything."

The two trucks barreled down country roads, around sharp corners, up and down valleys. "Almost there," Nick said after he saw the sign for Hungry Point. He slowed down, and turned onto Double X. "Anything happening, kid?"

"I think they're walking away from the house," Michael said.

"Can you see where they are?"

Michael covered his face with his hands, and concentrated. "They're going to the river."

"The river," Nick said, "exactly what we want him to do. How about now? Still going to the river?"

"Looks that way," Michael said.

Nick pulled over to the side of the road on the edge of the long driveway to the cabin. Moses pulled up behind him, got out and walked to Nick's truck. "What's the plan?"

"According to Michael, they're walking to the river."

"He's doing just what we want," Moses said. "You feeling anything?"

"A little, but nothing's clear," Nick said. "We didn't do anything to make him go to the river. He's going there on his own, so let's be careful."

"You think he knows we're here?" Moses asked.

"That's likely; he's been a step ahead of us up to now," Nick said.

"It's your call, Nick."

"Okay, we'll go down the driveway to the front of the cabin, you go around, and down the old logging trail. You're with me kid," Nick said. "We know what he wants, but he's not going get it. Let's go!"

ENGAGE

Nick guided Michael down the trail. "Stay alert, kid," Nick said. "He can pop out from anywhere."

"I'm watching," Michael said, "but I feel I'm fading in and out, like into a dream."

"Stay a little in front of me, and keep your eyes forward, I'll watch the flanks and rear."

They moved down the drive a step at a time, stopping every so often to listen. There was a breeze and the usual sounds of the forest under clouds that floated in a dark blue sky.

Nick tried to connect with Michael. "You feel or see anything?" Nick asked. "Is it the same as before?"

"Nothing, Poppi," Michael said. "I think he's on the trail to the river."

"How's young Mike doing?"

"Still with Otto, but seems to be fine."

"Let's stop a second," Nick said, "and wait for Moses to get around us."

"I still don't know why he wants me, Poppi."

"He wants the missing pages, Kid, and he thinks you've got them, or know where they are."

"But I don't have them," Michael said. "Why would he think that I do?"

"Yeah, I know," Nick said, "but he doesn't know that. Let's keep moving. I'll take the lead and you follow, okay?"

"Okay, I'll follow your lead."

"Slow and steady, kid, slow and steady. Stop a minute," Nick said, and looked up, and around.

"See anything moving, Poppi?"

"No, looks quiet, but stay alert."

Then Moses walked out the front door of the cabin. "He's not here," he said. "He's going to the river."

"Let's find Otto, and get young Mike back. We'll split up and meet at the backwater where Singleton was killed. That's where he'll be waiting."

The sun was on the way to a late afternoon as they stood at the trails at the edge of the forest. "I don't see any tracks or clues that anyone went this way," Nick whispered, and shook his head.

"Nothing here either," Moses said. "How about on your trail Michael, see anything?"

"No foot prints that I can see."

They met on the trail, looked at each other with uncertainty, then split up walking down to the end where it met the river. As the forest grew thick, their view still obscured, the sound of walking vanished. Otto was in no hurry to run.

"What is it about this guy?" Michael said. "He keeps coming back, and it seems there's nothing we can do to stop him. We plan, show up, but he's always a step ahead. How does he always know what we're planning?"

He heard a dog bark. "Buster?" Michael said. "He's run off down the trail just like he's done before, got the scent." The river came into sight, and he stopped,

Young Mike was sitting on a log. "Should I wait for Moses and Poppi? What if he needs help?"

He approached with a calm step, looking all around, watching for Otto. "Michael, you okay?" he asked. "Are you okay?" he said again and as he was about to touch the shoulder of young Mike his body turned into scatter and he vanished. "It's just an image of him. He heard the sound of footsteps coming from behind, and readied himself for a fight, but it was Nick and Moses.

"Michael, what happened?" Nick asked.

"He disappeared, just vanished as I was about to touch him."

"Otto could have sent him to another dimension, to a different time," Nick said.

"How can he keep doing this?" Michael asked.

"I don't know, kid," Nick said. "I don't know. But we can't let our guard down now. Otto's still lurking around here."

"So, what should we do?" Michael said. "Just wait here?"

"Is that a boat?" Moses said.

"Sounds like a boat to me," Michael said.

They turned toward the sound. They watched the river and watched a fishing boat make its way up stream. "Looks like only one person," Nick said, "and I've got a good guess who it is."

The boat cruised into the shore, and hit land scraping a groove into the ground. Otto stood after it stopped and got out. "Gentlemen, so here we are again. This place must be special because we've met here before."

Moses and Nick started to move closer to Otto. "Now, now, let's not get anxious," Otto said. "We've got to talk about young Mike before you go ballistic."

"What have you done with him?" Nick said.

"I assure you he's in a safe place," Otto said, then moved toward the boat, reached in and grabbed a shotgun. "I'm sure you recognize this, gentlemen, it's the same weapon I used on Singleton, remember?"

"Okay, what do you want?" Nick said.

"You know exactly what I want."

"So, how's this going to work?" Nick asked.

"You give the missing pages to me, and you get the kid back," Otto said. "Simple as that."

"How can we trust you?"

"You'll just have to. You have no choice."

"How do we know you've got him?"

"Want to take that chance?"

"We need some proof."

"Sure, recognize this?" Otto said, and held up young Mikes pocket knife, then tossed it to Moses, who gave it to Nick.

"Okay, how are we going to do the exchange?" Nick asked.

"Just hand over the pages, and I'll tell you where he is."

"No, that's no good, we need a failsafe," Nick said. "It's the only way this is going to work."

"Okay, okay, we can play your game, but if you don't follow through, it'll be over for young Mike. You'll never see him again. I'll send him to the worst place I can think of. So bad he'll wish he were in hell."

"We're not going to do anything, we just want him back."

"You there, Michael, know why they want the kid?" Otto asked as Michael and he exchanged a hard look, then Michael turned to Nick, but didn't say a word. "He doesn't know. That's funny, he doesn't know. Don't worry, Nick, it'll be our secret."

"What the hell's he talking about Poppi?"

"I'll tell you later, kid," Nick said.

"Yes, by all means, tell him later," Otto said and laughed. "Enough talk," then he pushed the boat into the backwater. The kid will appear in the boat, at that moment we'll make the exchange. Do you have the missing pages?"

"I've got them," Nick said. "You do your part, and I'll do mine."

A shadow, then a form appeared in the boat, it was young Mike. He wasn't moving, and looked asleep.

"Is he alright?" Nick asked.

"He's fine, just sleeping. He's been on a long trip. Maybe he's got a little jet lag?" Otto said and laughed.

They approached each other. Nick took out some pages from his pocket, and held them up. "You can have the pages after I get him out of the boat," he said, glaring at Otto.

Nick walked into the water, and pulled the boat to the shore. He shook young Mike trying to wake him up, then young Mike opened his eyes. "Come on kid, wake up!"

Otto stood peering, grinning, and watching. "The pages," he said. "You have him, give them to me."

Nick held up his hand, and tossed the pages in the air. They landed on the water, and floated away. "All yours," Nick said. "Go get them."

Otto's body transformed to a shadow, then into particles that evaporating into the air, and he was gone. Gone just like a dream after we wake.

YOU ME WE

Michael walked over to young Mike, and helped him stand. "Are you okay?"

He wobbled a bit, and said, "I feel fine now, but had a strange dream."

"What kind of dream?"

"I can only remember parts of it, but felt like I was trapped, and there was a shadow of a man. Couldn't see the man's face, only a shadow, and thought he wanted to help me because I felt there was no way out. Don't remember any other details. It seemed so real."

"Don't worry, kid, it's okay. We're all here to take care of you. You're safe now."

Young Mike looked at Michael, and said, "Thanks, dad."

Thanks, dad, Michael thought it was strange to hear that. He looked at Nick. "Poppi, what did Otto mean when he said, I didn't know. What was he talking about? Know what?"

"Not now," Nick said, "later." Nick helped young Mike get comfortable. "Just relax, kid."

"Later," Michael said, his voice warped with concern. "Why not now? Can't you tell me what Otto meant when he said that?"

"Okay, it's complicated, but I guess you'd have found out sooner or later. You okay, kid?" Nick asked young Mike, then turned to Michael. "I'm not trying to keep any secrets from you. I guess it doesn't matter, because time is short. It's over now because Otto's must have, or knows where the professor is. He'll be hard to stop. Brace yourself kid because all of this might sound very strange."

"Go ahead and tell me," Michael said, and let out a breath filled with fatigue. "Just tell me."

"Remember when I told you stories about your mom and dad, and how they were killed in a car accident?"

"How could I forget," Michel said. "They died a different way every time you told me the story. I thought you were just getting a little senile. Forgive me, Poppi. I know you're not."

"Well, Michael, your mother and father didn't die in a car accident, or any kind of accident."

"How did they die, then?"

"I don't know," Nick said.

"I don't understand. What do you mean?"

"Young Mike and you are the same person, right? You're just from a different time and dimension, but he thinks you're his father. You and the man you think is your father are the same person . . . we are the same person from a different time. Three generations together from different dimensions."

"What? When did this start?"

"After I met the professor," Nick Said, "and seeing him talk about predicting the future using logical formulas. We met, and I asked if he had any way of knowing about a situation that could be predicted before it happened, and what might happen in the future using some kind of formula. If we could plan our operations knowing what would happen, we'd always come out on top."

"I thought you were telling me stories," Michael said. "How can this be? When?"

"It was back in the early fifties," Nick said, "when I worked for SSU. The professor wasn't interested at first, but later became intrigued, and began to come up with formulas predicting everything down to every last detail. He became so good at making predictions, showing that time could be altered, and the future or past could be changed."

"What about the stories you told me, were they all true, or made up?"

"They're all true, what we did, all happened. Almost like when you're watching home movies of yourself when you're a kid, but it's happing in real time, and you know what's coming next. Information from the past used to predict what will happen in the future. It's all pure logic, and sequencing."

"Where's the professor now?"

"Haven't seen him for quite some time, and I'm afraid, if Otto has him, we're really in trouble. Hopefully he's gone to some dimension, and could be watching us right now."

"Do we need him to help us? Can we get rid of Otto ourselves?"

"Don't think so. We need the professor. I don't see us stopping Otto without him because his formulas are the key to everything. All of this started with him, and will end with him, too."

"How can we find him?"

"We can't contact him. It's up to him to find us."

"There must be some way to make contact," Michael said. "There's got to be a way."

"I know he was there when Singleton was shot, and has been out of sight since."

"Maybe that's the answer," Moses said, "Something to do with Singleton."

"I don't follow you," Nick said.

"This seems to have started with Michael finding Singleton floating here in the backwater. Maybe this place has got something to do with all of this."

"This place could be the door to other dimensions," Nick said.

"But how do we test it?" Michael said.

"I'll do it," Nick said. He walked into the backwater, and turned, then gave a salute to Michael and Moses. They nodded, and Nick went under the water.

RIVER OF TIME

Michael, young Mike, and Moses watched the spot in the river where Nick had gone under. Air bubbles rose to the surface, some popped, and a few flowed down river. They kept an eye on the place as the waves of the river brushed the shore where they stood. It touched the soles of their shoes and left imprints of them in the sand. Young Mike moved back and sat on a piece of driftwood. Moses and Michael exchanged glances wondering what would happen next. Not a word left their lips, and the silence was filled by the sounds of the river flow, birds, and other living creatures. Moses and Michael joined young Mike on the log, and sat on either side of him.

Finally Moses said, "I guess we just wait now."

"How long do you think?" Michael asked.

"We'll know when to leave," Moses said, and it was quiet again for a time, then Michael started to whistle the theme song from *The Good, the Bad and the Ugly*. Moses joined in, then young Mike. After that they all laughed.

"The story is similar to our situation," Michael said.

"Yeah, and Otto is the Lee Van Cleef character," Moses said.

"Whose the Clint Eastwood character?"

"That's got to be Nick," young Mike said.

"And, what about Eli Wallach?" Michael asked.

"The professor?" young Mike said. "Maybe not."

"The professor is Sergio Leone," Moses said.

"Will it end the same way as the movie?" young Mike said. "This feels like a movie that's being replayed over and over."

"Yes, sir, it sure does," Michael said, "some kind of endless dream loop."

The surrounding trees waved in the breeze while what was left of the afternoon sun warmed their backs. The river flowed and time ticked away, and it was running out for them. But rivers and time seem never ending, always running, like fashion trends. They looked up at the sky and watched the clouds float in the same direction as the river. Soon a setting sun would paint the sky into a reddish hue, and night would soon fall. Now the river seemed to calm.

"Well, I don't know about you guys, but I think we should've brought some fishing gear. I bet the fish are biting," Michael said. "We could catch our supper since we're staying here waiting and not sure how long it'll be."

Young Mike looked up and smiled. "Yes, we should have brought poles," he said. "How long are we staying here?"

"Like I said, all night if we have to," Moses said. "Nick will be back, and he'll bring the professor. The professor's the only one who can stop Otto now. He knows his formulas and has perfected them."

"I hope you're right," Michael said. "We should get some wood for later to start a fire because it's going to get dark soon."

"Good idea," Moses said. "Let's gather up enough wood for the night, but don't stray too far."

They marched off in different directions, later bringing back wood cradled in their arms, stacking it near the riverside camp.

"That's a big pile of wood," young Mike said. "Looks like we've got enough to last for a couple of nights."

"Looks like a lot, but this stuff is dry, and will burn fast," Moses said. "Let's get a little more. I don't want to be stumbling around in the dark later."

The pile got bigger as Moses cleared a spot. Then put some stones in a circle, took out a lighter and got the fire going. "That should give us enough light to see what's happening."

"Is anyone hungry?" Michael asked.

Moses looked around, and said. "Yeah, it's hard sitting around a camp fire without food or drinks. You guys want to go to the cabin and get some? I'll stay here and keep an eye on things."

"Sure, I'll go to the cabin and get some food," Michael said. "Come with me Mike. You can give me a hand carrying the stuff."

"I'll hang out here," Moses said. "Keep alert. Bring a couple of flashlights back with you, and anything else you think we might need."

"I'll lead the way," young Mike said. "I know the trail better than you, I think."

"Better than me, I walked these trails for many years, but it seems that was long ago."

"Things change over time," young Mike said, "and it's getting darker."

"Okay, you lead the way."

"How long do you think it'll be before Poppi gets back?"

"Like Moses said, we really don't know. Just have to hold out till he shows up. I see the light on the cabin by the driveway," Michael said. "We're close."

"What else should we bring back?" young Mike asked.

"Food, water, beer," Michael said. "We'll need a grill for the meat."

"I know where one is," young Mike said. "We take it on camping trips. I'll get that."

Michael knew exactly what he was talking about. "Alright, I'll get the food and drinks."

They gathered everything, and met in the cabin. "Well, that should do it," Michael said. "You ready, Mike?"

"Yes, I am," he said. "Head back to the river then? I'm ready to catch some fish."

Moses sat thinking and watching the river, then heard voices.

"We're back!" young Mike said.

"Let's cook some of this food," Michael said. "We might be here for a while."

"I'll see if I can catch anything," young Mike said.

Later after eating, drinking, and fishing, Moses said, "Why don't you guys get some rest, I'll stay up and keep watch."

THE DOOR

People of the world live in a dream-filled place, where shadows disappear from sight with every blink as they enter a different space and time. With open eyes after sleeping the night away, some wake to a new dimension looking similar to an image of the world they saw the day before. The changes are subtle, small, and unrecognizable at first, but are there to take note of. And once recognized, the changes experienced make us feel differently, and affect all senses, feelings, and beliefs. People might be able to change the world using the information they've stumbled upon during this time.

And with the professor's formula perhaps people traverse dimensions, and cross time itself, forward, backward, and shift into new worlds. Could this be where ideas come from? Great moments of inspiration from a lost memory carried through another dimension unwittingly traveled to at some point. In a way people seem to know certain things, but at the same time don't understand, the what and why, until it's worked out in their mind.

The professor perfected his formula step by step while learning more about the hidden world most people can't or don't see. And along the way he was not only able to predict future events, but could change the cycle of ongoing spinning time. The beginnings and endings are muddy or lost when someone arrives where a distant memory resembles a dream.

Bedtime Stories and Dreams—Memories of Michael Colt—The Fight Begins

In the dream a kid walked down the hill to where the driver waited. The driver asked how it went with Otto. The kid said that Otto knew what was going to happen. He knew him, and that he'd be there. More than likely knew all about the plan, and the kid had to get out, and go back to the dimension from where he came, now. The driver said they didn't have any time to waste, and to go find the missing pages. First they went to the park where the kid first woke in this dimension.

"The driver was there," Michael said.

"Yes, he was."

"Why go back to the park?"

"He told the kid he could travel back to the dimension he came from. He just had to find the spot where he came in; and said it works like a shadow, and is a door back to the last dimension. This is what they said."

'Okay, I think I remember the place,' the kid said. 'I should be able to find the same spot. How many times have you traveled back and forth between dimensions?'

'A few times,' the driver said. 'If you go to another dimension from a different spot you'll be sent to another place, and that makes it hard to get back to where you really would like to go.'

'That's it,' the kid said

'Yes, as easy as that,' the driver said.

'There's the fountain,' the kid said, 'and that's the bench I woke up on.' They walked closer. 'What should I do now?'

'Sit on the bench,' the driver said. 'Don't know when we'll meet, but I'll see you again, I know it!'

"The boy sat on the bench and closed his eyes. His body changed into droplets of water that evaporated into the air. The driver backed up a few steps, stood still a moment, then held up his arm to wave. The kid tried to open his eyes, but was in a dream state, then vanished."

"Then what happen?" Michael asked.

"Now back at the château, an older man stepped over pools of blood from the bleeding bodies of family, servants, and visitors. He walked through the first floor of the château leaving a red trail of stained footprints. He had charge of his family's vast fortune, and in the process of controlling the professor's formulas.

"Everyone was dead?" Michael asked.

"Yes, and there was only one person left to eliminate," Nick said.

"The older man thought and stopped a moment with his gaze seeking any sort of movement. Then the walk continued up the stairs, his sights on the office door at the top. He stood quietly in front of the door before opening it, grinning, a hunter ready to enjoy the prey. After the door opened young Otto looked up, then stood behind the desk. Without a word he stepped back, and looked for a way to escape."

"Did he get away?" Michael asked.

"No, and the older man entered the office where young Otto waited, and said, 'My, my, so this is how it was back in the old days. I just strolled through the carnage downstairs, and have to say, you do fine work young Otto. I'm proud of you. But there can only be one of us, so I'm afraid you'll have to join our dear departed family.'

"He met his younger self?" Michael asked.

"Yes, and was going to absorb him. He looked at young Otto. 'Do you know me?' the older man asked.' and young Otto said. 'No, who are you? Who am I?' The older man's diabolical laugh filled the room, then moved closer to young Otto. 'I'm surprised that you have no idea who I am,' he said, and his voice grew powerful. 'Look at me,' he yelled as he walked closer, then grabbed young Otto by the shirt, and pulled him close until they were nose to nose. 'Look at me carefully. Study my face. Guess who I am!'

"What happened next?" Michael asked.

"Young Otto was silent, his arrogant, and tough mind-set withered after gazing at the older man. He made no sound; his breath had been taken away. It was like looking at himself in a mirror of the future."

'Do you see a resemblance? You are me!'

'How can that be?' young Otto said.

'Yes, and now that you've done the work, I have no worries about this family of ours getting rid of me.'

"He wanted the energy of his life," Nick said. 'There's only one more job to do,' he said, and as his power grew he tossed young Otto across the room into the wall. A painting of their grandfather fell to the floor. The older man raised his arms in the air and let out a growling scream, and his eyes widened as he walked toward young Otto who squirmed on the floor.

'Wait, wait!' young Otto yelled. 'I can help you.'

'How can you help me?' the older man said.

'There's no one who can help more than me,' young Otto said. 'You'll need someone to watch your back.'

'I don't need anyone to watch my back, and I can't leave you here. There's only one way where we are together, forever.'

"What did he mean by together forever?" Michael asked.

'There can only be one of us,' the older man said.

"He picked up young Otto, embraced him, pulling him closer, then absorbed his essence until they became one.

The room changed, moving forward in time flowing into the future. Then, older Otto walked behind the desk and sat in the chair feeling satisfied. 'Now, only have to take care of the Colts, and the professor.'

"Then what happened," Poppi?"

"Time for bed Michael, Nick said. "I'll tell you tomorrow."

"Good night, Poppi," Michael said, then closed his eyes, and fell asleep.

INSIDE THE NOTEBOOK

Otto looked around the château, the memories of his life coming back as he sat in his father's and grandfather's chair. It was old and worn with time, but would last for years to come. He squeezed the chair's arm rests, and ran his hand across the surface of the desk. His arm dropped down to open the drawers, and inside were papers written and signed by him years ago. On the desk an old Japanese piece of slate carved into a slight *S* curve used as a paper weight fit perfectly in the fist.

Across the room arched windows overlooking the city draped the room in a soft light, and it reflected throughout the room. Priceless works of art in ornate frames adorned the office. Paintings by renowned artists that had never been displayed in public hung on the office walls, and bookshelves filled with first editions reached the ceiling. Then he focused on the notebook. "None of this compares to what's in this one notebook," Otto whispered. He held the book in his hands, caressed the cover, and turned the pages gently, then put it in his coat pocket. "Time to get a crew together."

Otto climbed the stairs to the roof of the chateau, and walked in a circle looking at the horizon for the door back to the previous dimension. He opened the professor's notebook to the last page, looked at the formula, but couldn't make sense of it because the last five pages were missing.

Geometric Relationship

A=60°,B=120°,C=85.3°,D=69.4°,E=34.7°,F=49.9°,G=45.1°,H=55.3°

Here are four of those relationships:

C/A ~ \/2, B/D ~ \/3, C/F ~ \/3, A/D~ e/pi

To explain the notation, if a and b are positive numbers, then a ~ b will mean that a and b are approximately equal.

Relationships involving ratios of the above angles and ratios of consecutive terms in the sequence of square roots of positive integers:

\/1, \/2, \/3, \/4, \/5, \/6 , \/7 .C/ A~.\/2 /\/1.....................(.5%)

H/G \/3/\/2.......................(.11%)

D/A \/4 /\/3.....................(.17%)

H/F~\/5/\/4.....................(.27%)

F/G ~ \/6 /\/5...................(.4%)

A/H \/7/\/6......................(.45%

C/A ~ \/2....................(.5%)

B/D ~ \/3..................(.17%)

$D/E \sim \backslash/4$ . . . .$(.0\%)$

$I/G \sim\backslash/5$ . . . .$(.45\%)$

$C/E \sim \backslash/6$ . . . .$(.35\%)$

$B/G \sim \backslash/7$ . . . .$(.6\%)$

There are several relationships involving the number gamma

$D/B \sim$ gamma . . . .$(.2\%)COT(A) \sim$gamma . . . .$(.025\%)$

$F/C \sim$ gamma . . . .$(.75\%)2SIN(A) \sim 1/$gamma $(.025\%)$

Relations involving natural logarithms.

$D/I \sim ln(2)(.3\%)$

$F/G \sim ln(3)(.1\%)$

$A=60°$

$B=120°$

$C/A= \backslash/2$

$B/D=\backslash/3$

$A/D=e/pi$

$C/D=e/\backslash/5$

$C/B=\backslash/5/pi$

Knowledge of some kind of hyper dimensional physics.

A message encoded, a kind of Physics involving more than three dimensions and that this kind of Physics furthermore can somehow explain the locations of dimensions. Suppose one considers just 12 points. If you draw all possible line segments between such points, you will have 66 such line segments. The number of triangles that you can form using these line segments as sides (i.e. any three of the 12 points as vertices) turns out to be 220. Each such triangle has three angles and so one gets a total of 660 angles. (If it happens that three points are on a single line, then some of the angles may coincide.) If instead one starts from 25 points, then it turns out that one can form 2300 triangles and therefore one gets a total of 6900 angles, all between 0° and 180°.

A law of sines for The Bell and the space of all shapes.

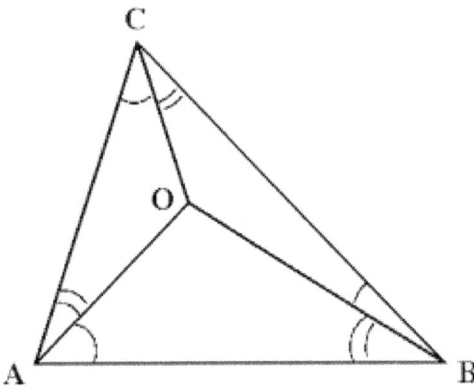

A corollary of the usual _law of sines_ is that in a tetrahedron with vertices O, A, B, C, gives us this below.

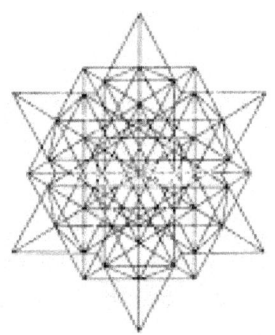

THE RIGHT PERSON

"I need to get to the professor," Otto said. "In the end we all have to die, but I won't because I'll have total control after I go back in time and terminate every dimension of Colts. I need the missing pages."

As Otto sat back he opened another drawer and removed a brown leather-bound book with a gold etching of a lion's head, a sword, and a crown on the cover: the family crest. He glanced over at a silver frame enclosing a family picture sitting on top of the desk, the same family that was now lying in blood-soaked clothing scattered throughout various rooms of the chateau. Otto seized and held the picture.

"I need some help to finish this once and for all," Otto said, "to help send the Colts into extinction once and for all. My family has political connections and power. Why not use people who work for the company to get the job done. I'm sure for the right price; I can get some of them to join me. Money is a great convincer."

Otto looked through the family record and history of his family. Memories of growing up and of his parents began to set him on an emotional spin, so he slammed the book shut.

"Of course these people I choose will have to be brought up to date; they are stuck in a dimensional time lag. I'm sure they'll be able to make the leap to the future; even a small child can learn to use a computer by themselves. Timing will be important. It'll have to happen at the precise time when the Colts are most vulnerable, and that's when at least two or more of them are together. Two or three generations gone will leave an enormous gap and stop their passage of knowledge between them." *I've got to figure out the timing, that's what's important, and get the people together to raise hell to get this over with.*

He opened the book again. "How elegant and smart you all thought you were," he said, then let out an obsessive laugh, and leafed through the book, scanning it page by page, reading the break-down of the Voritch Family Empire.

He walked to the window and looked out at the city and said in a nonchalant way, "Oh my, almost forgot about the bodies. What shall I do with the bodies? Can't just leave the family, servants, and assassins lying about; the odor would be horrendous. How will I clean this up before anyone notices what's happened?" He laughed when the idea came to him, then blurted out. "FIRE! That's it! I'll burn the place to the ground. I'll take what I need and put a torch to the place."

Otto thought about what he would take, and how much he could carry, then grabbed the Voritch family register off the desk, and filled a small bag with things he thought would be useful later, in case the items weren't available in another dimension. After that he walked out back and into the garage where there were containers of gasoline and a storage tank. He filled the containers, carried them up the stairs to the top floor, then started pouring the gas out. One by one he emptied the containers and tossed them down the stairs, after the last one he watched the gas spill down the halls and into the cracks and corners. He repeated the process on the second and first floor until the the chateau was bathed in gasoline.

"Well, I think this will be quite a show for the town," he said as he stood in the arched entryway in the main hall, then breathed in the fumes. "Oh, a lovely smell. I'll never forget this day." Then he took out a lighter, dropped it, then with a big grin on his face slammed the door shut and walked out.

He made his way down the hill on the narrow street that was lined with small shops. There he watched people standing in front of the shops chatting as smoke rose above the chateau. They were pointing and surprised at how fast a gray cloud was forming above chateau. Otto continued walking, then waved a taxi down. One stopped, but before he got into the car he had one last look. "Easy come easy go," he said as the flames danced in the sky.

"Where would you like to go today, sir?"

Otto took out a piece of paper, showed it to the taxi driver, and said, "Take me to this address."

As the car drove away Otto looked back once, then turned his attention to the list in the register. The wail of sirens made him look up for a moment, but he soon got back to the list of names.

"Very nice day today?" the taxi driver said, but then he pulled the car to the side of the road. "I wonder what all the noise is about. There's a fire, and here come the trucks. I wonder if anyone's been hurt."

"I'm sure someone has," Otto said and smiled, "Yes, it's truly a wonderful day."

"There's a lot of smoke," the taxi driver said. "It must have happened close to where I picked you up."

"Oh dear, you're quite right," Otto said. "Fortunately I just got away in time."

There was an explosion, then another one, and one more.

"What could have caused all that?" the taxi driver said.

"I'm sure I don't know," Otto said, "something flammable I gather."

The cloud grew in size and began to engulf the city, and more fire trucks and emergency vehicles were on the way.

"Are you in a hurry," the taxi driver asked. "I know a short cut."

"Good," Otto said. "I like someone who takes the initiative."

"Might save you some money," the taxi driver said, "but perhaps it's not so important to you."

"Oh, but it is young man," Otto said as he leaned forward, and patted the taxi driver on the shoulder. "On the contrary it shows that you are a man who wants to get ahead in the world. Of course the money means nothing to me because I have so much of it, but I like your way."

"Some people just want to make things better or easier if it's possible."

"Yes, that's what I want to do," Otto said. "Make this world a better place."

"Looks like I ran into the right person," the taxi driver said. *Maybe this is the break I've been waiting for.*

Twenty minutes later the taxi driver said, "Here we are. Where would you like me to drop you off?"

"This is fine, Otto said. "Just out of curiosity, do you like driving a taxi?"

"Oh, yeah, more than anything in the world," he said with a smirk. "Are you kidding? I'd quit right now if the right opportunity turned up. I'm a student in my last year of school, just driving a taxi to make a little money, and hoping to get a position after I graduate."

"Like I said, you're the kind of guy that wants to get ahead, and it just so happens that I'm looking for someone to help me with a project. Interested?"

"What is it? What's the project?"

Otto sat back, "Involves traveling," the tone of his voice sly, and mysterious. "Are you willing to travel?"

"Travel to where?"

"I'm afraid I can't go into the details now, but if you would like to make more money than you've ever imagined, park this taxi and come with me."

"What about the car? I can't just leave it here on the street."

"Why not? What will happen? I'll tell you what, nothing. Nothing will happen."

"I don't know anything about you."

"Last chance my young friend. Like to have you aboard, this is a great opportunity that I guarantee will never knock again. Can I count you in?"

"Can I change my mind later?"

"Sorry, this is all in, or all out. What's it going to be my young friend?"

"Okay, I'm in."

"You've made the right choice," Otto said. "And what would you be called?"

"Luke Paris."

"So, Mr. Paris, let's put you to work, park in front of that building, and come with me."

They entered a five-story stone building that had no sign or name to identify what it was or who owned it. The guard standing at the entrance allowed them to pass without any questions, a nod from Otto sufficed. Around to the right a stairway waited, soon they were on the top floor, and walked into the office at the end of the hall. Off to the left was another office.

"This is where you will work, Mr. Paris," Otto said. "Your first job is to watch, and greet anyone who comes in. Find out who they are, what they want, then tell me." Then Otto gestured and said, "You can have that desk."

"Anything else you need me to do?" he asked.

"Not right now, so just tell me if anyone comes in or calls. I'll be in my office for a while. After that I'll have something important for you to do."

THE DEVICE

After a time Otto came out of his office. "Anyone come in, call?" he asked.

Luke stood. "No calls, nothing happening," he said. "I've just been sitting here reading and studying."

"And what are you studying, Mr. Paris?"

"About logic, predictions, outcomes."

"I see," Otto said. "I'd like you to join me in my office, Mr. Paris. We've got some planning to do."

"Call me Luke."

"Luke?" Otto said. "I rather like Mr. Paris."

"Okay, I'm good with that."

Luke followed Otto into the office. "Have a seat," Otto said, and pointed to a black leather chair near a bookcase that reached to the ceiling.

"You've got a lot of books."

"Knowledge is power. So, you're interested in logic, and predictions, Mr. Paris?"

"Yes, I think the future might be known if it's logically thought out."

"Interesting! What I'm going to tell you doesn't leave this room," Otto said.

"I won't say anything."

"I've chosen you to help me retrieve something. I'm going to share something with you now that will sound outrageous and hard to believe. Let me begin."

Luke sat ready to listen to Otto's every word. "First, do you have any family, Mr. Paris?"

"No, I don't."

"What if I told you that you could see them again?"

"How can that happen?"

"I have a way."

"You can bring people back to life?"

"No, but I can take you to another dimension to where they are."

"How do you do that?"

"With King's Water," Otto said, and opened his shirt revealing a snowflake shaped ornament hanging around his neck. "This mechanism is called a Bell," Otto said. "Each triangle contains a drop of liquid called King's Water. It was created by man known as the professor. Someone you'll get to know."

"How does it work?"

"You have to enclose it with your hand, then think of where you'd like to be, and you'll go there."

"So, what do you need me for?"

"I have one last chance to get the missing pages of the King's Water formula because this Bell is almost drained. I want you to help me make more. Part of it vaporizes every time it's used. There's basically only enough for one more trip to another dimension."

"What do I have to do?"

"The people who have the missing pages know me, are expecting me, and are preparing to stop me from getting them," Otto said. "But, if you go in my place they won't be expecting that. They would never believe that I would give up the Bell to another person."

"Okay, what do I have to do?"

"You'll be going to a small town called Hungry Point. Look for a cabin just on the outskirts of the village. The person who owns it is Nick Colt. There's mailbox with his name on it near the driveway. I think he has the missing pages hidden in the cabin."

"Where in the cabin? Do you know?"

"Not sure where, but once you locate them, take this key, and go to the Post Office in Hungry Point. You'll see some lockers, put the missing pages in the locker."

"I just put them in the locker," Paris said. "What about the key?"

"You keep the key, and I'll find you."

"That's it?"

"That's right, after you follow the plan, and it works out, you can go anywhere and do anything you like. All I want are the missing pages."

"What if this Colt guy finds out about me, and I can't get the missing pages?"

"Then you'll have to deal with it," Otto said. "Colt is a trained assassin, so if he discovers what you're doing, he won't let you live. You'd better do your best to get them, you won't have another chance."

"So, I get them for you, then I get to see my family, friends, and relatives, but what about . . . money?"

"You will never have to worry about money," Otto said, as he took out an envelope. "Here's a number to a bank account that I've opened in your name. I only want the formula."

Paris took the paper with the bank information. "What's next?" he said. "What do I have to do now?"

"Let me show you," he said. "Come this way, and look over here."

They walked to the elevator. Otto pushed the button for the roof that opened to a spectacular view of the city, and a pool with crystal blue water. "This works better the first time in water. Jump in and think of where you'd like to be, which in this case is Hungry Point."

"That's it? Just think of Hungry Point?"

"Stay under the water until you think you can't breathe," Otto said. "You'll wake up in Hungry Point, and look for the Colt cabin."

Luke stepped closer, and stood near the pool, his toes dangling over the edge. "I don't know about this," he said.

"You said you'd go through with it, there's no backing out now," Otto said as he moved behind Luke. When he turned he saw a revolver in Otto's hand.

"You have two choices, my friend," Otto said. "Jump, or get shot." He raised the gun and pointed it at Luke's head. "Basically you have no choice. Don't think about taking the gun. Well?"

"Okay, okay, just give me a second to catch my breath. I'll jump, I'll go. Wait, wait, I'll jump."

Otto gave him a nudge in the back with the barrel of the revolver. "Remember, don't panic after you jump. Just stay under the surface, wait for it, and it'll happen. You'll know when it's right."

"I sure hope you know what you're talking about, here goes," Luke said and jumped. He sunk down to the bottom of the pool looking up at an obscure Otto, who was giving the thumbs up. Luke opened his mouth, and bubbles floated to the surface. Then there were no bubbles, and he began to fade, and in a flicker he was gone!

HUNT FOR THE FORMULA

Luke Paris dragged himself out of the river coughing his guts out, and spitting up water before collapsing face down in the sand. He stood silent a moment, feeling lost, looking the area over, then he walked away from the river. He stayed there near the shore for a time. It was quiet, waves washed in, an occasional fish jumped, and clouds covered him in shade until they floated away in a slight breeze. Then he fell to the ground, and blacked out!

The sun warmed his face. "How long have I been out?" he mumbled, shaking his head and coughing as he watched a big bug crawl by his face. He lifted himself off the ground from the prone position, and for a moment sat quietly, then wiped his eyes, looked around, stood, then brushed the sand from his clothes.

"I'm dry, not wet at all," he said, and turned toward the water. "Must have been out quite a while. Where am I?" His memory felt like it had been erased, he was confused. There must be a road around here that leads somewhere, he thought. "What am I supposed to do?" he said as he tried to remember why he was there, then a name came to him. "Colt, I'm looking for Nick Colt's place, and the notebook." *Hopefully it's there*, he thought, and walked down a path in the woods. *It's been a while since I've walked in the woods, reminds me of when I was a kid.*

He looked up when he heard the sound of a truck go by, but couldn't see anything, and followed his ear. "The road is near," he said, and his strength came back little by little. Now he moved with ease through the woods, brushing away branches, and taking longer steps. "There it is! I made it, now which way do I go?" he said as he stood at the edge of the forest next to the road. There was another wood line across the road, and from where he stood the road curved off in both directions, "I'm guessing Hungry Point is to the right," he said, "so I'll go this way." He stepped off to the left and followed the road. As it became narrow he saw a sign with a double X. "This is the right way. I'm getting into the country."

Paris walked along the narrow rough ribbon of asphalt. "Aren't many cars on this road, guess that's good. I don't have to worry about explaining who I am. There's a mailbox up ahead. Could it be the one I'm looking for?" he said, and ran to it. Up close he saw black letters that read, C-O-L-T. "Found it! The cabin must be down this way." Luke followed the overgrown driveway as it twisted round, left and right, then he stopped. "The cabin," he said, and looked around to assess the situation. He only heard sounds from birds, bugs, and a gentle wind blowing through the trees, making them talk in tree language. Paris approached the cabin, slowly, alert and listening.

"Anyone's here?" he said, and stepped onto the deck while trying not to make too much noise. "Hello, anybody around?" he said, then looked through one of the windows. He walked into the cabin, scanning the room, thinking of where the formula might be hidden. There was an old desk in the corner, and some pictures hanging above it. The picture in the middle was the biggest, so he took it from the wall, and turned it over. He ripped off the cardboard from the back, and took out some papers that were folded in half. He held them wondering if he should look at them. *Why not,* he thought, and looked over the pages. "What is this? Lot's of complicated formulas. What do they mean? And what are these diagrams? I've seen this before, but where?"

Luke looked around checking the area, then went back to checking the pages. "I know what this is, but what does it mean?" he said, and studied what he saw.

"Better get out of here before someone comes back," he said, and made his way to the road through the woods. After he left the wood line he walked along the road into Hungry Point. Then an old pick-up truck drove by, stopped ahead, and pulled over. The driver's arm popped out of the window and waved him to come, so Paris walked faster up to the passenger side door.

The window was down, and he could see the driver. "Hello," Luke said.

"Hey," the driver said. "Where are you heading?"

"I'm going that way," Luke said, and pointed toward Hungry Point.

"Want a lift? I'm going that way," the driver said. "Hop in, I'll drop you off."

"Thanks, that would be nice."

"Haven't seen you around here, passing through? Related to anyone?"

"No relation around here, just passing through. I'm trying to make it back to my hometown."

"Where's that? Where are you from?"

"England."

"I thought I could hear the accent. Where in England?"

"London, but I moved to France. Lived in Grenoble."

"I've heard of it, good for skiing, right? I think I remember reading the winter Olympics were held there back in the sixties. I've been to France too."

"You were living there?"

"You could say that. I was in the service. How did you end up here in this place?

"It's long story," Luke said. "One of those unplanned things that go out of whack. Was hired to do a job. Not sure it was the best thing to do though, but don't get me wrong, it's been a great experience."

"What did you do in France?"

"I was a student,"

"What did you study?"

"Logic, algorithms, and how the future can be predicted using formulas."

"Interesting," Moses said. "How'd that go? Were you able to predict how your trip here turned out?"

"Not exactly, but I'll be able to be more accurate in time. Is that Hungry Point up ahead?"

"Yes, it is, that's the place. Where do you want to be dropped off?"

"I need to go to a post office, got a letter to send. Can you drop me there?"

"Sure, no problem, Post Office is on the right. I'll put you in front of it. Where you heading after that? Got any plans?"

"Next town, I guess, then head back home."

"Well, there's the post office." Moses pulled in front of the Post Office and stopped.

"Thanks for the ride."

"Good luck on your trip, and your way home. By the way, I'm Moses."

"I'm, Luke Paris," he said, and reached out his hand.

As they shook hands, Moses said, "Your name is Paris, and you lived in France, interesting."

Luke opened the door and stood there a moment after he shut the door.

"Happy trails, Luke," Moses said. He raised his hand to his brow like a casual salute, and drove away. Luke waved back.

Luke stood in front of the post office a moment thinking of what he had to do, then went in, and made his way for the lockers. "Any locker is okay," he whispered, and opened one. Then hesitated as the thought of keeping the papers he'd found grew in his mind. He unfolded and opened them to look once more. The writing became more and more familiar to him. "I know why I'm having these feelings. This is my handwriting. But how could that be? I don't remember writing any of this. None of it! And the dates are in the future. What is going on here? What is Otto trying to do?" Then he tossed them into the locker and turned the key, but not before tearing the papers into small pieces. Paris walked out of the post office thinking about what to do as he felt the crystal ornament that hung around his neck.

"I've done my part," he said as he walked back to Nick's place. Instead of going to the cabin he walked through the woods to the river. Once he got there he just stood at the bank of the river. "The view here is spectacular," he said. He realized who he was, and what he had to do. "I have to finish what I started."

THE BODY

"Look over there," Sue said. "See that thing floating out there. What do you think it is?" Michael couldn't see it at fist. "Over there, see it?"

"Oh yeah, I don't know what it is," Michael said, "but it almost looks like a body."

Something odd was definitely floating in the water. They watched whatever it was bob around in the waves, but it more or less stayed in the same place and wasn't coming to shore. They continued to watch the mysterious bulge float back and forth, up and down, twisting and spinning round.

"Maybe it's caught on something, so it won't wash ashore. Let's swim out and see what it is," Michael said. "How about it?"

"You really want to do that?" Sue said. "I'm not sure that's such a good idea."

"What else can we do?" Michael said. "It's stuck on something, so it'll never come ashore."

"Can't we just go and tell someone, and let them go out and get it?" Sue asked. "If it's really a body we should call the police, or someone."

"It might float away by then," Michael said. "The river's pretty strong and carries everything downstream. "If it's a body we might help solve a crime. You wait here, and I'll go out to get it."

"I don't know."

"I have to see what it is," Michael said. "It'll be fine."

"Okay, Michael, I'll wait here, but if you get in any trouble out there, wave or signal, and I'll get help."

"Don't worry," Michael said, "I'll be fine." Off went his shoes, socks, shirt, pants, and he stepped into the water. He walked out until the water was chest high, then started swimming out to the hulk bobbing in the water. He looked around and up to the sky at clouds hanging in the same place, not moving. Across the water the waves pitched over his head as Michael swam farther out. He turned back to give Sue the thumbs up as he made his way out to an object that started to look more and more human.

Michael began to have flashbacks as he swam farther, so he stopped and closed his eyes, blinking faster as images from dreams appeared. He shook his head to clear them away, then heard a dog barking. He looked back again where Sue was standing on the shore, but only saw his dog Buster barking and jumping, agitated by something.

"Where's Sue?" he said, and looked around perplexed. She was nowhere in sight.

He moved closer to see the floating hulk in front of him, then grabbed, and pulled it ashore to where the dog barked. "Where is Sue?" he said again after making it back and looking around at the trees, shore, and backwater. Michael's focus went back to the body he'd dragged out of the water, then knelt down and turned it over. It was Singleton, the same guy he found the first time when he was just a kid, on the morning he took Buster for a walk to the river. Then he heard sounds of footsteps walking on brush, and branches breaking. Someone was walking out of the woods. It was an older man who stood at the edge of the forest with a grin, but said nothing.

"Who are you?" Michael asked.

"Think deeply, and it'll come you," the man said. "This is getting tiring."

Images of places, faces, and sounds flashed in Michael's mind. Generations seem to go by, and he wondered how this could be, and what was happening.

"I see by the look on your face that you're beginning to remember," Otto said, and he moved closer. "There's a key in the pocket of the body you just pulled in, and I want it."

"A key?"

"Yes, a key to a locker that holds the missing pages of a notebook."

Michael thought a moment. "What's in the notebook? Where's the locker?"

"At the Post office in Hungry Point."

"How do you know that?" Michael said.

"Because I'm the one who had them put there."

Then Michael thought, I remember finding the key.

"Yes, by the look on your face I think you're beginning to remember, but too much now. I had someone remove the pages from the cabin for me after they were found by you."

"How could you do that?"

"I think you know how."

Buster stood at Michael's side as he moved away from the body. "So, you want the key?"

"Yes!" Otto walked closer to the body, and went through the dead man's pockets. "Where's the key?"

"Can't find what you wanted?" Michael said, and moved toward the woods.

"It's not here," Otto said. "You've got it! I'll get it from you, then there's one more thing I need to do before I take it from you."

"What else is there to do?"

"I'm afraid you can't know that I was here, so this memory has to be wiped away, and there's only one way to that."

"How?"

"You know," Otto said.

Michael backed away, Buster's barking was frantic, Otto moved closer. "Just go," he said. "I can't do anything for you."

"I can't," Otto said. "I have to end this here. Getting rid of you is as important as having the pages of the formula."

Michael moved even closer to the woods, stood still a moment, then ran off with Buster following close behind, his breathing became quick, hard, and deep. This was a sprint for his life. He turned back to see if Otto was behind, but saw nothing.

"Got to run faster," he said, "faster, faster," he repeated.

Buster ran in front of Michael and took the lead. "Wait, Buster!" he yelled. "Wait!" but the dog vanished from sight. Michael stopped when he got to the edge of the woods, and fell on his knees out of breath. "Why is this so familiar?"

When he looked up he saw Poppi on the deck of the cabin. He got up and ran yelling, "Poppi, Poppi! He's here, he's here!"

Nick turned when he saw Michael, and stepped off the deck, then in a quick stride made his way toward Michael. "Who's here?"

"The man, the old man!"

"What man?" Then Nick realized what man. "Otto!"

Michael ran into Nick's arms. "It's okay, Michael, it's okay. I'll take care of this. Go into the cabin."

Otto emerged from the edge of the woods, stopped, looked the area over, then stared at Nick. This wasn't the Otto Nick remembered as he looked at an older face that was ruddy and rough. Not the young Otto he'd saved years before.

"Well, my friend, it's been a long time," Otto said, "or seems that way."

"I'm not letting you go this time, Otto. You'll never leave this place," Nick said. "It finishes here! It's done here!"

"I agree," Otto said. "I remember your kind gesture years and years ago from another time, and haven't forgotten what you did for me, for letting me go, but I'm sorry to say, I cannot let either of you go. So, let's get to it, then."

As Nick thought, memories from both their pasts flashed before them and seemed as if dimensions had locked and crashed into each other. They tried to erase each other's memories with their minds as they stared each other down by forcing energy from their bodies. It started when they were children, moved back and forth in time from the past to the present. They erased old memories from the past, and once gone they would never return even as a passing thought. They approached each other, walking closer, circling, attacking and erasing their old memories. Faster they moved, finally colliding, gripping each other by the shoulders foreheads touching. A glow of color and air waves moved outward into the trees like wind bending them away, both of them spinning like a tornado until they became a blur. Michael stepped out of the cabin, and stood on the deck watching Nick and Otto turning faster, the power strong rising upward and down, attracting and repelling. Michael began to age. He grew physically from a boy, then into a man, and Nick disappeared.

Otto floated up looking at a sky that was growing dark, light, then dark again. Otto looked down at a shadow where Nick had been stretched out on the ground. It was silent and still. He grinned with delight, and railed. "It's done, it's done! I win!"

Then there was the sound of a bell, one ring that echoed through breaking the waves of air, then behind Otto, Luke Paris appeared.

"The Professor," Michael said as he aged, became an old man, then a young kid again.

"Mr. Paris, how good to see you," Otto said. "Have you got my key?"

"Yes, right here," and opened his hand to reveal the key.

"I'll take that now."

"Sorry, I can't give it to you unless Michael comes with me."

"Mr. Paris," Otto said. "I'm getting angry. We made a deal."

"You can't take the key from me," the professor said. "You know it has to be given to you. Michael comes with me."

"You know what happens don't you?" Otto said.

"Yes, I do," the professor said. "I've rearranged what happens, and when you take the key you will know as well."

"Okay, he goes with you," Otto said. "Hand over the key."

"Come here, Michael," the professor said. "See you somewhere sometime again, Otto."

"Yes, Mr. Paris, I will see you again, and then that will be for the last time. I guarantee it!"

The professor tossed the key to Otto, then Michael walked to him, and took his hand.

"Professor," Michael said. "What will happen now?"

"A story, and a new life for both of us Michael," the Professor said, and they walked into the trees of the forest and disappeared.

The early morning sun rose as Otto stood in the woods looking around, observing, and thinking about where he was. He opened his hand, and saw a key which he recognized immediately. "Now to get the missing pages," he said, and looked for a vehicle, but there were none, and he began walking in the direction of Hungry Point, down the path through the woods and to the main road. Otto walked until a few more structures came into sight, then a sign that said, Hungry Point. *There's the Post Office*. He walked into the Post Office to the locker, and inserted the key. "Finally it's done! I have them!" He reached into the locker and removed the torn pieces of the missing pages. As he held them, they turned into powder. Otto's face went pale as he gripped what was left in his hands. "I'm stuck here in this dimension."

Otto left the Post Office an SUV pulled over, and the driver rolled down the window. "I've been looking everywhere for you, dad. Come on! Lets go home. The fire place is done. Colt finished it today, and he did a fantastic job. I think you'll really like it."

"Fire place?" Otto said.

"Yeah, the fire place, he finished today. Hey! What's that you've got there in your hands?"

"This?" Otto said, and held up his hands.

"Yeah, what is that?"

"A powder that contains the ways and means of time travel through dimensions past and present by just using the mind. I would have been able to change events in time." And Otto dropped what was left of the missing pages into the air, and watched as it floated away with the wind like a forgotten dream.

"Okay, dad, whatever you say, but let's go home first before you do any time traveling and have dinner." *The old guy finally lost it.*

Otto got into the SUV holding his hands together in a tight grip, squeezing them, and staring out of the window, wondering if he'd ever get the missing pages back or just grow older day by day and soon die.

HOME SWEET HOME

Michael sat on the river bank leaning against a huge old oak tree looking up through a canopy of branches and leaves that partially concealed a vivid blue sky. He watched balloon like barkentine clouds float by with the wind while key moments of his life appeared in passages like a movie through a window framed by the universe of time. After his mind unlocked, it was overwhelmed and flooded with ideas from another time. Everything he'd done, every move he'd ever made rolled on and connected into a flawless series of events. Some memories were things that he would have never recalled; things that would have been hidden forever, and things he realized had molded him into who he now was. The professor stood behind Michael and together they watched his life's events reflect off the water, rise and float in the air, then return back to a river that flowed without a beginning or end.

All of the good and bad that had happened revolved in front of his eyes. He wondered what he might change, and what he could do with this power he now had. Would it enable him to cut, paste, delete, and add anything to parts of his life and other's lives like a writer using a computer program?

The professor's task was to put everything back on an even keel and strike a balance that would last as long as possible. A newly built world solid as a stone structure, long lasting, to hearten, revere, enjoy, and last for the ages. The professor's top duty and task would be to stop anyone like Otto who had grandiose ideas of controlling the world. People who wanted to destroy others and control everything had to be blocked from doing so, and the professor would be the dream killer. Their life's memories would be sent to the underworld, and remain there forever locked in grim reality, buried, and never allowed to escape.

The professor walked closer, stopped, and looked around, taking in the surroundings, listening to the river flow and breeze blow. He smiled. "Think of it, Michael," he said, his voice filled in excitement, "being able to travel through time by just thinking of where you want to be or go. Making your dreams reality and stopping anyone who's planning to tear the world apart. This is not just some kind of legerdemain trickery; it's real, a true experience."

Michael stood and said, "I know and understand how you feel about stopping power hungry lunatics like Otto from destroying this world. As far as I remember I came to you, and initiated all of this. Because of you I've discovered things previously unknown to me, but do you really think we're the ones who should decide what becomes reality and what doesn't? Are we supposed to align the world however we see fit and mold it to our desire? Isn't there supposed to be some randomness to it? Some spontaneity?"

"But we can eliminate chance," the professor said, "and make certainty the norm, have all things just as we think and plan come true. We can do a lot of good, and right the wrongs in people's lives!"

"Are we sharing this great development with everyone?" Michael asked. "Will all people be able to do this mind travel stuff?"

"I believe we can only share it with a chosen few, the ones we can trust, and the people who we know who will use it for good. We'll be the gate keepers for anyone who breaks this aspiration because there's a need for us in a world with foul people like Otto. Others like him will follow, so we'll transcend with this power. We can't let this chance slip away. Someone must take on the role as gatekeeper and dream killer of the beasts in the world."

"Be the few to filter out who can and can't use the formula?" Michael said. "Choose what, or who's right and wrong? Sounds like a lot politics to me, and not sure I'd like or want any part of it, but if you feel it's your place, go ahead, I won't try to stop you. You're very dedicated, and I owe you a huge debt, but I've had enough of mind time travel for a now. Going through this whole thing with Otto's exhausted me."

"Like you said, you're the one who came to me, Michael. You started this years ago looking for ways to predict the future. And back then you understood that we had to control the events or someone like Otto would. What's changed since then?"

"So, it's all on our shoulders then," Michael said. "Are you so sure it was me who came to you first? Do we know that for certain?"

"However or whatever the reason for us meeting and doing this we are the chosen ones," the professor said. "It was meant to be this way by design. I'm not the one who created the formula, or this world as we know it."

"Then who did?" Michael asked.

"Michael, let me share something with you," the professor said. "I haven't mentioned anything about this because I'm not even sure about it myself. But there's a tribe of beings."

"A tribe of what?" Michael said, as amazement gripped his face because he couldn't believe what he had heard, then stared at the professor with a hard obtuse look.

"I don't know if they're men, or creatures from some far away place in the universe, but once while in a dream state I had a glimpse of them. They reminded me of wizards the way they were dressed."

"You saw these men, creatures, or wizards, who created this formula for mind travel?"

"Yes, I think so," the professor said. "And from that dream I know they're in trouble. I can feel it! One of them wants all the power. The others are trapped and need our help. We're connected to them somehow."

"Really!" Michael said. "We're connected to them? They have all this enormous power, but need something from us? Why? I don't think I want any part of of this anymore."

"Someone has to do it," the professor said. "We're a part of them."

"I think if I could," Michael said. "I'd just go back to a time when I was a kid on the river with my dog and a fishing pole, just enjoying the time day by day with Sue."

"Okay," the professor said. "If that's what you want you can make it happen. You can do whatever you like, and erase any memory that you want. Understand that you have the power."

"Can you control all of this without my help?" Michael asked. "Keep the world in check and help the tribe people all by yourself? Do you really need my help?"

"I'll continue to be the dream killer," the professor said. "I'll do my best to stop people like Otto. Some dreams aren't meant to come true. I'm going to stop anyone that I believe should be stopped. I'll find out what the tribe beings need, and figure out what to do to help them."

"Can there really be another Otto?" Michael asked.

"Time and space is an unknown place," the professor said. "It's vast and mysterious. If there's a way to determine what might happen in the future, you can be sure that someone is dreaming about conquest at this very moment, and they need to be stopped."

"So you're sure you don't need my help, and you can do this on your own?"

"We were put together to do this collectively, I know it, but maybe this is the way it's supposed to turn out for now," the professor said. "This could be the order, and the way it's supposed to play out. I don't think anyone can control everything."

"Is there a way to go so far in the future or back to the past to see what happens that we can prevent any kind of problem?"

"There are limits to how far I, you, or anyone who possesses this knowledge can go," the professor said. "It's just another lever, time is forever changing, and maybe it doesn't even exist as we know or comprehend it. Time seems to be a loop that goes and comes round again and again, and no one really understands it."

"I can't go on endlessly," Michael said. "I need this to end."

"Then it will end," the professor said. He interlocked his fingers, cracked his knuckles, and took a deep breath. "Your dream will end for now, and another will begin. I'll see you again in another of dimension. Goodbye, my friend!"

Everything became gray, soon turning black, then eventually every color in the universe, rotating, spinning, and after a moment they were surrounded by emptiness floating on a beam of light. The professor stepped off a light that was frozen in space, his face calm and expressionless a moment, then a smile appeared on his face as he faded into the darkness. A bell sounded and echoed, then he fell into the stars. A voice filled the air, and Michael heard him say, "A dream may not be what you think a dream to be, Michael. And there's always the possibility it could be better than you've ever imagined."

Michael raised a hand to wave, but the professor morphed into a shadow outlined by a glowing light for a moment, and soon after seemed to be absorbed into darkness, then burst into an explosion of light. Michael watched the brightest beam anyone could imagination. It blinding him, then spread over everything he could see. The light turned golden and broke into droplets floating gently through space, hanging in the air a moment, then finally falling to the ground leaving the earth covered in a glowing reflective diamond like substance.

In this substance all of Michael's dreams from the past flashed in front of him again, then he watched them vanished. He closed his eyes, and when he opened them he was a kid on the river. Buster was sitting at his side, and in front of him a fishing pole braced on a stick that was pushed into the ground. The dog jumped up, ran to the edge of the river, and started barking. Michael watched and his attention was caught by something as he looked out over the river. "You see something, Buster? What's that floating out there?" he said. "It's probably just a log. Let's go Buster. We'll show Moses the fish we caught, then clean, and put'em on the grill. I wonder what Sue's up to today. Maybe we can ask her to come over for dinner."

He gathered all of his things, and as he walked into the woods, turned once more toward the river, then paused a second watching a floating hulk, and looked at his dog. "It's nothing, let's go home!"

TEMPORAL ZONES

From years of systematically altering a series of plausible formulas by trial and error I've discovered a way to do more than just guess or foresee the future, now I'm able to shift into the past and future through dreams.

Used correctly by a person who has the capability to truly understand dreams, all events, thoughts, and ideas can become reality. Originally my work and method used logic to show the outcome of situations. The data studied circumstances, state, conditions, and involvement of participates. This resulted in showing the outcome.

It wasn't until later that I discovered a series of tones to unlock the dream state. This knowledge fell into my hands quite by accident, and the precious information in the missing pages from a distant time is what some desire. These tones involve a process to release a power giving the dreamer the ability to cross into another dimension or time. When the dream killer awakens the dreamer, they resume their life. But there comes a time for all when the dream killer doesn't come, and the dreamer doesn't wake, but instead goes on new journey beyond any imagination.

My travels have taken me to worlds that have disappeared long ago, and to places that have never been known to anyone. I stay vigilant, the ring master, keeping an eye on the present, past and the future, watching this three ring circus of what we call life. Remember, a dream may not be what you think a dream to be, and a mind has no limitation, leaving destiny in your hands.

Pleasant Dreams!
The Professor

Poetry

Inflexation
Fences
The Poetry of Food and Drink
Warblings
Are You Casablanca

Novels

ExPRESSION
AWAKE ASLEEP DREAMING DEAD
DREAM KILLER

www.jsiwicki.com

infojsiwicki@gmail.com